I0684881

Robert Chandler

FIFTY SHADES
of FORESKIN

Robert Chandler is a writer, filmmaker and sexual revolutionary. Since an early age, he dreamed of telling stories of adventure that readers would masturbate to, but put those dreams aside to focus on his cats and career. He finally worked up the nerve to put fingers to keys with his first novel, *Fifty Shades of Foreskin*. He is also the creator of the popular adult website, FantasticForeskin.com.

FIFTY SHADES
of FORESKIN

Robert Chandler

Published by
Chandler World Media

Fifty Shades *of* **Foreskin**

FIRST CHANDLER WORLD MEDIA EDITION,
FEBRUARY 2015

Copyright © 2015 Chandler World Media

ISBN: 098611930X
ISBN-13: 978-0-9861193-0-9

Book design by Robert Chandler
Cover design by Robert Chandler
Cover image © 2015 Robert Chandler

Chandler World Media
www.chandlerworld.com

This book is dedicated to all the gay men who have done porn, past and present. You've taken risks and made sacrifices to bring happiness and make fantasies come true. You deserve respect and admiration. You are brave and you matter.

And also to me. Because I wrote it.

CONTENTS

FIFTY SHADES
of FORESKIN

CHAPTER ONE
THE FINAL DAY OF MY BOYHOOD

I'm hot. No, I'm really hot. It's summer. It's Houston. It's hot. Sure, the air conditioner is doing what it can but it's a pretty old unit, older than me, I think. But it's still so fucking hot! When it's like this, I really don't bother with a routine or getting up early. In fact, it's a few minutes shy of noon and I'm not even out of bed. I figure I deserve it today. Despite the oppressive heat, I've never felt freer.

I'm due to become a "real" adult soon. Well, that's what mom had said at graduation last Thursday before my cousin Todd took me aside to awkwardly hand me a joint, trying to be all secret-like. But some bits of pot escaped the paper and fell on my graduation gown. Mom saw. Genius.

Don't get me wrong, I love that guy. Sure, he's a bit kooky, but… he gives one hell of a blow job. But I might biased because he was my first. He taught me everything I know. Being an only child, it's nice having an older cousin not too far away. I smoked my first joint with him and I sucked my first pole with him. He's my mentor in all things immoral.

All the excitement from graduating high school and all the attention and praise is still buzzing in my mind. I loved wearing the cap and gown. I loved seeing "JAKE LUCAS PARKER" written in script across that diploma. But the realization that I'll be starting real life soon is starting to nag. I'm trying my best to push it aside and enjoy life as a slacker today. Maybe it's time to get out of bed.

I stumble off the edge of the mattress, take a warm shower, shove on a pair of worn-soft purple and red plaid boxers, throw on some shorts and zap on the TV and then the Xbox. *Halo 4* is already in, so I decide to just go with it. Mom and Dad are both at work. I've got a two story house to use as my slacker paradise, but all I can think of is planting myself on the couch.

I reach my hands in my shorts to scratch my smooth balls as I trail downstairs. Todd's joint is still in my pocket. Hello, my little friend! He's just begging to be blazed.

I lean back in the family couch, fire that bad boy up and start the game. The first puff turns my brain a lit-tle marshmallowy. *Where does Todd get his stuff?* I get well into the game, and I'm doing pretty good, which is amazing considering how baked I'm getting. I'm blow-ing up aliens and… whatever else. Seriously, this stuff is really good. I've worked too hard in school and my "extracurriculars" these past few years. I can spare some brain cells.

It feels like a couple of hours pass, but I check my phone and I've only been up about twenty minutes. I'm starting to get hungry. I really, desperately want a pizza. With pineapple. And something else. I pause the game and I dial the pizza place, ordering a medium with pineapple and whatever tastes good with pineapple. Surprise me.

I settle back into my routine of shooting stuff. I'm vaguely aware that I'm seriously kicking ass. I don't know how much time has passed, but the doorbell is ringing. I pause the game again and jump up to answer the door. My shorts slide a bit as I get up and I realize I'm showing a lot of underwear for a suburban white boy. I'm desperate for that pizza now.

I open the door and I like what I see. The pizza guy. He looks about my age, maybe a few years older, redhead, and he's… well, *he's hot*. When did redheads get so fucking hot? Even in his navy-blue chinos and polo thickly striped in branded reds and blues, the guy still has it going on. His pale skin is flawless and stretched over chiseled features; high cheekbones, and a square jaw. His face isn't covered in freckles like you'd expect from a ginger, only a faint speckling across his nose and cheeks. He's like a college-jock Jimmy Olsen. But a Jimmy Olsen that even Superman couldn't keep his hands off.

"Parker?" he asks, holding up the pizza.

"Yeah," I stammer, forcing my brain away from the needs of my cock, which starts to twitch a bit in my shorts. I'm suddenly aware that I'm not wearing a shirt.

I motion him inside, and go to grab my wallet from the coffee table. My joint is sitting in the ash tray. When did I put it there? This stuff is definitely working.

When I turn back, Pizza Guy is standing in the doorway. He looks around curiously, his nostrils flaring. He smells my pot.

I giggle silently under my breath. "You wanna share?" I say with a raise of an eyebrow, holding up what's left of the joint.

"Well," he starts reluctantly, "I probably shouldn't while I'm working."

And suddenly I realize that I know this guy!

"Oh my god. You're Kevin Hollister's big brother! Uh… Tommy? Tony! Tony, right?" I stammer through trying to remember the guy's name. He was a popular jock at my school, which is the only reason why I vaguely know his name.

"Yeah, Kevin's my little bro." says Pizza-Guy Hollister with a roll of his eyes. "My name's Toby. Close, though."

"Kevin mentioned his big brother was going to be back for the summer. Looks like you found a gig pretty quickly," I say, trying to make small talk.

"It's just till I go back to school. College is crushing me. I'm not really the book-type. Football, yes. Books, no. I wanted something mindless and stress-free to do over the summer. And I could use the cash."

Well," I say, picking up the joint and firing it up again with a flick of my lighter, "You're very welcome to share the rest of this with me. You could use a break, right? It doesn't get much more mindless than this!" I laugh almost involuntarily. I realize I'm not being the slightest bit witty and that only makes me laugh more.

Toby Hollister seems to struggle with himself for a second, before reluctantly taking the joint out of my hand and giving it a long drag. He can obviously see I'm in a very good place. I can see he wants to be there with me. "Shit," he murmurs softly when he breathes out, "Where do you get your stuff?"

"My cousin got it," I say, taking a drag myself. "I'm definitely gonna be asking him," I add with a laugh. "I never buy my own stuff. This was a graduation present. And a very excellent one," I laugh.

Toby Hollister chuckles too.

"Sit down if you like." I motion to the couch. I decide to swap out *Halo* for a bit of *Grand Theft Auto*.

"Thanks," he says, plopping down next to me with a heavy sigh, clearly relieved to be off his feet.

We eat pizza, smoke the joint to a nub and blow up some cars. I hardly ever bother with starting missions on these things anyway. Neither of us seem to really know how to play anymore, but we're having a fucking great time anyway. Toby Hollister is telling me about his first year at college and life in Ann Arbor, but I swear he's sneaking glances in my direction. Am I imagining it? Is it wishful thinking?

His eyes drop away from the TV screen, and I'm sure this time he's looking right where my shorts dip below my boxers.. No, that can't be it. I mean, sure, he might be looking in my direction, but that could mean anything, right?

Except, he *is* looking at my crotch. He's staring. He's just high enough that he probably doesn't realize it. He looks at me, then nods down at my crotch meaningfully, as if he were directing me to look. I'm confused, but at the same time, I feel my face growing hot. Sure, I've been sporting a bit of a semi since he arrived, but I don't think it's noticeable through my shorts.

I steal a look down. Oh. I got pizza sauce on my shorts. "Shit," I say, wiping the stain down with my hands, which only makes it worse. "I'm a total mess in every way possible!" We both laugh hard.

"Maybe you should take 'em off," suggests the college boy next to me.

My cock seems to agree with him, because it decides to stiffen even more. Goodbye, semi. Hello, full-on boner. I'm a buzzed gay-boy with a hard-on for the pizza boy. Toby Hollister's eyes are back on the game and he looks quite engrossed. Is he shy about the suggestion he just made or is he completely uninterested in the tent I'm pitching between my legs?

Fuck it. I'm too fucked up to care. I'll bet he and his college buddies sit around together in their boxers all the time. I breathe deep, then I quickly pull down my shorts. My boner springs up in my boxers. Please, boner, don't slip out of the pee-fly! I dive for the pizza box and put it on my lap.

I swear I saw the Toby-the-Red smirk out of the corner of my eye. Should I make a move? I'm horny. I'm always horny. But I'll play it cool. He's going to have to get back to work soon, so this thing will get figured out one way or another.

When it's my turn with the controller, I throw a car into the water absentmindedly. Fuck, I'm so high. Or horny. I've never been with a ginger before. I wonder what his pubes look like. Are they really, really red? I'd love to find out, but I don't want hot pizza in my face if it turns out I have the wrong idea.

Then Toby Hollister shifts and gets up from the couch.

"I gotta get back to work. I'm probably in trouble already. Thanks for the break," he says, holding out a hand.

I stand up and try to hide my disappointment. I reach over to shake his outstretched hand. Disappointment, successfully hidden. Boner, not so much. Toby clearly notices and he doesn't shake my hand. Instead, his hand misses my hand and moves downward. His fingers close around my hard cock through my thin boxers.

I moan in surprise and the sensation causes me to slightly lose my balance, forcing me to support myself by grabbing his shoulders. A fire spreads from my cock through my whole body. Every nerve ending tingles with pleasure.

"Maybe I should take care of this first?" he whispers huskily, smirking at my loss of control.

"I..." I mutter, now unable to form coherent sentences. My words don't seem to be working. But who needs them? I give him a big smile and that says everything.

He pulls my boxers down with two thumbs stuck into the front of my waistband. The feeling of the worn fabric over the tip of my uncut cock almost makes me cum. I breathe and clench. Not yet, boy! His pale hand squeezes my fully grown shaft at the base, causing my hips to thrust forward through his fist. My cockhead slips through the opening of my foreskin a bit. It's very wet. How long have I been pre-cumming?

"Hmm…" he says thoughtfully, as if he were looking at a painting at an art gallery.

I look up. "What?"

"I've never seen an uncut dick before."

I feel my face go red. All of the teasing I had to endure through junior high and high school came flooding back, and disappointment washes over me. I'm the weird white boy with the anteater dick again. Apparently, my foreskin a human oddity.

The ginger moves forward and whispers in my ear. "I like it."

My heart leaps along with my rock-hard dick in the pizza guy's hand. It looks like the graduation presents keep on coming. He begins to move his hand up and down my member, hesitantly pulling the foreskin back and forth over my hardened flesh.

"Is this okay?" He asks shyly.

"Yeah, that's good," I reply breathlessly. It feels so good I want to scream.

I realize I'm completely naked while he's still in his pizza delivery uniform, visor and all. I feel vulnerable and exposed. Time to even things up. I fumble with the zipper on Toby Hollister's pants, but he swats my hand away. I give him a whine in protest. He laughs softly and lowers himself on his knees. Keeping his eyes firmly locked with mine, he lets his lips and tongue explore my foreskin. Then he just looks at it very closely. He pulls my hood over my cockhead, then retracts it. Back and forth. He stares like he's a zookeeper who's just discovered a new species or a unicorn or something. Then he licks the thick pre-cum spilling out of my prepuce, causing me to moan as I feel silky wet heat of his tongue against my throbbing, moist cockhead.

He licks my shaft before continuing down to investigate my heavy balls below. He fits them both in his mouth, licking gently with his tongue. I love having my balls played with and he's so good at it.

He moves back up to take my dick into his mouth, sucking on my foreskin while he teases the small opening with the tip of his tongue. I can tell he's having a little bit of a challenge with my dick. I'm not sure if it's my size or if he's inexperienced. But either way, he's doing well enough. I'm leaking pre-cum so bad. The curious attention he's giving my foreskin is driving me crazy! I tighten my hold on his thick crimson hair, my hips jerking forward again. He takes it like a champ.

Now I want to see what he's got packing between his legs.

"Please," I say through my uneven breaths, "Let me do you too."

My personal Jimmy Olsen looks up at me. I see my pre-cum drip down his chin. It makes my cock leak even more.

"I will," he says, standing up slowly, one hand still stroking my cock clumsily while fidgeting with his belt then unbuttoning his navy chinos with the other. He lets them pool around his ankles and continues, "If you show me what cock-docking is like."

My eyes light up, and if it were possible, my dick gets even harder. I eagerly pull down Toby Hollister's white Jockey briefs and find a decent sized, rock-hard cock nestled in a bush of rust-red pubes. They're brighter than his hair, almost like they don't match. And it doesn't look like he's ever trimmed. Maybe he hasn't seen a lot of action up until now. It's hot. I decide I want to see what he looks like all over, and pull off his work shirt to reveal a light dusting of crimson hair trailing between his navel and cock.

I trace this path teasingly with my finger, down, down, down to the shaft. His straight, more-thick-than-long cock gives me a throbbing bounce. I smirk as it responds to the small attention I give it. I rub some pre-cum off the tip of my foreskin and use it jerk him off slowly, earning a moan from my new buddy. He grabs hold of mine even tighter, causing me to grind into his hand with a growl, sliding in and out of my fleshy sheathing.

"Here." I move our dicks close so that the tips kiss, causing us to both to moan loudly. I pull my foreskin gradually over the head his cock until it's completely covered. It's a struggle to keep us together, because we're both already so ridiculously slick with cock juice.

"Mmm! That's good," whispers the ginger near my ear. The sound of his excited voice causes me to shudder. I can tell he's trying not to make too much noise. Like me, I'll bet he's always played with himself while his parents were in the house. You learn to get very turned on very quietly. But we're all alone now. It's safe to let it out.

We both moan in frustration when his cock slips away, breaking our connection, dripping with slippery pre-cum. We both stand and watch our dicks drip for each other, silvery threads glistening as they drop from our cockheads. I love that he's as turned on as I am.

We move together again. I pull my foreskin apart with two fingers on each side and over the knobby head of his cock. I feel his throbbing dickhead against mine, pulsing inside my foreskin. Oh fuck! It's an amazing feeling. Anyone who says a foreskin is useless extra skin should feel what I'm feeling right now. My cock tingles with pleasure, like Spider-Man's spider-sense going off. It's warning me that I'm not going to be able to keep from cumming for much longer. The pleasure rush causes us to thrust our hips against each other, making his cockhead slip out of my skin again. I think I would have shot my load if we kept docking another second.

We just chuckle at the hopelessness of keeping our cocks joined in my wet foreskin for very long. Docking may be difficult, but it feels so fucking good to try! We're now covered in each other's juice. It's all over my hands and stomach. I want to lick it all up.

I kneel down to Toby's red-maned little monster. I'm face-to-face with his six-inch meat. I love when I'm with an older guy and I have the bigger cock. It evens things up a little. I lick his shaft and let my breath blow over his cock. His eyes close tightly and his fists clench. I smirk, loving the effect I have on him. I take him in my mouth and slowly move down and up, letting my tongue move over his tasty, smooth shaft. Has Toby ever been sucked before? It's hard to tell. Either way, I want to give him a cocksucking he'll remember long after he's back on the football field in Michigan.

I move my free hand to take care of my own slick and wet hard-on. I stroke my sensitive foreskin over the hard flesh in sync with my mouth moving over Toby's boner. As my fervor increases, I take him deeper and deeper into my mouth and down my throat. The pizza guy whimpers as I swallow his pepperoni. I slow down my hand on my own cock so I don't cum, then I begin to twist my wrist at the end of each stroke. I can't get enough of his medium-size meat-lover's delight!

Toby Hollister suddenly pulls out of my mouth, lifts me up and pushes me from where we're standing to the couch. He fall on top of me and grabs my arms with his left hand, pinning them over my head and pushing himself up. He grabs our leaking cocks with his right hand and begins stroking them together.

"Ohhhh, my fucking god! Fuuu-uck." I groan incoherent nonsense as my hips move in and out of the small space between the pizza boy's hand and cock. His hips are moving with mine too, completely out of control, rutting against me. His cock leaks against mine.

He releases my wrists. His finger moves down my body and I feel it tease the valley between my butt cheeks, pressing deeper and deeper until it circles my tight hole.

"Mmm! Yeah, right there. Right in there." I don't know what I'm saying, but Toby Hollister seems to understand. He pushes his fingers inside me and I yell, seeing stars. All the blood is flowing to my throbbing cock stroked in Toby's other hand. I think I may pass out but I don't. The pot and the sex-rush blend together to make me feel connected to the universe.

I lean up and squeeze my hand over the hand Toby's using to stroke us, causing the friction between us to intensify. I can see on his face that he's feeling as good as I do. We move our pelvises together until they become a blur, pulsating together at a violent and desperate pace.

"Oh god, Parker. I'm gonna…! Oh, Jake! I…"

I respond only with increasingly loud grunts and panting. All I can think of is the throbbing in my cock and Toby's finger in my hole. So close. My cock feels like it's generating enough heat to burn down my house. He keeps exploring my ass and finds just the right spot. Toby's about to blow and I can't hold back any longer. His hand is pumping out cocks together faster and faster.

"Uuuugh," we groan loudly in unison.

We both cum and we cum hard. Ropes of milky white jizz shoot between us in spurts again and again, covering us both until we're a sticky mess. Spunk keeps flying with every stroke of our fists. We're both panting so hard, so excited to see the other release. We don't stop our thrashing until we're drained and truly milked. We slow down. A final squeeze releases the last drips from our hard tubes. Our bodies convulse and he drops on top of me. His jock body crushes me a bit but I love it.

"Fucking hell, man!" he lets out.

"Yeah!"

"What's that on your butt cheek?" he asks. "Is that a tattoo?"

"What?" I twist my head and torso around to look at where he's pointing. "Oh, that. It's a birthmark."

"It looks like a cat's paw print. Mrrrrow!" he teases.

I give his cock a hard squeeze. A tiny drip of his spunk rolls out.

I look around, and suddenly I'm very aware of the mess we made. I have to clean up and make sure nothing got on the upholstery or my mom will have my balls in a vice.

"Don't move a muscle," I say before cautiously reaching over to the coffee table and grabbing a stack of logoed napkins Toby brought with the pizza.

"Start wiping," I say authoritatively.

It takes the entire stack of napkins and the better part of a paper towel roll, but the sofa, the hardwood floor and the fronts of our bodies are clean, albeit a bit sticky. I put the gooey wipes in a bag and into the waste paper basket. The pizza guy gets dressed and I put on my boxers, still very moist from my pre-cum.

I grab my wallet from the table and gather the cash for the pizza. When I hand it to Toby, he shakes his head. "Dude, after a year away at college, I never thought I'd have my first experience with an uncut cock back home in Houston. This is on me."

He stretches out his hand again. This time, it *is* my hand he shakes.

"Thanks for this," he says again. "If fooling around with uncut guys is always this good, I think I've found a new hobby."

I blush and laugh shyly. "Thanks!"

With that, he leaves, passing a woman down the driveway.

I do a double take. It's my mom! Thank god we thought to clean up. How long were we fooling around? She's carrying groceries. It's a good thing she needed to stop on the way back home from work. I hope this good fortune stays with me all summer. Now, where the fuck are my shorts?

CHAPTER TWO
GIVING MY ALL FOR THE COACH

My room is boiling by the time I finally go to bed at 2:30 AM. But that's Houston in June. Some comic books and Netflix helped me to squander away the night. It's amazing how many *South Parks* I can binge watch. I could really get used to this in-between life after high school and pre-real world. I tear off my clothes until I'm down to my thin underwear. It's way too hot for anything else.

When I'm undressed, I look around my room, at my walls, my desk, my bed. I've slept on that twin bed almost every night of my whole life. That's going to change to tomorrow. Everything is going to change completely tomorrow. I won't be sleeping here. I won't even be here.

I leap onto my bed with a bounce and stretch out. I'm nervous, but I'm also totally excited for what morning brings. I rub my hand over my smooth chest. With graduation behind me, everything is different now. I'll never get up and race off to my high school again. I'm so glad to be done, but I'll miss seeing my friends every day, school plays the basketball games. My basketball coach. I'll *really* miss my basketball coach.

I vividly remember that day six months ago. I had just turned eighteen. Coach Russo was one of those few Phys Ed teachers who actually lived by his lessons He was forty-five and fit. Really fit. His entire body was covered in thick, tan muscles that begged to be admired and touched. His chest was sprayed with dark, furry hair that showed through the neck of his polo shirts. He wore nylon shorts just about every day that showed off his hairy muscled legs. Sometimes, those shorts showed the ribbing of his jockstrap. It made me want to rub my face in his crotch. He drove me wild.

His wife was one lucky woman. She was a substitute Spanish teacher at my school. I used to see them leave for lunch together whenever she subbed. They always looked really happy together. But Coach didn't always get what he needed at home, as I learned that day.

It was my turn to clean up the gym after basketball practice. I grabbed every ball, cone and discarded practice jersey and brought them back to the locker room. The rest of the team was already showered and changing. I got a "goodbye," a "see ya later," and a few pats on the back as they filed out. I still had cleaning to do. I was all alone in the locker room, except for Coach. He looked up from the paperwork on his desk and saw me standing there by myself.

I was nervous when he came out of his office. He could be very tough on the team. Tough but fair. I wasn't at my best during practice that day. I was worried that he was going to yell at me. "Parker, you still here?" He was smiling. He leaned against the frame of the door and crossed his arms over his massive chest.

I shrugged. "Just about to shower, Coach."

All I was wearing was my jockstrap. I was tempted to cover up, but I thought that would draw more attention to my lack of clothing. And I'm knew he'd seen hundreds of his players in jocks and less. No big deal, right? But I got nervous around Coach. Every time I saw him, I felt my dick plump a little. And that jock strap wasn't helping my cock stay down.

"Jake, I wanna say something."

I stopped at the use of my first name. Coach never called any of us by our first names. It was a monumental moment.

"I want you to know that you've been doing a great job on the team. I'm, uh, gonna be sorry to see you go at the end of the season."

I was stunned. Coach didn't give out many compliments and I never saw him get sentimental. Not even during our current winning streak.

"Thank you?" I didn't know what else to say. I knew immediately after I said it how stupid it sounded. But it was too late.

Coach chuckled. "Well, I hope you keep playing when you start Dallas State U in the fall. That team deserves a player like you."

I blushed. My desire for him increased with every word he said to me.

"Thank you, sir. That means a lot." I lowered my head shyly. I've idolized this guy since he started coaching me sophomore year. I knew he was near my father's age, but I was drawn to everything about him. I looked up again, right into his face. His lips were full and his face was darkened with stubble. He kept his hair so closely cropped that it almost seemed like a continuation of the stubble. Maybe it was to cover up some balding, but it only made him hotter to me.

Coach pushed off the door frame and approached me. "Got any plans for the night, Jake?"

I shrugged, trying very hard not to show my nervousness. Or the boner growing in my jock. He stood so close. It took all of my willpower not to reach out and touch him.

"Not really. It's my birthday," I told him.

"Happy birthday." He squeezed my shoulder. It sent tingles through me. At the time, I didn't think he realized the kind of effect he had on me, but now I'm not so sure. He may have.

It was a full minute before he pulled his hand off my shoulder. I was sad to see it go.

"I'll leave you to shower," he said in a hoarse whisper.

I smiled back. This conversation left me feeling very nervous, but a good kind of nervous. I wondered if my attraction could be mutual. I thought it was unlikely, but I've never seen Coach so open with any of us players.

Coach took a step back and turned away, heading for the exit. As soon as his back was turned, I peeled off my sweaty jockstrap. My cock bounced up rock hard. Did I have a full-on boner the entire time Coach was in front of me?

"Fuck," I moaned. As soon as it was out of my mouth, I regretted it.

Coach wasn't out the door yet. He turned around and saw me, naked, with my hooded dick standing up straight pointed directly at him. Pre-cum was welling up in the ridge of my foreskin. He was only twenty feet away from me. I should have waited for him to leave before I took off my jock. I could feel my cheeks heat up and go red. Really, really red.

But Coach Russo just smiled and walked back toward me.

"There's nothing to be embarrassed about," he assured me. His eyes were on my cock. "Trust me, I have a degree in physiology." He gave me a wink.

I could smell him. He smelled like locker room, so manly. I loved his smell. A glistening drop of pre-cum spilled from the tip of my foreskin and dropped onto Coach's sneaker. I felt the color drain from my face and my heart stopped. I was mortified. Beyond mortified. Would the coach kick my ass, or would he still be understanding? A million thoughts ran through my head, but I sure as hell didn't anticipate the actual reaction I got.

Coach Russo chuckled at me. "Relax. You're a good kid, Jake. We all get boners."

 I didn't expect the smile that spread across his face. It was reassuring and… lustful. The intensity between us made it impossible for me to look him in the eye.

That's when I noticed Coach's shorts. The lines from his jockstrap were far more prominent than ever before. I couldn't believe it. I wasn't the only one with a hard-on. He caught me looking.

"We all get boners, Jake."

I looked back up in Coach's eyes and smiled nervously. I was still embarrassed that I couldn't control my unruly cock. There was no hiding how much I wanted him. But why even try. He was hard too. Really, what did I have to lose?

I took a deep breath and asked the question I wanted to ask for three years. "Can… can I feel it?" I looked back down at his shorts so there would be no doubt about what I meant. My eyes got stuck there. I couldn't look away even if I wanted to. Which I didn't.

"It's your birthday, Jake," Coach said. His voice was quiet and confident. "Let's celebrate."

"Holy shit," I thought. I couldn't believe this was actually going to happen. A part of me thought I should walk away. He was much older. What if he laughed at my inexperience? What if he changed his mind? What if somebody walked in? Maybe it would just be better to leave well enough alone and call it a win.

Yet my fingers wouldn't have listened to my brain even if I wanted them to. I've been trained to follow his orders for most of my time in high school. I'm a good player and now I was being moved into the big leagues. I tentatively reached forward and lightly brushed against the nylon green fabric at the front of his shorts. It felt thick. Coach didn't knock my hand away. This was really happening! I inched closer and pressed my entire palm against it. Coach shuttered and leaned into my touch. I felt his cock throb. I wanted to drop to my knees right then and there and swallow his cock in my mouth, but I was too nervous to move. So I continued to explore the front of his shorts.

I wondered if Coach had ever thought of me like this before. Was he just waiting for me to turn eighteen to try anything? Or was this the first time he ever thought of doing anything with a student? Maybe it was the first time doing something with a man!

I felt the thick mushroom head on top of a good-sized cock. I felt a set of heavy balls held tight in his jock strap. Coach grabbed my shoulders with firm hands as my fingers continued rub the length of his cloth-covered cock. His eyes shut and he moaned quietly.

He made the next move. He pulled his hands off my shoulders, pushed his shorts down and pushed me to my knees. I was face-to-face with his dick-stuffed jock. Its smell filled my nose and made me high. He smelled like pure man. I couldn't get enough.

I peeled his jock down to the floor. I loved what I saw. His dick was softer than mine. Much thicker. His cock didn't have foreskin like mine. The head was a dark red and incredibly smooth, like the skin was stretched to the limits. He was leaking pre-cum. Actually, oozing pre-cum. I held my tongue under the drop and let it fall. It was better than anything I ever tasted. I had fantasized about coach before, alone in my room with my own cock in my hands. But I never imagined his cock would smell and taste so fucking good. My nervousness was gone. All I could think about was how badly I wanted him.

Coach grabbed my head and tangled his fingers in my thick hair. He forced my mouth further down his cock. Panic hit me when my lips moved past his head. I didn't think I could fit that whole thing in my mouth! Strangely enough, I took it. Little by little his thick cock filled my mouth. I opened wider than I'd ever opened in my life. Once he got it all in, he started fucking my face. Slowly at first, then he sped up. I never could have accommodated a cock this thick, but with Coach, anything seemed possible. I could feel his engorged cockhead pounding at the back of my throat.

He closed his eyes and moaned. I buried my nose in this thick pubes as I swallowed his manly meat. He was rock hard. I loved that I could turn him on. It made me feel so fucking hot.

I started to stroke myself with my right hand and my left grabbed his tight ass. It was perfect. His furry butt was tight and muscular but still soft enough to get a good grip. My mouth worked over his mushroom head as my tongue danced across the piss slit His salty pre-cum flowed into me and drank it all down.

"Good boy, Parker!" the Coach praised me through his moaning.

Pleasing Coach Russo turned me on more than anything. His words ran through my body and into my cock. My dick felt like a volcano ready to erupt. It was hot and ready to go. My body started shaking. My moans were muffled as I took the coach's cock like a champion. My head got light. And I exploded. My cum was shooting and spilling all over the cement gym floor. Gobs of spunk ran through my fingers. It felt like it was never going to stop. Coach saw me score, and pushed his cock all the way down the back of my throat.

"Fuck," he gasped as he fucked my face hard. I felt like I was choking on his thick meat, I didn't want to pull away. My jizz was still flowing as I took him pummeling. I loved the way he was using me. It was the greatest feeling in the world. At that moment, I only existed to give him pleasure. I couldn't get enough of him. I wanted to feel his cum down my throat.

His hold on my hair got tighter. I felt a throb in his thick cock. His dick ballooned, hot and full. I almost gagged, but I refused to let my coach down.

"Get ready, Parker!"

He pulled my head into him and I took his cock to the base. His body tensed as he shot down my throat, load after load, thick and salty. Fuck, that man could cum! It filled my mouth and I swallowed as quickly as I could. I refused to let a single drop spill out of my mouth. I drank his warm cream into my stomach, as fast as he unloaded. I wanted to be filled by the coach's seed. I wanted everything he had. He must have wanted the same thing. He didn't pull out until every drop was in me.

Once spent, he pulled his still-stiff cock out of my sore, but satisfied mouth. For a second, I was terrified that he was going to pull up his shorts and leave. I didn't want that. I grabbed his ass to hold him still. Then I began to clean him off. Every drop of cum I sprayed on him, I licked up. I licked it out of the thick black fur surrounding his cock. I licked it off his shoes. It seemed to turn him on, because his erection didn't soften. I felt like a winner. He dropped down to his knees and shoved his tongue down my throat. He was rough and everywhere. I'm sure he tasted his own cum in my mouth. He pushed me down to the floor and climbed on top of me. His hands moved over every inch of my young, athletic body. I was laying in slippery puddles of my cum, getting wet and sliding underneath Coach's hard body. His mostly-hard cock pushed against my leg, getting harder by the second. I would have expected him to be completely soft from his orgasm. Coach reached between us, grabbing my cock and giving it a firm squeeze. He looked me in the eye and smiled as he stroked me. He seemed to be amused by the way my foreskin glided over my sweaty cock. That's when I realized something awful.

I hadn't showered yet. I had given my all on the court, and I still hadn't showered. I was covered in sweat, and not just sex sweat. *Fuck.* I probably smelled.

I pulled away from Coach's kiss looking embarrassed. "Shit, I'm sorry, Coach."

"For what?" he asked.

I told him I was a sweaty smelly mess, expecting him to get grossed and leave. But he didn't say anything. Instead, he kissed me once and lowered himself down my body. Every inch he passed, he left a light, barely-there kiss. He didn't linger anywhere for long. He just kept moving until he hovered above my hard cock. He held his head there, staring and breathing me in. I didn't know what he was going to do. Then he shoved his face right into my bush and bathed my balls with his rough tongue.

"Oh shit!" I definitely hadn't expected that. But I hadn't expected anything that happened to me that day. I threw my head back and covered my eyes with the palm of my hands. All I feel was his mouth on my sack.

It was glorious. He sucked gently on my right nut. His tongue darted around and licked me like a scoop of ice cream. Then he used his warm lips to lightly nibble my tightening sack. I loved that the most. I closed my eye tightly and saw stars. The pleasure was so intense that I was getting wobbly. Coach grabbed onto my waist and held me tight just before he gave my left nut the same treatment.

Fuck, I felt so good. He hadn't even touched my cock yet, but I was all ready to cum again. My balls got very tight and I didn't know how much longer I was going to last. I wished Coach had made his move sooner in the school year. Could we have done this more often? But maybe that was just the day that everything aligned.

I finally pulled my hands away from my eyes to stare at him. The look on his face was fucking incredible. He seemed so happy to have his nose buried in my sweaty pubes and his mouth on my ball sack. It was pure heaven. He lifted my balls and licked under them. Then around them. He moved on to my dick. He took my foreskin into his mouth and sucked on it as his tongue played with the folds of skin. I threw my head back again. I couldn't look anymore. It was just too fucking much.

His tongue danced across the sensitive skin of my cockhead, dipping inside the folds of skin around it to explore. He was so interested in my foreskin. I wondered if the coach had ever been with an uncut guy before. I wondered if he had been with any guy before. His lips gently wrapped around the puckering tip of my foreskin and lightly nibbled. He worked my cock hood thoroughly. My dick had never felt that good. Fuck, I had never felt that good, *period.*

"Come on, kid," Coach said, indicating with a nod. "Let's hit the showers."

Coach turned on the water as hot it could go, filling the entire locker room with steam. Then he began washing me down. His fingers massaged my skin with the soap from the canister mounted on the shower wall. Every part of my body was lathered and washed. My head fell back as my cock bounced, excited by his touch. After Coach finished cleaning me off, he gripped my shoulders and spun me around so my chest was pressed against the wall, water spraying around me. He pushed his chest into my back and ground his meaty cock against my ass.

"I've always wanted to do this," he said right into my ear. I let out a moan and rubbed my backside against his dick, begging him to take me. He just laughed. "Patience, boy."

I wanted to feel him inside of me. I had never been fucked before. Sure, I'd jerked off with a few friends during sleepovers and my cousin taught me how to suck a cock. But my backside was unexplored territory. I couldn't think of anybody I trusted more with my virgin ass than Coach.

He slid down by body until his face was against my rear end. I didn't know what he was doing. Then I felt something hot and wet against my hole. I gasped. I couldn't believe it. He spread my ass cheeks and was licking the outside of my hole. Fuck, his tongue was awesome.

I pushed my ass hard into his face until he grabbed my waist to keep me still. Coach was in control. His tongue kept a solid rhythm licking around my hole while his hands held firm to my sides. When he plunged his tongue past my ring of muscle, I almost nutted again. This was the first time I had felt something in my asshole and it was the greatest feeling ever. I tried again to push back, make it go deeper, but his grip wouldn't let me. He was using his tongue to open me up. I knew he was going to fuck me. I was so eager for that to happen, especially as his tongue moved in and out of me. If his mouth felt this good, I knew his cock was going to change my life.

He stood back up and kissed the back of my neck.

I've seen the way you've looked at my these past few years, Jake. Don't think I haven't noticed," he whispered deeply in my ear. "I've had my eye on you too. You've become a great player and a fine young man."

His soaped-up finger massaged my boyhole. Then he slid the tip in. I moaned. So far, so good. Slowly, he put his whole finger in me and kept it there without moving. I held my breath.

"Breathe, sport. Breathe."

As always, I trusted my coach and did what he told me. I breathed in deep and released. Then again. He moved his finger inside of me. It hurt but it also felt so good. Coach was opening me up as only he could.

"Keep breathing, Jake," he instructed as he slid another finger in.

"Ouch!" I let out.

"You can take it, Jake," he assured me as his fingers moved in and out of my tight hole.

The coach knew my body and its limits better than anyone. If he think I can take his fingers or his thick cock, then I know I can. The pleasure blended with the pain. I'd never felt anything like this.

His fingers moved out of me as I heard him soaping up his cock with his other hand.

"I've been thinking about this a long time, Jake." He kissed my neck.

"I have too, Coach."

Then he gave me what I wanted so badly. He plunged his thick cock straight into my ass. I yelped in pain as tears started to fall and wash away with the shower water. It was excruciating when he finally started slowly fucking. Coach wasn't exactly easy on my virgin hole. He grunted and started fucking faster. And faster. His cock felt impossibly thick as it relentlessly pounded into me. I didn't know how much I could take. I felt like I was going to be sliced in half. I wondered if this was all even physically possible. I clenched my eyes shut and tried to keep breathing. The pain was awful, but there was no way in hell I was going to stop. I trusted that Coach knew what he was doing and I trusted that he knew what I could take. Pain slowly gave way to pleasure.

It was like nothing I had ever felt before. I feel him deep inside of me. I felt the contours of the shaft and the round fullness of his mushroom head as it burrowed into me over and over. I felt the slickness of his pre-cum lube me up as he took me with every thrust. I felt his hot breath and stubble on the back of my neck. I was so glad

Coach was the man to take my cherry. I'd wanted this since the first day of tryouts. And now he was filling my ass, making me a man!

He bent me over a bit and spread my legs farther apart. It gave him better access so he could drive deeper into my hole. My ears filled with the sound of the running water, my non-stop moaning and the slapping of his heavy balls against my smooth, wet ass. We could have been caught at any moment, but I didn't care. If anything, it turned me on more. The idea of somebody walking in and seeing me fucked by my coach only got me harder. Up to this point, I didn't even know I if was a bottom. But it felt so right to be taken by my coach. I wanted everyone to know that I was his. My body was his. My my anal virginity was his to take. I bit my lip and focused all of my will power on not cumming again. It was getting harder and harder with every poke from behind.

He pulled out with a loud pop and I almost begged him not to stop. But I didn't get the chance. He grabbed me and spun me around. Then he gripped my waist and hoisted me up in the air, resting my back against the tiled shower wall. I wrapped my legs around his sides as he pushed inside of me again. This felt even better. My back was against the wet wall and my rock-hard cock was caught between our bodies as Coach supported my body in his strong arms. Every time he pounded into me, my cock rubbed against the wet hair of his firm stomach. It was pure ecstasy.

I clawed at his shoulders when he covered my mouth to cover my screams. I didn't know how to not scream. How did Coach manage to just grunt? He leaned forward until his jaw was resting at the crook of my neck.

He nibbled at my skin as he started to force himself in me harder and harder. He was touching places in me that had never been touched. If felt so turned on, so alive. He was so deep in me that he became a part of me. No, my body became an extension of him and he held me and guided me over his throbbing cock. I could feel his shaft swell in me. Knowing Coach was about to cum again sent a fiery wave through me. He was going to fill up my insides and I was ready for it. No. I needed it!

He drilled hard. Harder! Harder! Then I felt the warm explosion in me. He was panting in my ear as he gave me his seed. It poured into me and filled me. I'd never felt so complete. One final shove and he stopped. I felt his cock expand inside me as it gave me the last of its rewards. I felt so connected to him in every way. I felt the heat of his cum and his cock inside me. It was all I could take. Without a hand on my cock, I erupted all over the both of us. I howled louder than I did when I made the basket that won us our last game. To this day I'm surprised we weren't caught. Hell, I'm surprised they didn't hear us all the way to Dallas.

Coach kissed me and pulled out of my ass, dropping me to the wet, tiled floor in a heap. My legs were just too damn weak to support me. My hole was so sore. It felt broken and damaged. I didn't care. I just lay there and let the water wash the cum from my body. Coach knelt down between my legs to clean up my cock and ass. He was so thorough, he made me cum again. I didn't think I had anything left, but Coach alway knew how to get the best performance out of me. He ate every bit of my load before the shower spray could wash it away.

When my legs were strong enough to hold me up, Coach helped me to my feet and took me back out to the changing area to get dressed. Before I pulled my boxers on, he kissed me again on my lips. Then he kissed me deeper than I've ever been kissed. He tasted so good, so manly. I almost got hard all over again. What a fucking great eighteenth birthday!

We never talked about what happened after that day. Basketball season went on another three months but it never happened again. I played better than I'd ever played before. I wasn't going to give Coach anything but my best. I was disappointed he never fucked me again, but every once in a while during practice, when nobody was watching, Coach would look over at me and give me a little smirk. Every time he did, I felt his cock inside of me again.

I'm panting as I lay in my room, memories of my afternoon with my coach fading away. I glance at my phone and squeeze the power button. It's two thirty in the morning. I have to wake up early, and I finally feel relaxed enough now to sleep. It takes me a second to figure out why. I look down at myself, and realize that I sprayed a load of jizz without ever touching myself. I'm soaked in a wet puddle of my own cum. My boxers are drenched. I should have known. That happens when I think about my encounter with Coach. I smile as my cum dries on my lean, tight stomach. Then I close my eyes and let sleep take me.

CHAPTER THREE
FIRST-CLASS SERVICED

BEEP! BEEP! BEEP!

Slowly my eyelids flutter open and I fumble to get to the alarm clock on my phone. Silence fills the room once more and I'm tempted to go back to sleep. But if I let myself, I'll never wake up and I'll miss my flight. I'm not going to let that happen.

Today is the day I leave for London! I told my parents that I wanted to backpack across Europe for the summer and, even though they didn't necessarily want me to go, they eventually gave in. I pleaded my case. I reminded them that I've always been a good kid. I pointed out that I've been killing myself to get good grades for years. I brought up that I gave my all to theater and basketball without letting my grades slip. It took a while, but they eventually agreed. They worry. They're parents. It's what they do. I appreciate it, I guess.

I check my phone again. 8:00 AM. I sigh heavily. After last night, I could really use another two hours sleep. My flight doesn't leave until 12:55, but I have to be at the airport three hours beforehand and it takes an hour just to get to the airport. Ah well, I guess I can sleep on the plane. It's a thirteen hour flight with the layover in Philadelphia, so I should be good.

I take a swipe across my eyes as I hop out of bed. My morning wood is at full mast, just like it is every day. I grab the underwear I wore last night and shove them in the back of my drawer. I don't want mom dealing with my cummy underwear. Ugh. Those two things should never mix. Firewall! As I pull on some basketball shorts, I notice I'm still covered in my dried fluids from last night. I smile as I think about what my memories of my first fuck does to me. My cock responds with a little bounce. I'm glad Mom has already gone to work. That could have got embarrassing.

On my way to the bathroom to shave and shower, I hear what sounds like a faucet running from my parents' master bathroom. It must be my dad. He's taking me to the airport. I decide to delay my shower for now to say good morning. I love my mom, but I've always been closer with my dad. I always enjoyed when we did things one-on-one; like when we went to the Morrissey concert two years ago, or all the times he took me camping or just played baseball with me in the backyard. Those were some of my favorite times. Hopefully, graduation and what's to come doesn't mean time with Dad has to end.

When I cross into my parents' room, I can see the door to their bathroom is half open. My dad is turned toward the mirror, getting ready to shave.

My dad, Travis Parker, is in excellent shape for a forty-six year old man. He's bulkier than me, but unlike other suburban fathers his age, his girth is from muscle. There's no fat on him. He also has a head full of hair and he's handsome. I always admired my father's looks and physique. I hope the genetic overlords allow me to look as good as he does when I'm his age. Actually, I hope to be like my dad in a lot of ways when I get older. I admire him and look up to him. He's a lawyer and his job takes a lot of his time, but he always puts me and Mom first. I don't know if it's cost him money or promotions, but he's never missed a school play or a basketball game. He's always been there for me. They both have.

As I approach the bathroom, I get a better look at my father. He's standing stark naked in front of the mirror, shaving. My eyes drift down to the massive cock in between his legs. It must fall halfway to his knees! My dick has really grown over the past few years, but my dad's is still bigger. Has to be at least three quarters of an inch longer. And thicker too.

Is there something primal in me that causes me to respect him for having the superior cock? I think that's how things work in the animal kingdom. I mean, sure, most of the admiration I have for my father is based on all that he's done for me, for giving me a life based on kindness and love, for the values he instilled in me, and for all the encouragement he gives. But there was just something right, something natural, about my dad being bigger than me. Like it makes our roles that much clearer. That primal shit must be programmed into us. Though I can't be sure. They sure don't teach the anthropology of cock size in Texas public high schools.

It's not that I was exposed to my father's impressive dick all that often. There have been a few instances, but they were few and far between. There was that time when I was eleven and saw my dad in the locker room after we played tennis together. Or the time we changed into our swimsuits in the car when we went to Crystal Beach. I remember peeing next to him at a urinal and taking a glance when I was thirteen. (Is that weird?) There were a few others, but it was before I hit puberty when I first began to admire the hair on my father's chest and legs, and especially the thick patch of curly pubic hair that framed his cock and balls. I couldn't wait to look like that myself.

I'm not all that hairy. I got excited when my first pubic hair finally grew in because I was terrified that it would never come. I was always a bit self-conscious about being a late bloomer. I even told a friend at school about it and he told me not to worry. I have a bit of body hair, but not nearly enough to let people know I'm a man now and not a boy. Hell, everything about me looks like a boy, from my shaggy hair to my slender hairless build. But, who knows? Maybe my summer abroad will be able to put some hair on my chest, both literally and figuratively.

I stare at my dad's manly body one last time, wondering if I should announce my presence. After a minute or two, I decide to give him his privacy and take my leave. I'm sure he's completely unaware that he had an audience. The sound of the running water masks my departure.

I head into my bathroom and climb in the shower, turning the water on as hot as I can handle to wake me up. It nearly scalds my skin as I step under the spray, but I don't turn it down. The warmth washes away the last vestiges of sleep left in me, at least temporarily. Quickly, I begin to wash my hair and soap up my body, taking extra care on my rock hard cock. Hello, my friend!

I give myself a squeeze as I clench my eyes shut tight and lean my head against the wall of the shower. I know the clock is ticking and I have to leave soon, but I don't stop. It just feels too fucking good.

Slowly, I work my hand over my shaft with barely-there touches between pulsing squeezes to my tapered head. I dip my index finger deep inside my foreskin. My mind flashes to the pizza boy cock-docking me yesterday afternoon. I rub my finger in small circles over my dick-head. *Fuck!* It's like Toby Hollister is in my foreskin all over again.

I slap my free hand against the wall as I work my throbbing cock harder and harder. I bite my lip to keep from crying out, lest I announce to my dad what I'm doing. My arms start to shake and my knees start to buckle as I push myself closer and closer to orgasm. I see Toby's hard cock and red pubes is my head. Mmmmm. I see my dad shaving nude in my head. No! Rewind. Come back, Toby. I tell myself that I'm not imagining my father's tight naked body as I jack my cock off. No. I'm not picturing my father standing in front of me with the same hungry look in his eyes, so much like mine, as he strokes his own massive monster. That's not what I'm thinking about. Nope. That would just be weird, right?

And I certainly am not imagining him pushing his hard, uncut cock into my tight ass as I cum all over the shower wall. Uuugh! Load after load pumps out of me. I'm a fucking cum factory!

I lean harder against the wall, letting all the soap slide off of me. That didn't just happen. I didn't just fantasize about that. I tell myself a hundred times that didn't just happen. I do not fantasize about my dad. That would be messed up, right? Those things are separate. Firewall.

"Fuck," I breathe out.

I point the shower head at my jizzy load on the smooth shower wall and send it all down the drain. Wiping a hand over my closed eyes, I quickly turn the water off and step out of the shower. I dry myself off with a fluffy white towel, brush my teeth and shove my basketball shorts back on. Off to my room to get dressed and grab my things. I've already packed everything I'm going to need for my trip. It's all shoved in the large backpack my parents gave me after they told me I could go on this trip. I grab my iPhone off my desk and plug it into its dock. An old REM song starts playing as I pull on some gray Hanes boxer briefs, a pair of comfortable jeans and a dark green T-shirt. I run a brush quickly through my mop of hair as I take one last look around my room. I've slept here my whole life. Now, I won't see it for quite a while. I'm excited for the trip, but I know a lot is about to change. It's a little scary, to be honest. Am I really ready for all this? Only one way to find out.

Goodbye, room.

I leave my doubts in my room as I grab the backpack and close the door behind me. I can handle this. I just have to remember that I'm prepared. "You're Jake Parker, dammit!" I say it like it means somethings and I laugh. I'm not sure I can pull off talking about myself in third person like a comic book character. Maybe someday.

I shove my brush into my pack as I rush downstairs. Dad's already waiting for me, dressed casually in a pair of faded jeans and a white button-down shirt. He always looks good, like Don Draper without all the alcoholism and repression. He smiles at me. "Ready to go?"

I nod. "All set."

Dad lifts my backpack and the two of us head out his car. Since mom wasn't able to get off of work, she said goodbye to me last night. Still, I wish I could see her one more time before I leave. It's nice dad was able to clear some of his appointments to see me off. His clients can wait. Today is my day!

As we pull out of the driveway Dad turns to me. "Hey, you hungry?'

"Starved."

"What do you say we stop by Jack in the Box for breakfast?"

I can't help but chuckle. "I don't think we're supposed to be eating that."

"Don't tell your mother."

"Deal." I laugh again. Then I turn my head and stare out the window, my thoughts whirling around in my head.

I think about how good I've had it. As an only child, I guess I've been a little spoiled. My folks always gave me what I needed. And I got just about everything I wanted: Xbox, new basketball shoes every year, nice computers. They even gave me a bigger allowance this year so I wouldn't have to work, allowing me to focus on school and sports. And everything else. And there's all the unconditional support they've given me. Not once did they ever doubt me. They always believed in me and always encouraged me to go after what I wanted.

I know how it is out there. I was the lucky one among my friends. When their families were falling apart with divorces, affairs or just neglect, I never dealt with any of that. My parents were my rock. And as dad grabs the bag with our breakfast sandwiches from the drive thru window without ever asking me what I wanted, yet still knowing exactly what I like, I realize something. Despite all they've done for me, I never actually thanked them.

Should I? I mean, isn't taking care of me kind of what they signed up for? But then again, how many of my friends wished they had parents like mine?

I decide not to say anything right now. Not because I'm not grateful, I am. But because I know if I start getting emotional now, I'll start crying and I don't need to start my trip with puffy eyes and a runny nose. This is my first trip alone. My first trip abroad. I'm a man now and I'm not going to start my manhood by acting like a baby. I have a lifetime to tell my parents I'm grateful. And I can show them that I appreciate all they've done by being an exceptional person and making a difference.

For the rest of the trip, my dad quizzes me on different things related to European culture. "What are the names of England's royals?" "What's the name of Europe's currency?" "What countries still use their own currency?" "What kind of government does France have?" "What's tipping etiquette in Holland?" For the entire hour, he drills me. It's a game we play. My dad is really smart and he wants me to be curious about the world around me. He's quizzed me on pop culture, current events, literature and even movie trivia. When I told him that I wanted to backpack through Europe he brushed up on European history so that he could make sure I was prepared. It's actually fun, especially when I get an answer right and throw a question at him. He doesn't miss, but I still try.

"What European city has the highest population?" he asks.

It takes me a few minutes to come up with the answer. Dad looks at me smugly, thinking he's finally stumped me. I smile at him. "Rome."

His smile widens. "Not even close, kid. Where are you landing?"

My grin fade for a second. "London." Damn it, I should have known that. I can't help but laugh. Even with all my preparation, he could still get me!

"I wasn't that far off!"

Dad shakes his head. "Sure, you were only off by about five-million people. Not that bad."

We both laugh. I'm a little nervous about leaving. It's nice to laugh.

"You'll be fine, Jakey," Dad says when he sees how uncomfortable I am. "Look, you got your iPhone, and there's WiFi all over. Always make sure you know where the closest embassy is and know that you can call us for anything. Call collect if you need to. Most of all, you're a smart kid. You'll be fine. Your mom and I are so proud of you."

Fuck, Dad! Why do you gotta be so damn nice now? He's making this harder than it has to be. I will not cry,

I will not cry, I will not cry. You're Jake-Fucking-Parker and you will not cry.

"Thanks, Dad," I finally say. It comes out quieter than I expected. Dad just pats me on the knee.

We pull up at the airport and dad parks in short-term parking. He walks me into the airport, to the kiosk where I check in and waits with me in line headed to security. He doesn't leave my side until he absolutely has to.

"Well," he says as we're standing in front of the TSA agent. This is the farthest a person can go without a ticket.

"Yeah, well…"

Dad chuckles, and then pats me on the shoulder and messes up my hair. I'm about to head through when he pulls me toward him and wraps his large arms around me and my backpack. He keeps me close with his chin resting on my shoulder.

"Be good, son."

Did his voice quiver? What the fuck? My dad isn't a cold person, but he sure as hell isn't the kind of guy who cries easily. It hits me once again that I'm leaving. I wrap my arms tightly around my dad.

He squeezes me one last time before he finally pulls away and he kisses my cheek. "See you in a couple months, Jake."

I nod and hand my ticket and passport over to the agent. When I turn back around, dad's gone. I keep my head down as I move through the rest of the line. I try to wipe my eyes without anybody noticing, but I don't know how well I succeed. I don't think of myself as a hyper-macho guy but I am a guy! For so long, I was just so excited about this trip. I was finally getting out of Houston, and going to Europe. But now that it was happening, I keep thinking of everything I'm leaving behind: my parents, my home, my life.

The agent takes my e-ticket and passport and my passport. He looks at me and looks at my very handsome passport photo.

"Jake Lucas Parker?"

"That's me!" I smile.

He doesn't smile but he does stamp my passport and hands it back to me. I take it and walk to my gate. There's something different on this side of security. A feeling washes over me that I didn't expect. I realize that I'm truly on my own. I'm my own man. I don't have parents or teachers watching over me or telling me what to do. I don't have homework that needs to be done. I can make my own decision. I. Am. On. My. Own. Sure, it's a bit terrifying, but it's also fucking exciting!

With a bounce in my step, I make my way through the massive airport and the throng of people, looking for my gate. Once I find it, I stop by the nearby Chili's To-Go and grab a large sweet tea. This may be the last I'll have for a while. I don't think I'll be drinking much iced tea in London. What *do* they drink there? Is it all just hot tea? I take a seat, gulp my tea and chill out.

It takes about two hours before I can finally board the plane. Ugh! I want to be in London. Now. What is the point of getting to an airport three hours early if I'm just going to sit around at the gate? I'm not good at waiting.

I'm so hyped that I feel like I could run all the way to London. Except for, like, the ocean and the physical impossibility of it. But other than that...

A disorderly line forms to get on the plane. My section is called nearly last, but I'm thrilled as I walk down the aisle to find my seat. I take my place in economy class near the back of the plane. One of the worst seats on the aircraft. I'd say this trip was going to be filed under "unpleasant" until I see something to brighten my day. Or should I say someone? His name tag reads "Tim." He looks to be somewhere in his early forties with a light tan complexion and dark brown hair, the kind of dark brown that could easily be rounded up to black. Through his uniform, I can see a lean body with lines of solid muscles. He looks like the kind of guy who never misses a day at the gym. He catches me staring at him and smiles. I look away, slightly embarrassed.

As the flight streaks away from Texas, most people are miserable in their cramped seats, but I feel like I'm riding in first class. Tim gives me some special attention. I'm never without a Coke, I get a hot towel instead of a dry napkin and I enjoy a few extra packages of snacks. During meal service, he brings me the cheesy pasta and shrimp meal, even though they apparently ran out of it and I'm sitting near the rear of the plane. And when everybody is eating their dry shortbread cookies for dessert, he brings me a piece of moist cheesecake and a glass of the champagne they served in first class. Fuck, yeah. The passengers around me probably despise me by now, but what a way to start a trip to Europe!

Things get better as we fly over the Atlantic. Most of the passengers are already asleep, the lights are dimmed and most of the windows are shut. I'm too excited to sleep right now. I look around the cabin and see Tim down the aisle. He nods and points at me with a smile.

"What?" I mouth surprised. "Me?"

"Yeah," he mouths as he motions for me to come.

What's he mean? Where does he want me to go? I'm not sure, but he's got me curious. And I wouldn't mind stretching my legs.

When he walks by me, I unbuckle my seatbelt and follow behind him. He doesn't say anything as he leads me to a hatch that says "Employees Only." It leads down below to a private area near the cargo hold. I can hear a few suitcases that weren't secured well tumble around.

"What is this place?" I whisper.

Tim grabs me and starts pulling my shirt off. "Storage room. Don't worry, we're safe. The other attendants use this place when they find a hot passenger too. It's a special lounge for our special guests."

He laughs before he kisses me. I stop thinking and pull him closer, shoving my tongue deep down his throat.

His hands are all over my body, grabbing and squeezing. His hands reach the edge of my jeans and he roughly push them down. I nearly fall over when they catch around my ankles, but Tim keeps me up. My fingers go straight for the buttons of his uniform shirt. I can feel the chest hair beneath my fingertips as the fabric pulls apart.

Once I've undone every button, my hands slide to his shoulders and push the shirt away. He lets it fall without breaking our kiss. Then I start working on getting those fucking pants out of my way. Once they're gone, I do away with his flannel boxers. I pull away to admire his firm body up close. Tim is beautifully covered in hair: his legs, his chest and a perfect bush around his thick six-inch achingly-hard cock. Mine may be bigger, but that cut piece of meat look like perfection to me. My cock twitches and starts leaking pre-cum.

Tim notices and smiles. "Ready to join the Mile High Club, sexy?"

I nod my head. "Don't ask, just fuck me."

Then I pull him in for another kiss.

He grabs onto my dick and brings his own cock beside it, grinding them together. I let out a moan as I stumble again. But this time, he doesn't catch me, he comes down with me. He pulls my jeans and boxer briefs off my ankles, freeing my legs. He positions his knees inside my thighs, spreading my legs apart. His arms pin mine and I can't move. Not that I want to. His hard cock grinds into mine. My pre-cum is flowing. It lubes us up making the motion between us slick and smooth.

The pressure in my cock is hard to hold back. My muscles clench and I have a hard time breathing. I feel like I'm going to cum already. I need to slow this down. I don't want it to end just yet.

I grip Tim's shoulders and push him away from me gently. He takes the clue and climbs off. "What's the matter, baby?" I almost explode just from the sound of his warm, smooth voice.

I take a deep breath to try and get some control over my renegade cock. I look up at him and smile. "You've been servicing me all day. I figured I'd return the favor."

A shit-eating grin spreads across his lips. He lays back and props his head up in his hands, like he's caught in mid sit-up. His legs stretch and spread to give me better access to his glorious cock.

I crawl over him and inspect his hard rod. I don't touch it at first. I want to learn all I can about it before I do anything. It bounces, fully erect and pointing the ceiling. I inspect it closely. It juts straight with no curve. It's circumcised, the head is smooth and dark pink, shaped like a perfect mushroom. The shaft is darker under the head, the result of circumcision and the skin is tight. A thick purple vein runs on the underside from the base all the way to the tip. A single drop of pre-cum oozes out of his cockhead, down his shaft and onto his balls. Another drop spills down and is lost in his pubic hair.

My mouth is watering. I want to suck him off to slow down my desire, but it's only increasing with every second. My tongue darts out and wets the swollen knob. I savor his pre-cum. Tim inhales a sharp breath and holds it. I watch as his muscles start shaking. I feel a rush of satisfaction. Looks like I have some skills! I move the tip of my tongue all around his cockhead and lap up all of his fluid as it drips from his piss slit. He tastes sweet. I thoroughly wet the mushroom head and engulf his entire cock in my eager mouth. Tim lets out an intense, but muffled moan. Using my left hand, I start fondling his shaved balls. Tim throws his head back and moans again.

"Fuck, you're good at this."

I smile around the stiff meat in my mouth and suck even harder. He pushes me away from his groin and pushes me on the floor. His dark eyes look around the floor and he reaches over me to grab something out of his pants. When his hand pulls out of his pocket, I see a small tube of lube. I smile again. "Need that often?"

He shrugs. "One can hope."

Tim takes his place on top of me again, legs spreading my thighs. He looks down on me and shoots me a handsome smile as he fumbles with the lube. Then I feel a cold finger press against my tight hole. I gasp and lift my hips up to give him better access. I want to feel him inside of me, I want to feel my ass swallow his cock, I want to feel the pain.

His finger warms itself up by sliding around my sphincter until I can feel my muscle ring begin to pulse. He doesn't enter me right away. He teases me first as his finger massages outside my hole. I want it so bad. I'm whimpering now. Right when I think I can't take him toying with me anymore, he shoves his finger inside of me all the way to the knuckle.

I suck in my breath as he begins to stretch me out. It's been a little while since anybody's fucked me. Tim takes it slow. He knows how to open me up and it feels so good. Little by little his whole finger is in me. He slides it in and out. It moves easily as the lube coats my insides. I get just used to taking his index finger when he slides a second digit in.

I push my ass toward him, hoping to push the intruders deeper in my ass. Tim stops me with his other hand.

"Patience, little boy. Let me show you what an experienced man can do."

He massages the inside of my hole and my cock jumps. It feels so good. He's right. He is good. But that only makes me want his cock inside me more.

"Fuck me. Please, just fuck me."

Did I just say that out loud?

Tim laughs and pulls his fingers out of me.

"So eager! I like your enthusiasm."

When his fingers pull out of my ass, I'm left with an empty feeling. Tim grabs the lube and pours a few drops on his cock. He rubs it up and down his shaft. I love watching him do this, like I'm spying on him as he's alone and jerking himself off. But this time he's getting it ready to fuck me.

His knees spread my legs and he leans above me, supported on one arm. His other hand works his cock and guides the head into my hole. I feel something much thicker than a pair of fingers push into me. One more thrust and he's all in. I can't stop the bark that erupts from my mouth. It feels so fucking good.

I grab onto his shoulders. My fingers dig into his bare skin as he starts to slowly move in and out. He moves deliberately, but it's rough. He pulls his cock all the way out of me, teasing me before thrusting back in. I love being fucked by an older, experienced man. He knows what he's doing. I give myself over to him completely.

"Shit, fuck, son-of-a-fucking-bitch! You feel so good inside of me."

Tim gives me a cocky smile and laughs. I know I'm not the first boy he's fucked in the air. His expert cock pounds into me again and again. We stare into each others eyes, kissing occasionally. Tim is panting harder and harder as his fucks. My tight hole is driving him crazy.

His cock is hitting me in all the right places. I'm worried I'm going to cum. I cover my eyes with the palms of my hands and try to steady my breathing, but I can't ignore the amazing feeling in my ass or the handsome face looking down on me. I feel so full with him inside of me. I need to cum and I want to feel him cum inside of me.

I want to keep going forever, but I can't hold back much longer. It hurts in such a good way as he plunges through my ring of muscle as his balls slam against my ass cheeks. It's too much.

His legs spread my ass wider and his cock goes deeper in me. Oh, fuck. He starts moving faster and I can tell he's about to cum. His movements are less controlled, becoming more animalistic. He's getting rougher and I'm loving every fucking minute of it.

He starts stroking my uncut cock like he owns it. His gentle grip feels so good moving my foreskin up and down. He's fucking me so hard. So fast. Then he stops and lets out a quiet roar. I can feel the heat pour into my backside as his cock balloons and fills me with his seed. I feel it rushing inside me. It's all I can take and I shoot a huge load of spunk right into Tim's face. And another. It hits him hard. And tingle runs through my whole body as he squeezes the last bit of juice out of me and fucks his remaining nut into me.

He licks my jizz off his cheeks and chin.

"That's what I love about younger guys," he notes as he swallow my cum down.

He drops down on top of me. And I lick the remains of my cum off his face. He rolls off, laughing.

I sit up and immediately notice that my chest is also covered in my spooge. I grab my boxer briefs to clean off with, but Tim stops my hand.

"Don't."

He leans forward and licks my cum off of me. Every bit of it. I watch and it gets me real hard again.

"Thanks, kid," he says as he gives my foreskin a tug.

"Thanks for the first-class service." I give him a big kiss and we quickly dress. Tim leads me back up to the cabin and disappears before I reach my seat. I pass out before I can buckle my seatbelt.

***

I managed to sleep for the rest of trip and don't wake up until the plane touched down in Heathrow Airport. It's 10 AM and I feel rested and excited I grab my backpack out of the overhead and follow the line off the plane. Just as I reach the hatch, I catch Tim's eye once again. He gives me a sly smile. "Thank you. I hope you enjoyed your flight."

I smile back. "I'm already looking forward to the next one."

Before he can say anything, I'm out and heading toward the main terminal. I feel giddy as I take in my surroundings.

"Hellooo, London."

CHAPTER FOUR
STRIPPED BARE AND SEARCHED

I make my way through the busy airport to the Underground, checking out all of the guys around me. I do it at home all the time, but it's different here. These guys are different. They're less worked-out than the guys back home as a whole. But there's something casually fit about them. All those English guys I've fantasized about for so long: Andrew Garfield, Hugh Grant and Morrissey (in their prime), Prince Henry, Harry Potter, Harry Styles. These types are all around me. My dick stiffens as I drink them all in. If they knew what I was thinking, I'd probably get arrested for some British sex law. I can't help myself. All the guys look so foreign and I find that so hot.

But then I think: Wait! They're not foreign. I am. I'm the fucking foreigner here. So cool! Jake Parker, exotic foreigner! I like it.

As I move through the Londoners, I consider how all the guys around me are probably uncut like I am. Basically, I'm the only uncut guy I know back home. Except my dad, of course. And a few Latino guys I checked out in my high school locker room. I'm finally around my people! But I better focus on making it to my destination before I end up totally lost. There's time to be boy-crazy later. I adjust my backpack more comfortably on my shoulders and head for the nearest escalator.

I catch the underground from London Heathrow airport into the city. It's easy that way and I had it all planned out even before I arrived. I've become really good at planning. But then I know I better be more than good if I'm going to survive this summer!

After a quick tube ride (the call their subway "the tube" and I'm determined to fit in) I check into a youth hostel. This is going to do just fine for now. It's basic but kind of cheery. The common area has bright orange plastic chairs and accents among its sea of white. I make my way upstairs to find my room. I get a bunk bed in a room that fits six. I wonder what the other guys are going to be like. The newness of all of this gives me a rush. But I won't be spending much time in my room. I have a meeting soon. I also want to take in some of the city first chance I get.

I pull my travel bag out of my backpack and then stuff the backpack into my locker in the room. I head down the hall to the shower. Since it's a hostel, I get to share the shower with a few other guys who are staying there too. I hear a barrage of accents as we all exchange friendly smiles and versions of "hello" while we wash. Some of the guys are from around Europe and I spot an American. I can tell by his cut dick. But maybe he's Israeli. I won't know until I hear them talk. I notice a few of the guys giving me a glance or two. I return the courtesy and glance back. I love naked men on display!

There are a few different body types among the five of us in the shower. I love variety. I guess someday I'll settle down with one man, but right now it's the farthest thing from my mind. At this moment I'm using all my concentration to keep my uncut cock from raging upwards. I notice a guy across from me, a blond in his early twenties with lean muscles like a swimmer. His cock, even soft, hangs low down. His ballsack looks like it's carrying two rugby balls and swing proudly beneath his long shaft. His cock tip streamlines and tapers to the tip of his foreskin. Beautiful.

There's another guy to my left. He's black and built like an ox, but he has sensitive sleepy eyes. So hot! He seems totally unselfconscious about the thick monster on display between his thighs. He finishes washing and struts past where I'm showering. I get a closer glimpse of his muscular, firm round ass. The flesh there is milk chocolate-colored, like the rest of him, with a little fur scattered around. I swallow hard with repressed desire.

I look away quickly before the thoughts in my brain become a twitch in my cock. A time and place for everything, I remind myself as I summon inner strength. I hope I'll be getting some action one way or another during my stay in London. But it'll have to wait.

After a good cleaning and toweling off, I return to my room. I pull on the first pair of underwear I find in my bag, some loose black jeans and a white T-shirt. I'm set to head for my all-important meeting, my whole reason for being here. I take a deep, deep breath. I'm ready for this! I grab a look at my reflection in the mirror before I leave. It's the same me but I can't help wonder how I appear to others around me here. I've never been outside the United States before today. Is it obvious? Do I look out of place, different? Even if I do, do I seem exotic? There's something exciting being a fish out of water. I feel more open to possibilities that I ever did at home. I feel vulnerable in a way that gives me an edge. I feel excited. I remind myself that I'm the guy with the sexy accent here. I fucking love that! I leave my temporary new room and the hostel. I'm ready.

I start the short walk to my destination. I take in everything along the way: the people, the architecture, the flowers, the park, the men, the men's bulges, the butts on the men as they walk past me. Nothing gets by me. I come to a pretty nondescript building, a storefront with a "For Let" sign in the window. I pull a key out of my pocket and I look around carefully before using it.

This meeting, I know, will change everything for me. I feel my heart begin to pound faster as I open the door and walk into the structure. I make my way past empty retail space and into the storeroom in the back. It's very dusty and all abandoned-looking. Another victim of the crappy global economy? You'd think so.

But even the dust can't hide what I know to look out for. Just at the end of the corridor, there's a door. Beside it there's a keypad on the wall, like some outdated, forgotten security system. Or so you'd think. I memorized the 23-digit code weeks ago. I punch it in, getting it right on the first try. Awesome! Off to a good start, I think confidently. There will be time for congratulations later. There's work to do now.

The door slides open to reveal a concealed elevator. I get in and it heads down. Quickly. I brace myself to keep my balance. Nobody mentioned this to me. When the door opens seconds later, a large, underground room is revealed. It's a huge contrast from the shabby, neglected storefront above. My eyes widen at the hi-tech surroundings beyond the small lobby. Metallic walling and modern gadgets run along both sides of the room. People move through with focus and intensity. The best that science and technology have to offer is right here in front of me.

As I step out of the elevator, a few men begin walking my way. I count three of them, two at least six feet or taller. The third one is stocky, broad shouldered and strong-looking. They're dressed in all-black uniforms, their outfits obviously not your everyday wear: snug shirts made of something durable, patches on their right sleeve and dark pants tucked into darker laced boots. They're moving toward me quickly. I'm struck by their intimidating appearance, their hard bodies and their harsh, good-looking faces. Then I notice their weapons.

They're all armed. Machine guns? No. On closer inspection, I see that what they hold are top-of-the-line blasters using the latest laser and plasma technology. I'm glad now for all those hours I spent familiarizing myself with munitions. One blast from those guns could do some serious damage. They're power tools of the scariest kind. I've read about them, but I've never been around one. These guys don't fool around. I can tell from their expressions that they would easily take me out if they had to. They don't seem all that friendly.

Without a word, two of them firmly grasp my arms and lead me through one hallway after another while the tall one, the one with the mustache leads. There are desks in every office room we pass, always manned, always by uniformed men busy on their consoles. This wasn't the greeting I was expecting. Where are they taking me? My curiosity grows as we finally stop at the entrance of what looks like an interrogation room.

What the fuck? My hesitation is met with a little shove into the bare, white-walled room. The only furniture in view is a plain metal table and chair. I turn around to face the three men, their strong-looking faces give me no clue or comfort.

This isn't exactly how I thought things would go. I didn't expect the red carpet treatment, but I didn't guess there'd be this cool hostility. I feel my chin lift defensively as I face these large, tough men and try not to be intimidated by them, no matter how much their muscles bulge bigger than mine.

"Can you tell me what's going on? I'm *supposed* to be here," I inform them with calm firmness.

"We're well aware of that. Standard operation, Mr. Parker," the one in the middle coldly shoots back. The clipped tones of his British accent sound sharp in the sterile room. His thick, dark mustache hides any expression on his lips. He has the identical impassive look of the other three in his gray eyes, but a certain air of authority. He's the oldest of the three, likely in his early forties. I'm guessing that he's in charge of whatever's going on here.

"This is your first time here. We can't be too cautious," he says. "I'll have to ask you to strip down for us. Would you please do that now? "

I get that the "please" is just a courtesy. They aren't asking. Strip down? I thought I knew exactly how this was going to go. Where's my contact? Is this a test? Is this to keep me from being too comfortable? Has something gone wrong?

Am I in trouble?

With a quiet and deep sigh, I pull my white T-shirt over my head, pull off my shoes, unbuckle my belt and let my pants drop. I kick them off a few feet away as I stand in my white briefs and white socks. Fuck this underwear! I wish I wore something that made me look cooler and not just the pair of briefs my mom got me at JCPenney. They're white, store-brand Y-fronts with a dark blue and gold stripe around the waistband. So embarrassing! Maybe I should give a little more thought to what I wear under my pants. But then I didn't exactly expect to be put on display like this. Now I'm stuck here feeling, and looking, ridiculous. I really wanted to be cool about this whole thing. Yet here I am, three pairs of eyes looking at me like an insect beneath a microscope. Except insects never make the bad decision to wear stupid department store underwear bought by their insect moms. Lucky insects! Am I off to a bad start already?

"Strip all the way please, sir," one of the other armed men, the bald one, instructs.

Oh man! So much for worrying about my underwear choices. I try to play it cool as I shed the socks and chuck off the last bit of my modesty. Goodbye, JCPenney briefs! Hello, nakedness.

I see the guards glance down toward my middle and then raise their eyebrows. All three have slight smirks on their faces. What could break their Palace-guard stoniness? I look down and realize I have a semi. I'm beyond embarrassed right now. I suddenly miss those dorky briefs. Would I get shot if I tried to put them back on right now? Do most first days at work go like this?

Two of the security guys holster their weapons and tell me to lift my arms. There's something about their clinical, detached tone that makes my nudity seem all the more cruel and humiliating. Hearing those deep, rich voices with their English accents cause my dick to go completely stiff. Three men in uniform and me in nothing. I feel vulnerable and on display. But why am I so turned on? I try to think of world hunger, chemistry tests and John Boehner just to get my mind off the three large men viewing me in my birthday suit. Anything to make my boner go down. Grrr! Go away, boner!

The two well-built guards begin deeply and thoroughly inspecting every crevice of my body to make sure I'm not carrying any kind of weapon or recording device. They wear black fingerless leather gloves that feel smooth as they rub against my skin. None of this helps with my boner elimination efforts. Whoa! Does he need to go that deep up my ass?

The inspection continues without anyone mentioning my state of arousal. Thankfully. They finish, finally satisfied that I'm unarmed and unwired. Phew. But my relief is short-lived.

"We got ourselves a bloody healthy one here, mates, The brown-haired and stockier of the three comments. "Right fit."

I glance around to see that their formerly stern faces now have full-on smirks. The tall guy with the mustache suggests, "Looks like he might require a more thorough inspection."

Uh. What's that? What could be more thorough than the probing I just received. I don't suppose I could ask to speak to someone in HR?

I know I'm in deep shit when they all lock their guns in a cabinet. At least I know I'm not going to get shot. Then, before I can object, they're on me, all three of them this time. They're groping at me and once more, inspecting my body parts. But this is different from before.

"Hey, look guys…," I protest, trying desperately to keep from panicking. "I'm just here to do a job." But the pre-cum flowing out of my foreskin calls me out as a liar.

"Oh, we've got a job for you to do," says the stocky one, a leer on his broad, handsome face.

What the fuck? Are all British guys crazy? My heart is pounding in my ears, almost deafening me. The touch of their big, rough, gloved hands on my body sends a combo of arousal and adrenaline running through me. I feel more vulnerable than ever as the bald guy pins my arms from behind and the other two poke and prod, squeezing my nipples, spreading my legs and fingering my foreskin. They roll me to the ground. The floor is cold on my back. The moment I feel one of them grab my cock, I jerk violently. I'm so turned on. I feel like I should resist, but my cock is fighting my brain on this.

The mustache-man says, "Nothing in his bits except some slippery boy-juice. All good here, men."

The other two laugh. Is this funny to them? I'd be so fucking mad if I wasn't so fucking turned on! Another of them, the one with the shaved head and lean body, twists my torso, taking hold of my butt cheeks and wedges them wide. "Nothing in his arse. Yet."

What? Safe to assume this routine inspection is over and there's something else going on here. Just what have I got myself into? I'm confused yet insanely aroused. "Look guys…Wait!" I exclaim, again trying to object as I think I should. But I'm beyond petrified about how much harder I've become since the unexpected "attack" began. How can I be enjoying this? I have to be pretty fucked up to want this, right? But I do. I want it bad.

"On your knees, mate," I hear one say as all three stand. His tone is authoritative, brooking no argument. They're surrounding me, hands reaching for their zippers. With the sound of those metal teeth opening, I feel a shiver run through my naked frame. Should I object again? What's the point when my cock broadcasts how much of a willing participant I really am? They don't undress. Instead they just pull their cocks out. Otherwise, they remain clothed in their uniforms. It's just me naked. They stand in front of me, a blur of cock-stroking and leering, sweaty faces.

"Can we talk about this?" I ask unconvincingly, one last attempt at being the good boy even as I'm lifted to a kneeling position. Suddenly, seven-and-a-half-inch, thickish, uncut British cock is in my face. *My first foreign dick!* It's the mustache guy. The team leader gets the first crack at me. The dude has lots of coarse, wiry, black pubic hair to match his mustache. Part of me is relieved that I don't have to keep going with my half-assed objections. My lips instinctively wrap around the invading, musk-sweet pole. Mmmmmm. I just realized I love the taste of English cock. He gets even sweatier as he continues to fuck my face. The smell makes my head swim.

These guys are all imposing, even the one who's on the shorter side, obviously the youngest of the three, maybe late twenties. He's on my right, burly and broad shouldered. His brown hair is swept to the side. His strong, furry right arm flexes as he strokes his wide and imposing cock from the base, letting his thin foreskin do the work.

The third one is completely bald and totally hot. He reminds me of the guy in those "Transporter" movies. I place him somewhere in his middle-thirties. His cock is an uncut monster. It's not as thick as the other two but very long. And it's completely hairless. I wonder if his whole body is smooth. He slaps his cock against my face from my left while his large hands run through my hair and guide my sucking on his commander's cock.

"Nice," Commander Mustache observes. He rubs the side of my face. "Skin like a baby's. Soft and warm. I bet you'll be soft and warm deep inside, too." I imagine his cock out of my mouth and up my ass. The pre-cum drips faster from my own member. How much of this stuff can I possibly have in me? Am I going to dehydrate if this keeps up?

I look up through all the cock and see their faces. They look tough, like they've been battle-tested. They're the kind of guys I'd want to have my back if I was ever in trouble. Now I'm thinking they may have my backside instead. They're rough with me. I'd be surprised if they weren't. I guess it goes with the job. Or they want to teach the new American kid his place. My stiff boner and my eager cocksucking make it clear that I'm all in. My throbbing dick keeps spilling its slick pre-ejaculate, forming a puddle on the floor. There's no hiding how aroused I am. I'm way past the point of trying to pretend I want this to stop.

I give into my hunger and focus on the cock being shoved in my mouth. I breath in the sweat from the older man's dark, unshaved pubes as they bash into my face. I breathe deep and I get high from the smell. I grip his upper legs for balance. If this guy wants his cock sucked, I'm going to show him what an American cocksucker can do. I glance up and see how turned on he is. His eyes are clenched shut. I'm guessing he's struggling not to cum.

My mustached man pulls out with a chuckle, and says, "All right, Hamm. Have a go."

The shorter one with the stocky build lines his cock straight with my lips. He doesn't waste any time, slamming his cock into my waiting mouth. He lets out a manly purr as I take his whole schlong in my mouth. It's not easy. His dick may not be as long as the other two, but it's challengingly thick and wide. His soft brown pubes tickle my face while his fingers in my hair are brutal. His grunts fill the room as he shoves me onto his broad shaft again and again.

He tugs at my hair harder and my scalp wants to scream. I'd say, "Watch the hair, man!" if my mouth wasn't stretched to its limit. I gag as his thick, hooded dick jams deep into my mouth. My eyes sting with sweat. My body floods with sensation. The other two are down with their hands exploring my body. Fingers jab into my ass, making me want to squeal. But it's not going to happen with this chunky pole in my mouth. Whose hand is that? It doesn't even matter any more. There are hands everywhere and the constant touch sends me to a higher level of pleasure than I've felt before. I feel my dick being stroked by a leather gloved hand. What a feeling!

Hamm's banger throbs as my tongue wraps around the bulbous head under his foreskin. I feel his cock getting even bigger and warmer. Looks like this guy is going to be first across the finish line. I savor the taste of his flesh, allowing my nose to get rammed into his patch of chestnut pubes as he pumps his hips quicker and quicker into my mouth. He's so close. His grunts grow louder with mumbled declarations of pleasure too hard to make out. I twist my head to work every surface of his too-thick cock with my mouth. His body starts to rock and with a great, sudden roar, he begins to pump load after load of cum down my willing, hungry throat. My first taste of Brit jizz is delicious.

"How's that for a welcome-to-London, boy?" Hamm mutters with a small grin, pulling his husky pipe out as I wipe an errant trail of cum off my chin. I don't get a chance to reply to his rhetorical question before I'm grabbed under the armpits by the other two and placed on my back, on top of the long metal table. It's cold.

The mustached dude indicates for the bald guy to move toward my head. "How's about you have a crack at him, Jasper?"

"I'd say it was doable," Jasper replies, nodding his rugged, smooth head. "You're always full of the right ideas, Will."

Jasper approaches me from the side of the table. I'm face-to-face with his uncut dick, his cockhead barely poking out of the tight foreskin and staring at me like an eye. It's not a particularly thick cock, but probably eight-and-a-half-inches long. Yikes! As I see the long pipe bobbing so close to my nose, my mouth waters. I still have the taste of Hamm's first load on my tongue. I'm hungry for more.

"Yeah, suck that knob," Jasper pants. I do as I'm told. "Feels fucking brilliant!"

I think so, too. I feel completely submissive and at the mercy of his lengthy cock. I suck him like I'm starving. I shudder all over, wanting to savor every moment of this. I let Jasper's oversized prong rub the back of my throat, clamping my aching mouth around his dickhead when he pulls back, working his foreskin with my mouth.

As I service Jasper, I feel my cock and ass being explored by unseen hands. I don't know if it's Will or Hamm or both. My face is full of smooth crotch and cock. I close my eyes and just *experience*. A fist pumps up and down on my foreskin, jerking me hard. My balls are cupped and pulled. I breathe and focus on not shooting my load. I'm on the edge and I like it there.

I'm still slurping Jasper's wood when someone positions himself between my open legs. I can feel my ankles being grabbed from where they dangle over the edge of the table and spread wide. Someone just stuck a wet finger up my hole. Then two. I moan, my throat constricting around Jasper's cock.

I hear someone say, "Fucking tight arse on this one."

I love the way he says it. I've never heard my asshole complemented with an English accent. I think it's Will taking charge again. I try to struggle and get my legs free from Will's grip, just because it seems like I should try to resist. But there's no point. He's too strong and I want him too bad. He shoves my legs as high back as they can go, his fingers tight around my ankles. I know what's coming and I try to relax as much as is humanly possible. I feel the head of a cock brush against my exposed butthole. Then, without warning, he spears me. Just like that, a hard cock is forcefully pushed up into me. My body stiffens, electrified by that first thrust that sends Will balls-deep into me. My eyes bulge. I cry out, unable to help it, but the sound is muffled by the long cock fucking my face.

My feet are high up on Will's shoulders now. I feel wide open to him as his cock continues to invade deeper in my hole. Through the side of my eye, I see him giving me a little smile. "That's right, Parker. Show us what an American lad is made of. My fat cock is going to open you wide. Take it as a compliment, boy."

I can't reply. Even if my mouth wasn't full of cock, I think I'm in too much pain to say anything anyway. Will must be almost eight inches and he's very thick. He's not the longest or the thickest of the guys, but he's got enough of both to challenge my aching asshole. I feel the mustached man's throbbing lump of flesh filling up my hole, pushing, pushing, pushing forward inside me. *What the fuck, it hurts like hell!* But beneath the pain is a deep, driving pleasure that intensifies as he pushes deeper inside me. I wasn't expecting the intrusion but the sting from the entry soon starts to ease. Not that he's gentle, far from it, but he's lubed up good and his cock slides easily inside me. It feels nice to be fucked by an uncut dick. I like how it slides in and out of its sheathing while inside me.

"Damn, that's a tight, fit arse," Will growls through his mustache. I'm now certain he's the one in charge of this security team. He's been guiding this fuckfest from the beginning. It's probably why he's the one who gets to have his way with my ass.

He fills my body so completely with each thrust. It feels so good even though it feels like I'm being split in two. Jasper continues to pound my mouth. Hamm has stopped stroking me for the moment, but my foreskin glides over my moist cockhead as it bounces with each slam of Will's cock. It feels like my every nerve ending is on fire. There's a powerful surge in my balls and I try to concentrate on holding it back. I don't know how much longer I can contain my load.

I've had fantasies like this but I didn't even imagine how good being in the center of a boy-bang like this could be! My mouth! My ass! My cock! I'm experiencing so much at once. These guys are pushing my body to its limits and I never want it to stop.

Keeping my cock from exploding feels more and more impossible with Jasper aggressively feeding my face. My lips never release his cock as my hands wrap around the inches at the base. Now I have both hands around his long cock. I reach my tongue out and lick on his cockhead, the foreskin draws back every time I pump downwards on his shaft with my fingers. I watch his pointy cock tip appear and disappear inside its fleshy hood until, with a grunt, he shoves his cock impatiently past my lips.

"Just suck it, mate" he growls, holding both sides of my head as his hips thrust into my face. I oblige him as much as I can, but the sheer length of his pecker... I've never had such a long tool in my mouth. And my lips already ache from being stretched out by the girth of Hamm's cock. Even trying my damnedest, I can't quite get all of him into my mouth.

Will's cock feels fantastic inside me now that I've re-laxed more and I'm a bit loosened up. It darts rapidly in and out of me. The hot pleasure-pain of his fuck is making my muscles constrict around his shaft. He isn't going to last much longer, not at that jackrabbit speed. I can feel his dick start to pulse inside me. My sphinc-ter clenches around his fleshy tube. I feel his cock swell more, getting even thicker as it throbs. He's panting hard and lets out a little whistle as he breathes through clenched teeth. He grips my hips so tight and his thick fingers dig in. My lower half bucks while my lips are tightly wrapped around Jasper's cock. I focus to keep from biting his dick as my ass is pounded by Will's bru-tal fucking. My whole body vibrates with his spasms. He's about to shoot his spunk deep inside me. His body jerks and releases a powerful stream of cum, filling me with it's warmth. It feels like it's never going to stop!

My ass drinks in all Will has to give as Jasper fucks my face harder. As he watches his superior unload his final blasts of sperm in me, his own cock moves faster in and out of my mouth. He grips my hair and controls the movement of my head. My mouth waters thinking about his load. I open wide for Jasper's nearly-nine incher, and I'm rewarded with a hard slam into my mouth. He explodes as Will pounds his last drops up my hole. My cheeks widen to accommodate Jasper's huge release of salty spooge. For a second I think I may choke, but I don't. I swallow it all up in three gulps. My own dick is on fire, ready to explode.

"He's been such a good sport, hasn't he?" Hamm teases, his hand starting to jerk on my cock again, thumbing the pre-cum seeping from my piss slit. My hips buck into his hand. I'm still sucking mindlessly on Jasper's dick, not wanting to miss a drop of his tasty cum.

Will's cock pulls out of my hole but it feels like he's still in me. I feel his cum slowly run out of my hole. He's left me so full. Jasper withdraws from my lips, satisfied that I've swallowed every last drop of his jizz. I look around at these men, spent and satisfied. Rugged faces. Intimidating bodies. The last drops of cum dripping from each of their cocks, each of their loads shot into my hungry mouth and ass. I see Hamm's gloved hand bobbing up and down my shaft. He pulls my foreskin all the way back and then all the way up. All eyes are on my cock. With Hamm's single stroke, all the spunk I've been holding back this whole time finally floods to the surface. My whole body tingles and my face feels warm. I go off like a roman candle. I howl as I climax, my orgasm hitting me like a freight train. It goes on for a full minute. My jizz shoots straight up and falls in large drops all over me. It even hits the guys. I see them wiping cum off their faces and off their uniforms. My little revenge, small as it might be.

I feel Hamm scoop up fingers full of my spooge from my tight stomach, bring it to my lips and feed it to me.

It mixes with Jasper's load in my mouth and I swallow it all down. Then he feeds me more.

They help me stand and instruct me to get dressed. I think I'm going to be feeling Will's cock up my ass for a few days, like a phantom limb or something. As I pull my dorky briefs up, I think to myself no one mentions how my cock is bigger than any of theirs. I realize how little that matters. I was happy to give myself to them. I guess their experience trumps my inches.

I'm surprised that once clothed, I get a handshake or two, some pats on the back and even a hug here and there. I guess this is finally the welcome I was waiting for. Then Will's large hand falls on my shoulder.

"If you ever need anything, you call on us," the bossman declares with a mustachioed grin. "We're your brothers now."

I like the sound of that. I love feeling accepted as much as I love the lingering, salty taste of their cum in my mouth.

"He'll be in to see you shortly, Jake."

They're calling me by my first name now! I made it through their crazy initiation and now they see me as one of them.

The guys leave me alone, and I sit gently on the chair, feeling the aftermath of my ass workout. I'm slightly nervous and very excited by what's to come. Playtime is over and it's time to get to work.

CHAPTER FIVE
NAKED BEFORE DESTINY

I sit alone, waiting in this sterile room. I should be spent after the workout I just got, but I have enough adrenaline flowing through me and keeping me wired. I still have the taste of foreign cock, well cocks, in my mouth. Damn, they're not foreign. *I'm* foreign here. If I don't remember that, I'm going to come off just like another stereotypical ugly American. That's the last thing I want.

I think I'm really going to enjoy my time here at The Agency. It's not just the surprise gang-bang. I'm genuinely excited about what's to come. It's not going to be easy, but I know I have what it takes to get the job done. Right now, I just have to get through this next meeting. I've heard so much about this guy, mostly about what a hard-ass he is.

I look around and realize that multiple cameras are monitoring the room. They're tiny. That's why I didn't notice them before. Oh, man! How many people were watching me get plowed? There are no mirrors in the room, but I'm pretty sure I'm red from head to toe right now. I just hope that if anyone was watching that I gave them a good show.

I shouldn't have missed the cameras before. Sure, those three security guys didn't give me much of a chance to think, but that's exactly what I'll need to be doing if I hope to stay alive. Gotta keep the skills sharp. I stand up and do a 360 assessment of the room. I realize that all my months of training are definitely paying off. Not only has it firmed up my lean body, but it's made my mind that much sharper. I pinpoint the weaknesses in the set up here. If I really wanted to leave, I could prob-ably disarm the cameras in less than a minute. But then, I'm not sure how far I'd get. These guys taught me ev-erything I know. I'm sure they have contingencies. Any-way, I can't think of anywhere I'd rather be right now.

I hear the door open and a buff older guy enters through it. He's attractive and reeks of confidence. He introduces himself as Colonel Jason Anger and shakes my hand. But I already know who he is.

"Have a seat, Parker."

Somebody brings in a chair for him and he joins me at the table where I was naked on my back just seven minutes ago. Colonel Anger informs me that he's in charge of the young recruits division for The Agency, the Shades. I'm certain he knows that I'm aware of this. I guess it's a formality. The colonel seems like a very formal guy. His clothes are similar to the security guys I just met, but he has long sleeves and no gloves. He looks put together and rugged at the same time. He speaks softly but firmly as he instructs me to pay close attention to everything he says. I take in his deep British accent and I feel my cock twitch, as I start to think of some boss-employee fantasies that I'd like to fulfill with him. I discreetly admire the broad shoulders and barrel shaped chest that fill his tight uniform. I wonder how the dark stubble would feel while he was kissing me. I notice how his military-short brown hair is just starting to show hints of gray and how his stern face shows years of experience. I can only imagine where this man has been and what he's done.

"Do you understand me, Parker?" he barks.

I totally missed what he was saying but I respond anyway.

"Yes, sir!"

This is definitely a bad time to get all boy-crazy. I quickly see why he's the colonel and I'm just a recruit. This guy could scare a Texas death row inmate. I know I gotta focus, but this guy is really sexy. I let my cock know that he's had his time in the sun today and now my brain has got to be in charge for a while. I want to please Colonel Anger and not just in a sexual way. I have to earn his respect. I want him to know I can be one of the top young recruits, one of the best Shades.

"I hope the security team didn't shake you up too much," he says, not giving me a clue if he knows what just happened in here.

But he must. I'm sure nothing gets past this guy. He's seeing how I'll react. He's sizing me up.

"I wasn't expecting to be detained or searched, but I understand the need to be careful, sir." I don't show any signs of weakness or embarrassment. I'm perfectly cool.

"The security team are dedicated agents who have risked their lives dozens of times and they'd give their lives without asking why if called to do so," the colonel informs me. "They work hard and they play hard. I let them blow off steam when appropriate, show them that they're appreciated. They deserve it. I hope your experience wasn't uncomfortable. You're going to be one of us now."

Going to be? Despite everything I went through back in Texas, the colonel doesn't fully see me as one of them. I feel like I've proven how serious I am already. I did everything required of me and I did it better than just about anybody else. I'll never forget that crazy day in Texas that changed my life. It's hard to believe it wasn't even six months ago.

I was walking out of school, just having bombed at a surprise math quiz. My Advanced Quantitative Reasoning teacher, Mr. Brown, didn't believe in letting us relax just because senior year was half over. I didn't end up failing or anything, but I knew I could have done better. College was on my mind and I was feeling the pressure. To get my mind off of school, I was planning on going home and beating off until my dick went numb. There's no better stress-relief. My parents had just bought me a new laptop three weeks before for my birthday. It had a 15.5-inch screen and it looked sharp. I had already spent way too much time searching for vintage gay porn. I probably should have been doing more Advanced Quantitative Reasoning and less Michael Lucas Fire Island videos.

As I was walking, I noticed a handsome guy wearing a dark suit approaching me at a deliberate pace. I bit my lower lip in anticipation of what he might ask me. It was looking like I might not be jerking off alone that afternoon. I was in shock, when his first words to me weren't "Let's hook up," but "Do you want to make the world a better place and do things most of these assholes will only ever dream about?"

"What're you talking about?" I wondered if he might be crazy.

"Come with me," he said.

I hesitated and looked around the schoolyard. I noticed that nobody would see me go off with this stranger. I figured this had it's pluses and minuses. If I'd never been seen again, nobody would have known why. They probably would have figured that I freaked out about some pop quiz and offed myself, another tightly-wound teen tragically gone before his time. But if anybody did see me go off with this handsome guy, they probably would have assumed it was some Grindr hook up that went bad. I wondered if I was too old to yell "stranger danger."

Curiosity got the best of me. I decided that I might as well see what's up. I grabbed my bike from the racks and followed him. He took me down a back alley to a waiting black van. I had visions of this being one of those bang-porno vans and I'd end up naked and bukakked all over for everyone to see on the Internet. I was also calculating the odds of this handsome guy going all *Dexter* on me and chopping me to bits. Still, I let him take my bike and he tossed it in the back. He guided me into the passenger seat and I willingly jumped in. My sense of adventure overruled my caution. He started the van and we took off.

He knew so much about me. He asked about both my parents by name and mentioned some specific events in my life. Creepy! I wondered if I had a stalker, which would have been kind of flattering.) Or was this all some crazy dream. I kept glancing down to see if I was wearing clothes still. If all of a sudden, I'd been naked and surrounded by the high school basketball team, I would have known that this was just another one of my vivid wet dreams. But it was very real.

The handsome stranger eventually made a left and turned into an industrial park not far from my school. We parked in the back of some nondescript complex. He hopped out of the van and so I followed. He walked me up to the door. He didn't say a thing, but as his suit jacket pulled I noticed his pecs looked pretty nice in his fitted shirt. He opened the door that had "Merrick Insurance Agency" lettered on the glass.

"Oh fuck. Are you gonna try to sell me insurance?"

He almost laughed but then caught himself. "Don't worry, Jake. This is *much* better."

As we walked through the entrance I saw a number of people working. My eyes adjusted to the annoying fluorescent lights that lazily illuminated the blandness of the space. There were a number of small cubicles and everyone seemed to be working, absorbed into the monitors in front of them. I pinched myself hard to check that I wasn't living out my worst nightmare. I didn't have any desire to end up in a job like this and I started to question my decision to follow this guy. He planned on changing my life with career in the insurance industry? Fuck that!

The handsome stranger escorted me through a maze of mindless cubicle drones and into a store room. It was private. I figured I'd come this far. Maybe I'd get a blowjob out of this. We went through the back door of the storeroom to another series of offices that looked a bit nicer. He opened one of the doors and told me to take a seat in front a fake wood desk. He took his place behind the desk, removed his suit jacket, sat down behind a keyboard and started tapping away. My curiosity went into overdrive.

A door opened and another stranger entered, looking similar to first guy: handsome, middle twenties, short hair and kind of all-American. He was also wearing a white long-sleeve shirt and a disarming smile on his face. It hit me at that moment that I wasn't there for any kind of insurance. I figured these guys as Mormons who were going to try and convert me. I frantically looked around the room for a window to jump out of.

The new guy sat on the edge of the desk, looked me right in the eyes and said, "Jake, we want to offer you a job."

"As a Mormon?" I asked with confusion and repulsion. "How do you know my name? You said I could make the world a better place. How? By passing out books of crazy door-to-door? I'm not looking for any work. But thanks. I'm going to college in the fall to study computer science. You can keep your homophobic superstitions and fairy tales. I don't think I'm what you're looking for."

He leaned even closer to me and said, "You're exactly what we're looking for."

His tone turned a bit seductive. I got a little flush in the face. It's not often I'm caught off guard, but I wasn't used to getting propositioned by Mormon guys in the back of an insurance agency.

"Oh, wait! You guys want to fuck me?"

The original stranger seated behind the desk ignored my question. Instead, he started explaining everything to me and assured me they weren't Mormons. He told me how the two of them are in charge of recruiting the best and brightest young people from around Texas and the South. He explained how they're specifically targeting young men and women who have a certain potential for greatness in them.

I interrupted and explained that there was really nothing all that special about me. Sure, I got good grades, but I wasn't like I was going to be valedictorian. They both laughed. The guy behind the desk explained that they know all about me and my 3.8 grade point average. Then they assured me that I am exceptional and that I would succeed in this position.

I found myself rolling my shoulders back and sitting a little bit higher in my chair. My ego inflated at their suggestion that I could be a part of something that only the elite few are part of. But I still didn't know what it was they were talking about. I looked at both of their firm, lean bodies and started to feel that I'd likely do anything for them. They were cute and I was horny. I was feeling open for anything. I crossed my legs to hide the growing erection in my jeans and the guys pulled out... paperwork.

I had to know what it was that I'd been chosen for, so I scribbled my signature at the bottom of the confidentiality form and I finally got some answers. The two of them explained together that they work for an inter-governmental peacekeeping agency. This agency is responsible for taking care of threats that individual governments are unable to deal with on their own. They also have the autonomy to handle threats that many countries aren't even aware exist. They told me all about their young recruits division that they want me to join.

"The members of the young recruits in The Agency are called Shades. Like the disembodied spirits they get their name from, they're able to walk into dangerous situations without drawing attention. You'd be sent places where more seasoned agents couldn't blend in effectively. It would mean intensive training for six months and, if successful, you'll be taking on you first mission come summer."

They told me that I'd be paid well if I passed training and was selected, and that I'd have access to tech that very few in the world have ever used or even heard of. They also told me I'd be a part of making the world safer for my family and friends. I was so excited by what I was hearing. This is some major shit and they want *me*!

With very serious looks, they explained that by agreeing to join The Agency that I couldn't tell anybody about it. Not my family. Not my friends. Not even any future boyfriends.

"Not even my parents?" I asked.

"No! No one."

They told me that if I did, there would be serious repercussions. I would immediately fail the training. They might even take drastic steps to discredit me, even making me look insane and having me committed.

"This is serious, Jake. We don't mean to be harsh but it's important for you to understand what we're telling you. There are lives at stake, brave men and women who risk their lives to make the world just a little safer. We're sure you can understand the situation."

I gave them a nod to let them know I got what they were telling me. "I'm in. Let's do this!"

They both grinned and shook my hand. "Welcome to the program, trainee. We'll contact you with more details soon."

They lead me out of the office, back through the storeroom and through the large crowd of worker bees, and dropped me back off at school. As I rode my bike home, I wondered if that all really happened. I figured I was either crazy or about to start the most incredible adventure ever.

A few weeks later, I got a text to meet back at the fake insurance agency. I hopped on my bike and pedaled faster than I ever had before. When I arrived, I saw a group of guys waiting in the storeroom. Some I knew attended other nearby high schools. I'd seen them at basketball games or Academic Decathlon tournaments. Other guys there were slightly older and completely unfamiliar. We all seemed to be in the roughly eighteen to twenty-four range. I counted around seventeen guys altogether.

After orientation, the days quickly started to blur into one another. Every day, I'd have to keep up with school and lie to my parents about where I was spending my after-class time. This lasted right up until the last week of high school. I was living a double-life and it was exciting! In training, we'd learn about the history of "The Agency," as it was called. It doesn't actually have a name. It's completely secret and off the books. We had training in intelligence-gathering technology, learned about some potential threats facing the free world and trained in the basics of fighting. We were warned never to completely rely on technology in the field. We'd need to know to handle ourselves in a fight. Machines fail and we were constantly reminded that our greatest weapons are our minds and bodies.

The guys all trained together and female recruits were in a completely different location. I love women as friends, but I really loved the idea of going through this intense experience around so much male energy. Especially when the physical training began. We had an accomplished fight instructor named Todd who pushed us all hard. He made my basketball training seem like a cake decorating class. He was definitely the toughest of the instructors there, but I knew that's what I needed if I was going to make it through training and into the final phase. There was no way I was going to get cut.

Some of the other guys groaned at the idea of having their first fight. I was excited about getting to interact physically with some of the hot bodies in the room. I was stoked as I found myself stripped down to a pair of tight running shorts and standing in front of Cole. Cole, a fellow recruit, was taller than me and also from Texas. Unlike me, he had a strong Southern accent. He was in his first year of college and had shaggy blond hair and darker blond fur on his chest. We were both getting results from our physical training, crazy cardio sessions and an insane amount of push-ups and sit-ups. My body was starting to fill out a bit from the exercises, without losing it's leanness. It had given me a boost of self-confidence too. Cole had come into the program with a classic football-player body. At this point, he was looking even stronger and bulkier. It looked good on him. He was my first opponent in fight training. I couldn't wait to see how my leaner twink frame would do against his bulkier physique. I was also curious how I'd do against someone who outweighed me so much. As I faced him on the mat I watched as a trickle of sweat made it way from his neck, down between his pecs and then slowly down each one of his defined abs before it disappeared past the waistband of his shorts. The whistle blew and he came at me like a bull.

He had the strength, but I had the agility to outmaneuver him. I crouched down, knowing that I'd have to use my brains and speed to beat him. We'd been told time and again that it's the split-second decisions that win the fight. I easily blocked his attempt to nail me with his right hook. I responded with a swift kick that knocked him off balance. I followed that up with a few quick jabs into his left kidneys. He recovered quickly and came right at me again. I suspected that he'd try to pin me and I did my best to hold my ground. He surprised me with a head butt. Then I felt his full weight on top of me. He easily pinned me to the ground.

I struggled to find a way to escape. I tried to pinch a pressure point on his body, but he slammed my hands to the mat. I felt his hot breath on my neck and I tensed up knowing that my cock was starting to grow. He flinched and got a weird look on his face. I knew that I had my chance to knock him off of me, but I wanted to see how he would respond. He ground his body closer into mine. He made it look like he was just pinning his opponent further down, but he was really pushing his now-hard cock into mine.

His weight on top of me made it hard for me to breathe, but I didn't really care. All I could think about was licking the sweat off of Cole's body from head to toe and all the furry parts in between. Our eyes connected and I saw that his lust was as strong as mine. A whistle blew and we stayed in contact for a few seconds longer than necessary. We both rolled over, did our best to hide our erections and moved on to our next matches. We continued to make eye contact with one another throughout the training session.

During one of our scheduled breaks, Cole caught my eye and nodded toward the exit. I got the signal and discreetly left our assigned training space right after him. I followed as he kept walking. He seemed to be ignoring that I was behind him. Suddenly, he disappeared to his right. I jogged to catch up and noticed he'd entered a side room. I looked behind me to see if anybody had followed us and quickly entered the room.

It was dark and I didn't see Cole anywhere, but I heard the sounds of stroking. I followed the noise and saw Cole sitting behind some boxes completely naked. I raced to him and our lips connected. I kissed him as intensely as I could and I felt his hand guide mine down to his rock-hard cock. I stroked the shaft slowly, amazed by its girth. His chunky cock was the perfect accessory for his thick frame. I struggled to wrap my hand around it. He broke our kiss and looked down. He squeezed the tip of his mushroom cockhead and let the pre-cum ooze out as he exhaled with pleasure. He scooped it up with his finger and rubbed it along my lips. He pulled me close and our mouths connected, wet with his salty fluid.

I placed a second hand around his cock and began to double-pump it up and down. I broke the kiss and licked the sweat from his neck. He moaned loudly and I licked down to his shoulder. I moved my mouth away and blew cool air on the wet trail. His whole body shivered. I loved how sensitive he was to my touch. I steadied myself with my right hand and kept stroking with the left as I leaned forward to suck and lick on his nipples.

"Just like that, Jake," he instructed.

I licked down his body and noticed that he was starting to buck his hips. I could tell that he was eager for me to take his rod down my throat. I licked all the way down his bulbous head to his shaft and then straight for his furry balls. I sucked, kissed and licked them as I inhaled his musky scent. I was eager to fuck his hopefully-tight hole, but wanted to focus on pleasuring his cock first. I teasingly licked from his balls all the way up to his shaft and back down. As my tongue moved back up to the tip, he held me in place. I looked up and I could see the pleading look in his eyes. This guy wanted something and I was happy to deliver.

He surprised me by pulling me up from his groin. We kissed briefly and then he pushed me back to sit on the floor. I hoped that he would relieve me of my tight shorts and liberate my rock-hard, uncut cock. Instead, he pulled my right leg up. He removed the shoe from my foot, stuck his nose in it, inhaled and tossed it aside. He pulled my sweaty, sock-covered foot toward his face and started to suck on it. He kept at it for a few minutes. I was a little taken aback, but definitely turned on. I'd never had someone pay attention to my feet before.

He ripped off my sock and began sucking on each toe. I couldn't believe how much this was turning him on. I've done a few things in my eighteen years, but definitely not this. He looked up at me and gave me a wide grin. It's like he knew that this was my foot's first time and it thrilled him to be taking its virginity. He went through the same routine as he removed my left shoe. He pulled the sock-covered foot toward him, sucked, removed the sock and licked my other five toes. Then he moved my moist feet toward his cock and guided me to jerk him off between my feet. While my feet were enjoying their first cock, Cole leaned forward to finally remove my shorts and free my eager boner.

"Harrumph."

We both jumped up at the sound of a throat loudly clearing itself behind us. Due to the lack of light, neither of us could tell who was approaching. Cole quickly reached around to grab his shorts to cover up. I found mine and used them to try to hide my erection. Our hearts were both pounding so hard. Boom! Boom! Boom! We heard a few steps before we finally saw who the intruder was. It was our fight trainer, Todd.

"Stand at attention, trainees," Todd barked angrily.

I got myself up off the floor, shorts barely covering my hard dick. Cole who had been struggling to put on his shorts, dropped them, and stood beside me. Todd walked toward us and I felt desperately intimidated and fearful about how we'd be punished for leaving training. A former Shade himself, Todd was in his late twenties and had been training recruits for years. He stressed discipline and never tolerated anyone slacking off. I cursed myself for stupidly leaving training and wondered if I'd be kicked out.

"Trainees, you have disrespected me, my colleagues and the other young men in that training room. I will ask you one simple question and you will answer it: Why?"

I tried to speak but Cole beat me to it.

"It's my fault. I…"

Todd interrupts, "I believe you meant to say 'It's my fault, *sir*.'"

Then Todd slapped him across the face. Hard! Cole was stunned, but regained control.

"It's my fault, *sir*. These workouts get me all horned up, sir. I'm really attracted to Trainee Jake, sir."

I felt myself blushing and turned to look at Cole. What an idiot. What a totally awesome idiot! I also noticed that his cock was harder than ever. He just got a hand across his face and his dick was standing at full attention.

"Eyes forward, recruits," Todd barked.

He came close and walked behind us. I could feel his breath on my neck and it was starting to turn me on. Over the past few week I'd got myself off thinking about most of the other recruits and definitely the trainers too. Todd had several starring roles in my nighttime fantasies, many revolving around his hot bubble ass. He wasn't as tall as Cole or I, but his body was flawless.

I was shocked by the feel of a hand on my ass and I dropped my shorts. Then the hand began to rub my ass.

Todd whispered in my ear, "You ever been fucked, trainee?"

I was stunned. "Yes, sir. Actually, recently with my coach..."

"I wasn't asking for your autobiography, Parker."

"No, sir. Yes, sir," I babbled nervously.

Using his years of training, Todd had me on all fours in a fraction of a second with my ass in the air. He spit on my exposed fuckhole and began licking it ferociously. I looked back and saw that Todd's arm was out, stroking Cole's thick cock. Cole's bulged eyes connected with mine and we both gave each other shocked looks. This was so much better than getting in trouble! I focused back on the intense pleasure I was feeling from Todd rimming me. I wanted to reach down and stroke my throbbing uncut cock, but knew that I would shoot my load right away.

"Get over there, trainee, and feed Parker your cock," Todd ordered to Cole.

Cole walked up to me and pointed his crotch right in my face. What else could he do? I wasted no time and filled my mouth with his beefy meat. I struggled with his huge mushroom head, but managed to take it all in once I relaxed a little. This was by far one of the hottest moments in my life and I wanted every millimeter of that massive cockhead. Todd pulled his face out of my hole and I heard him walking away. Then I heard him unzipping his backpack.

"Dude, you've got lube in there! You gonna fuck Parker?" Cole asked.

I heard a smack and saw that Cole's face was red. Todd backhanded Cole even harder than before. I figured this wasn't going to be a friendly fuck.

Todd sternly replied, "You forgot to say 'sir' and you don't ask the questions, trainee. You're lucky I don't turn you in right now, 'dude.'"

I felt sorry for Cole, but he should've known the rules by now. We were there to train, not to question. I approached this encounter like I would any training session. I did what I was told and I gave it my everything. I kept sucking on Cole's cock hoping that it would take the edge off the sting of Todd's slap. But from the way his cock throbbed, I wondered if he might have *liked* it. It was then I felt Todd's lubed up fingers beginning to probe my anus. I felt one, then two fingers. Then he moved his fingers in and out of my tight hole. He removed his fingers and I braced myself for impact. I tried to relax more, not knowing what I was in for. Todd was so confident, so cocky, that I feared that a colossal, record-breaking cock was about to torpedo into me. But Todd's dick easily slipped in. He quickly forced himself all the way in and I felt his stomach pressing up against me. I estimated that there was less than five inches of cock inside me. But it felt good. Really good. Todd didn't need the biggest cock to dominate me. Or to make my ass feel great. He knew how to use it and hit my prostate with each thrust. This guy was good at everything. I was completely his.

"I think I'm gonna cum," Cole softly whispered, scared of irritating Todd again.

Predictably, Todd pulled out of me to stand up and give Cole another mighty slap. Was that Cole's intent? I stopped sucking him because I knew that the slap would send him over the edge. And neither of us had been given permission to cum yet.

Todd ordered Cole to lay down beside me with his legs up in the air. He instructed him to not touch his own cock. Cole quickly obeyed. Still on my hands and knees, I glanced back to see this muscular young stud with his legs up toward the ceiling. His cock didn't deflate one bit and I realized that he was eager to get fucked. Todd rubbed my fellow trainee's furry and exposed hole, loosening him up just as he'd done to me. Cole grunted loudly as the fingers entered and I wondered if he'd ever been fucked before.

I was feeling disappointed Todd pulled out of my ass. He was a masterful fuck and knew how to use his cock. His pounding had me on the verge of shooting my load. I went to stroke myself and Todd smacked my hand away. He hoisted Cole's legs onto his shoulders and began pounding away at the big guy. I was both jealous and turned on by the sight. Todd noticed the look of jealousy on my face. He pulled out of Cole and shoved himself back into my hungry hole. I turned and faced Cole and noticed the disappointment in *his* eyes. Todd's fuck must have had the same effect it was having on me. Then Todd pulled out of me and thrust into to Cole's waiting sphincter. He was fucking us both at the same time. He truly was a master. Cole and I locked eyes and felt so close in that moment. Todd continued to bring us each to the brink of orgasm before pulling out, never allowing us to touch our own dicks. Finally, I couldn't take it any more.

"Please, sir! I gotta fucking cum, sir!"

I immediately regretted this. Todd pulled out of Cole and was on top of me in a fraction of a second with his forearm pressed against my neck. I couldn't breathe. I looked to Cole for help. He just looked up at the ceiling, knowing that there was nothing he could do.

Todd shouted into my ear. "Know your place, trainee. You're here to learn and to serve. You will learn to take a command and serve your superiors."

I struggled to speak through his chokehold. "Yes, sir!"

He released his grip and pulled me to a standing position. He guided Cole to his feet too and turned our heads together.

"Now, kiss, recruits."

We're both shocked but we didn't dare question his order. Nor did we want to. We slammed toward one another and passionately kissed.

"Finger each other's assholes."

We did as told. Our fingers slid easily into one another as our bodies pressed together.

"Let me hear some moans, recruits!"

Cole and I let out the sound of desire we'd been holding back. We kissed and finger fucked as our cocks ground together.

"Down on your knees, trainees."

At Todd's order, we disengaged and both dropped to the floor. Todd shoved his cock down Cole's throat. Cole consumed the whole thing easily. I was jealous again. Despite the sadistic way we were being treated, every part of me wanted to please my trainer. His confidence and authority turned me on. I soon got my wish. He pulled out of Cole and slammed his cock into my mouth. I comfortably took it all in. His smaller size allowed me to do things with my tongue I'd never been able to do with a bigger cock. He grabbed the sides of my head and started face-fucking me. It was a perfect fit and I never wanted him to stop.

"Suck your fellow trainee's cock," Todd breathlessly ordered Cole, who was panting hard.

I felt Cole engulf the tip of my uncut cock as I took Todd's balls in my mouth along with his cock. It took Cole a few bobs up and down before he was able to take my whole tool down. I felt so good! My cock was close to exploding.

Todd ordered Cole to stroke himself. "You will both cum on my command, trainees."

"Yeshir," I mumble through a mouthful of cock and balls.

With his pants around his ankles and his shirt pulled up, Todd continued fucking my face. His obvious pleasure made him look less in control than I'd ever seen him. I let his balls drop from my mouth so I could fondle them. They were so tight, the universal sign of a load about to be shot. He was breathing so hard as he stabbed my mouth with his modest cock again and again.

"Counting down to orgasm, trainees. 5, 4, 3, 2, 1... *release!*"

Instantly, I felt Todd's load shooting down my throat. He was a gusher and I struggled to swallow the first two intense loads. He then began to squeeze out smaller loads. I heard Cole choking on my massive squirts down his throat. I had so much cum filling my balls and I wasn't sure if Cole was prepared for such a massive load. Cole must've pointed his cock toward me, as I felt a number of his loads splash all over my side.

Todd slowly pulled his cock from my mouth and instructed me to clean the spunk off my face. Then he stuck his cock in Cole's mouth and fed him the last few drops of jizz. Todd surprised us both as he bent down and started licking Cole's semen off of my body. Every last drop! I moaned at the feel of his tongue on my body. I was even more shocked as he engulfed my still-hard cock and cleaned it thoroughly, making sure to get every drop out of the folds in my foreskin. I could see the shock on Cole's face as our trainer proceeded to lick the last few drops of cream off his mushroom-headed cock too.

Todd quickly dressed, as Cole and I both just stood there staring at his fit body and taking in everything that just happened. We felt shocked and drained by our boot camp fucking.

"Break time is over, recruits. Back inside in ninety-seconds or you'll be running laps until you're on Social Security."

Todd left the room and we both got dressed quicker than we ever had. Cole and I didn't say a word to each other but, somehow, I ended up wearing his underwear home that night. Cole stopped me before I opened the door to leave and pulled me close for a sensual kiss. It was a nice surprise.

As we made our way back to the training area, Cole broke the silence and whispered, "That was fucking hot, Jake. Way better than I was expecting."

I smiled back, not sure how to reply. No one could have expected what just happened.

CHAPTER SIX
ARMED, DANGEROUS AND HORNY

"Parker? Hello?" Colonel Anger barks.

I shake off the memories and focus on my superior standing in front of me in The Agency's London headquarters. I don't blame him for being impatient. I know it's going to take everything I've got for me to stay alive through the end of the summer.

Colonel Anger puts a small pistol in my hand. It's lighter than I thought it would be. He explains to me that it's made of plastics and can get through most security scans. I like it. It's sleek and easily concealed. This is just what I need. I raise it up to see how it aims.

For a split second, I get a little queasy. I've never killed anyone. The idea is a little terrifying. I lay the gun on the table after I make sure to put the safety on. I don't need any accidents before I've even left base. I remind myself that I can handle this. I've had some pretty intense weapons training. I'm ready for this.

"You'll need these," the colonel puts a bag on the table.

I take a look inside. "Shoes? Uh… thanks! That's really nice of you."

"They're not a present. The trainers are for the mission, newbie," the colonel corrects me, referring to the running and CrossFit sneakers. "They have hollow soles where the gun can be stored after it's taken apart."

He shows me how to dismantle the gun and how to use the hidden storage in the shoes to hide it. He makes me practice until I can do it right and do it fast. I'm good at this! I think Colonel Anger is impressed, though he doesn't let it show.

The Colonel lifts his hand and beckons me with his index finger. "Walk with me." He's already moving before he finishes talking.

I quickly follow behind him and try to keep up. This guy is the real deal. He's worked his way up The Agency and has a reputation for getting the job done. I want to be as good as him someday.

"I know you've received a general briefing on your mission after training, but I want to go over some details with you. As you know, your assignment is to go after a young, international terrorist. Not much is known about him except a first name, Cody. He works for a shadowy organization known as SATYR."

"That short for something?" I ask.

"No."

Before I can say anything else, he continues, "They have their fingers in a lot of pies, including global banking and various religious organizations. Their goal is to bring down the international economy. They want chaos. They believe that they can take control and become the dominant global power. And they're doing a damn good job of it so far."

"That's not good," I chime in.

"Their influence has been on the rise since 1980. They've done incalculable damage to the global economy. We need to shut them down."

We finally stop at Colonel Anger's office. It's impressive. He leans over his desk to pick up a file. I take a moment to admire the man's firm ass before he turns around. I hope he didn't notice that.

"Here's what we know about your target," he says, handing me the manila folder

I take the folder. It's definitely light. Too light. "You weren't kidding when you said we don't know much about the guy." I look up with a nervous chuckle.

Colonel Anger doesn't seem to share my amusement. He glares until I look down again. "Our sources tell us he's recently enrolled in a summer session at a men's college in Holland just outside of Amsterdam. You'll be going undercover there to gather intel."

I nod, listening to what he's saying while trying to memorize everything in the file. There's a picture of my target paper-clipped to the inside flap. He's a good-looking guy. There's something familiar about him but I'm not really sure why. His hair is dark and his features are boyish with a little bit of edge. If he wasn't evil, I'd ask him out.

Colonel Anger snaps in my face to get my attention.

"I can't stress this enough, rookie," he says looking directly into my eyes. "This assignment is information gathering only. You are there to find out what Cody and SATYR are planning, report it back to us and get the hell out of there. You are not take any action. You are not going to try and take Cody down on your own. Now, what are you going to do?"

"I will find out what SATYR is planning, sir, report back and then get the hell out of there."

"Good!" He steps back.

I almost let out a sigh of relief. It's hard concentrating with such an intimidating man standing so close.

"Under normal circumstances, I would never trust a rookie your age with so little training to handle a mission like this. But, the blokes back in the States seem to think you'll be able to handle yourself," he tells me. "I hope to god they're not wrong."

"Thank you, sir."

"That wasn't a compliment, Parker." He sits down at his desk and starts going through his paperwork. "Dismissed."

I leave quickly. When the colonel tells you to do something, you do it. My dick is starting to harden just thinking about it. I find his natural authority a turn on. But it's obvious he's not that impressed with me. Yet.

It takes me a few minutes to find my way out of the base. I'm a little embarrassed in front of my new coworkers when I have to double back because I went the wrong way. I smile sheepishly when I see someone, trying to work my youthful charms. Eventually, one of the security guys who fucked me earlier takes pity on me and leads me back to the elevator. He wishes me luck and sends me off with a squeeze to my shoulder.

Once I'm back in the fake storefront, I make sure nobody sees me leave as I head out onto the street. My gun has been dismantled into four parts and hidden in my new shoes. I carry the extra pair and my old shoes in the bag Colonel Anger gave me. To anyone who doesn't know where I've just been, I look like an ordinary American twink enjoying the sites and doing some shopping. Inside I'm reeling. It's hard to believe that only a little over a week ago, I was graduating from high school, and now I'm in London with a mission to take down a terrorist organization. I try to appear calm and cool despite how excited I feel. I mean, I'm about to save the world. Well, help the world. I'll be a hero. It's the biggest thing I've ever done and I know I'm going to be awesome. And since it's an intel mission, it should be easy. It doesn't get any better than this.

I head over to the bus stop. London is an incredible city and I'm not going to get to see much of it. I might as well take in as many sites as I can before I have to leave. I'm so excited to be in London. When the bright red double-decker bus shows up, I almost applaud. I nearly knock an old woman down on my way to the top deck. The extra height give me the chance to see more of the city than the lower level could.

I get off the bus near Palace of Westminster, where the houses of Parliament meet. It's bigger than I imagined, and the brown stones set it apart from the light gray that surrounds it. It's one thing to see it online and in textbooks, but it's breathtaking to be standing in front of it. So big and so old! I take a bunch of pictures. Mom and Dad think I'm on vacation so it'll be good to send them some pics regularly. I don't want them to worry or suspect anything.

Next on the agenda: relieve my bladder. I have to pee like a racehorse. It takes me about ten minutes to find a public bathroom. It isn't the cleanest of places. Looks like London toilets aren't any better than Texas restrooms. I guess men are men everywhere. That's strangely comforting. I run to the closest free urinal, unzip my pants, pull my foreskin back a little and let it go. Ahhh! I piss so hard I think I might chip the porcelain. I feel better right away.

There's a guy at the urinal next to me. I steal a glance at his cock. His stream of piss travels through and out of his long foreskin. It's an interesting technique. I always pull my foreskin back when I have to piss. That's how my dad taught me to do it when I was a little boy. I wonder if it feels better to just let it flow through. Maybe it gives him better aim. I tilt my head up slightly to sneak a look at his face, wondering if it's as nice as his cock. He's staring right back at me. He gives me a small smile, then shakes and zips up. He's gone before I even smile back. He totally saw me checking him out. My cheeks heat up as I hurriedly finish up. Looks like my secret agent skills are a bust when it comes to cruising.

I head back outside and decide to walk around for a while. I wander around Parliament Square and act like a total tourist. With no one I know around I don't have to act cool. I love this stuff! I love the history and the stories. I'm a nerd in a jock's body. I wander around and take a million photos on my phone. I wonder how long it'll take me to blow through the hard drive at this rate. A few minutes later I'm staring up at a stone block with three British flags secured to it. There's a wreath carved into the side and the words, "The Glorious Dead" underneath it. Red floral wreaths decorate the base. I ask an older British man standing nearby what it means. He explains to me how it's there to honor dead British soldiers from both World Wars. I thank him and take it all in. A lot of those guys were probably around my age when they were sent off to war. I wonder what they were thinking before they went off to battle.

I keep walking and taking in the city. It's hard to believe how long it's been here. It makes me realize how new the United States is. I think about The Agency's global goals and they mean more to me than ever. There's a whole world outside of Texas. It's one thing to know that. It's another thing to experience it. But right now I want to experience some food in my stomach. I've been searched, fucked and briefed but I haven't had lunch yet.

Eventually I'm in front of a tall building with a café on the ground floor. It's a small sandwich and cappuccino bar that looks cool, very European. I sit down and I'm served by a gorgeous waiter with blue eyes and a scruffy face.

I demolish my turkey sandwich and Coke as I watch the people go by. It's so exciting being in another country for the first time. I want it to always be this exciting. I check the time and see it's getting late so I head back to the youth hostel. I pick up another double-decker at Trafalgar Square.

It's a quick ride back. As I enter the hostel I realize I'm exhausted. I've been up a long time and it's been a very full day. But I'm too amped go to bed right away. Instead, I take a seat in the common area to review as many Dutch phrases as I can, listening to a tutorial on my iPhone. So far, I can flawlessly say "Hallo," "Hoe gaat het," and "Kunt u mij vertellen wanneer de bus aankomt," which means "Hello," "How are you," and "Can you tell me when the bus arrives?" Thanks to my linguistics classes at Agency training, I shouldn't make a total ass of myself.

I'm about to delve deeper into my Dutch when two guys around my age sit down at my table. They're olive skinned with short dark hair and wide smiles. I can tell right away that they're brothers. They aren't twins, but they look too much alike to not be related.

"Buona sera," the taller of the two says. "Come stai?"

It's Italian. I recognize it easily as I pluck my earbuds out. But I don't want to let on that I know what they're saying. I'd rather come off as an average guy who hasn't learned some phrases in dozens of languages in spy training. He's asking me how I'm doing.

"Hi," I say with a wave and a dumb smile.

The taller one smiles wider. "Americano! Mi dispiace, I'm sorry. I'm Matteo and this is my brother, Leo. He doesn't speak much English."

Leo nods. "Buona sera."

"Buona sera," I repeat, making sure it doesn't sound too smooth.

"What is your name?" Matteo asks in a thick accent.

"Jake."

"Nice to meet you, Jake. Are you here alone?"

I only nod.

They ask me where in the States I'm from, what brings me to Europe and where I plan to travel. I lie about almost everything. I can't risk blowing my cover before

I've even gone undercover yet. That would be dumb. I tell them that I just graduated high school and I wanted to bum around Europe for a while before starting college. There's at least a sliver of truth in there.

I learn that Matteo is twenty years old, while Leo just turned eighteen. Matteo has a very strong accent, and he seems to continue his words once their done. My name becomes "Jake-a," and London turns into "Londonneh." Every once in a while he forgets about English and says something in Italian, especially when he gets passionate about something, like "futbol." It's really sexy!

After about ten minutes of chatting, Matteo says, "We have some vino in our bag. Would you like to share it with us?"

I almost ask them how they got alcohol, but I remember that we're in Europe and the drinking age is looser over here. I nod an enthusiastic "yes" and the three of us head upstairs to find someplace quieter where we can drink. On the way up, I catch Leo quietly saying something to Matteo, but I can't quite understand it. He spoke too fast and too softly.

Matteo answers, but again, softly and quickly. They smile at each other and laugh. I'm curious and I wish I was in on the conversation. Still, there's something hot about brothers having their secrets. Something about it stiffens my cock and I have to reach in and adjust myself.

After a few attempts, we find a small, unlocked storage room. Matteo pulls a bottle of Italian red wine from his bag. I'm not the biggest fan of red wine, but if offered, I'm game. Matteo pulls the cork out and takes a swig from the bottle before handing it to me. It's sweet and dry. A little rolls down my chin and I wipe it with my arm. The brothers laugh at me and I laugh with them. Before I can hand the bottle to Leo, he pulls out a joint and holds it up questioningly.

"Ti piace?" Leo asks.

"Leo!" Matteo yells. "Sediti é stai zitto!"

I flip through my brain files. I think that means "sit down and shut up." I guess Matteo is worried I'll turn them in or something.

"It's cool," I say as I hold my hand up to Matteo to reassure him.

Leo lights the joint and takes two puffs before handing it to me. It's good. Strong. A few hits of this and I'll be in a very happy place.

The three of us sit down on the floor and start talking again. Matteo's shorts ride up, exposing more of his hairy thigh. That makes it even harder for me to keep up with the conversation, which somehow turns to sex. At first I'm a little hesitant to tell them I'm gay. Even though it isn't a big deal back home for me, I know Italians are mostly Catholic. I'm having a nice time and I don't want things to get weird or tense.

"Amiamo sex with men," Matteo says with a smile.

I start coughing on the smoke from the joint. Did I hear that right?

"We love having sex with men, but back home we don't have many opportunities. Our family does not approve of omosesuali, and we have family everywhere," he tells me with a lot of hand gestures to clarify the Italian phrases.

"That's fucked," I say as I take a swig of the wine to stop my coughing. This wine keeps tasting better as I get drunker. I trade the bottle with Leo for the joint.

"Back home, my parents are cool with me being gay. But I don't tell them about the sex. I think I'd make them cry if I did!" I tell them and start laughing.

"You are very lucky, Giaco," he says calling me by the Italian version of my name. "Our family would never be fine with this." He takes the joint from his little brother and takes a long hit. "That is why we've decided to travel. This trip is a way for us to find ourselves. To find freedom."

"How long are you traveling?"

Matteo shrugs. "Who knows? We've been gone for a week so far. We're feeling happier than we ever felt back in Italia. We may never go home!"

We all laugh.

"Won't you miss your family?" I ask. I know I would. The idea of never going home is completely frightening to me. I'm excited about my mission and doing something thrilling and important, but I'll want to see my family once it's done.

"I have my brother by my side and the entire world in front of me. What else do I need?"

I shrug. "I'd say 'sex,' but I don't think you'll have any problem with that." I laugh at my own joke.

"Sì, Leo and I have managed to have sex much more than we could have dreamed back home." He licks wine off his lips and hands me the bottle again.

The wine and pot are really hitting me now. I stand up and grab the bottle, take another drink and end up falling into Leo. I feel too heavy to stand back up in our small storage closet hideaway. He doesn't push me away. I make myself comfortable, leaning against the younger of the brothers. He laughs and rests his hand on my thigh and starts massaging my leg through my jeans. His hand gets incredibly close to my cock. I'm half hard. It looks like Leo is the one I may end up with. But I would have been happy with Matteo too. They're both so hot.

Leo says something to Matteo in Italian and I'm too drunk and stoned to figure it out. Even if I was sober, it would probably be beyond the basics of my language training anyway. I just sit back and enjoy the sound of their voices. It takes my arousal up a notch. I've never met a real Italian before, much less two brothers. Much less two hot gay brothers! Hearing them talk softly to each other is really nice.

Matteo scoots over until his body is pressed against my side, opposite of his brother, and his tongue moves up and down my neck. "You like, Giaco?"

My only response is to moan. Matteo understands that this is universals for "fuck, yeah I do!" So it's looking like it's the older brother I'll be hooking up with. No problem there. I wait for Leo to make some excuse in Italian and leave the storage room so I can be alone with his older sibling.

Instead, little bro reaches over and covers my dick with his palm. He rubs my crotch delicately while his big brother starts nibbling my ear. I guess young Leo has no intention of leaving.

The guys put their hands on my chest and I feel myself shift. I grab onto Leo's shoulder for support as the two of them lower me on my back. I feel my T-shirt pulled up over my chest, leaving my torso uncovered. I feel four hands over my bare skin. Leo takes my left nipple in his mouth while Matteo takes my right. Is this really happening?

I take a deep breath and push my chest up into their eager mouths. It's not every day that I have two hot Italian brothers seducing me. I'm loving every second of this!

Matteo is definitely rougher than his younger brother. Leo's more soft and gentle. Matteo likes using teeth, while Leo is delicate with his tongue. Both feel incredible. It's wild having two completely different sensations on my nipples at the same time. I feel my zipper being pulled down and two hands reach into my white briefs. Both brothers have a hand on my cock. Just like with my nipples, Matteo is much rougher, squeezing and tugging, while Leo lightly fingers my foreskin. I groan and rub my fingers through each dark curly head of hair, pushing them closer to my hard nipples.

Normally I'm not into guys this young, but these brothers are driving me crazy. Maybe it's because they're my first Italians. Maybe it's because their lips are so full and tempting. Or maybe it's their hairy legs and the hint of chest hair I see poking out from the top of their soccer shirts. Or could it just be that they're two fucking-hot brothers and they have my cock out and their lips on my bare chest. Ding ding ding ding.

Leo says something to his brother before he leaves my nipple and moves down my body to take my rock-hard dick in his mouth. Matteo pulls away too and whispers a few words of encouragement in Italian to his brother. Then he strips his own clothes off. I take in the beauty of his naked, hairy body. His uncut sausage is rock hard and fucking huge. It looks like he's even bigger than me. I've heard that Italian men have big dicks, but this is the first time I've ever seen one. I reach out and grab it. My fingers can't get all the way around it. Matteo doesn't shave anything and I couldn't be happier. I love his full, dark bush. I want to smash my face into it.

I pull his tool forward and stuff it in my mouth. I can only swallow about half of it. He straddles my face and tries to push more of himself into my mouth. I feel Leo sucking on my foreskin just then. I groan and Matteo uses that as permission to thrust his dick all the way down my throat.

I grab his furry ass and squeeze while I wrap my legs around Leo's head, locking him in place. It all feels so fucking good. Matteo is roughly fucking my face, using me. His foreskin glides back and forth in my mouth. I can feel my own cock throbbing in Leo's mouth. He really knows how to work a foreskin. I wonder if he's had practice on his brother.

"Prepararlo per me," Matteo instructs his brother, not missing a thrust to my mouth. What? *Prepare him for me.* I feel young Leo's wet finger push into my asshole. Shit! I think Matteo's going to fuck me with his massive meat and he's got his little brother prepping me. I don't think this could get any crazier.

Leo pushes my legs into the air and pulls his mouth off my dick. I moan as I feel the cold air hit my warm penis. My cock misses the attention. Matteo seems to understand my boner's loneliness and, without ever pulling his dick from my mouth, swings around and swallows my cock. We're sixty-nining and it feels so good! My head gets even lighter, more drunk from pleasure than the wine. He doesn't struggle to get my cock down like I do his. He sucks my cock like it was a cannoli. I'm glad I have a mouthful of his massive meat, or else I'd me groaning so loudly that someone would hear us in here and we'd get thrown out of the hostel.

I'm ready to pass out from bliss as I feel Leo shove his hot, wet tongue right into my hole. His tongue easily glides in and out. I can't see, but these brothers' faces must be really close to each other right now. That really turns me on.

What's the story with these two? These brothers aren't at all shy around each other. I don't have a brother, but if I did, I don't think I could do anything like this with him. Still, they've barely touched. I wonder if that's because it's too taboo or if it's because they've fucked each other their entire lives and are now bored by it. I don't know, but they sure have no problem fucking somebody else together and being really close during sex. If they aren't going to do anything with each other, that leaves more attention for me.

I can't tell which sensation feels better: the mouth on my cock, the tongue in my ass or the dick down my throat. It all feels so fantastic, I'm surprised I haven't cum yet. Maybe all that wine is helping me hold back. Matteo feels like he may be close to exploding soon. I suck even harder, hoping to feel his cum fill my stomach. I'm eager to try his creamy Italian dressing. I figure a little ass play might send him over the top. I slowly work my finger into the older brother's furry hole as we suck each other's cocks.

"You are a naughty boy, aren't you Giaco," he says smiling, letting my cock slip out of his mouth. When I try to put a second finger in, Matteo groans hard and then pulls away before he can cum. He gets up off me and stands up. His huge cock looks like an overfilled red water balloon.

"You get me too close to finish," he explains. "I don't want to finish. I like you and my brother likes you."

"I like you guys too," I shoot back. The hard, wet cock bouncing on my stomach says it better than I do.

I look down at his little brother excitedly eating my ass. I push my heels into the ground and scoot my ass up give Leo easier access.

Matteo goes over to Leo, pulls him off of rimming duty and stands him up. He kisses the side of his little brother's forehead.

"You like my brother, Jake?" he asks.

"Yeah. I like you both. A lot!"

Matteo pulls Leo's shirt off and slaps his flat stomach.

"What do you think of my little brother now, Giaco?" I love when he calls me that. "He doesn't think the boys like him as much as they like me," he explains. "I tell him he's stupid."

"He looks nice," I assure him. "Anyone would love to be with him."

Leo just smiles. It hits me again how very weird this all is. But good-weird. Matteo unbuttons his brother's pants and pulls them down. Leo is just in his small black briefs with a thick waistband as he kicks off his shoes. He's much smoother than his older bro, with just a smattering of dark hair in all the right places.

"He's a nice boy, right, Giaco?" Matteo asks, knowing that the answer is obvious. I just nod with enthusiasm.

The older brother whispers in the younger's ear and Leo turns around. Matteo pulls his brother's dark briefs down. There's just a little hint of soft dark fur on Leo's butt. Matteo rubs his brother's cheeks with one hand. I sit, enjoying the show, wondering what's coming next.

"I'll bet the boys in the United States don't have asses as nice as this, Giaco. I think you would like my brother's ass," he speculates. Leo looks over his shoulder and smiles.

Leo does have a nice ass. Flawless, in fact. I'm not sure I'm qualified to compare it to every single rear end made in America, but I can see it's beautiful.

"Your brother's ass is hot, Matteo," I say through a big smile.

Matteo whispers a translation of what I just said and Leo nods and smiles right at me. It seems Leo's the more submissive brother. Or maybe it's just the language issue making Matteo take charge.

"My brother wants you to fuck his ass, Giaco. You want my brother's ass? I like to see my brother with a boy like you. You're same age," he rambles.

I'm not sure I'm understanding the logic of what he's saying. Maybe it's because he's pretty drunk. Or maybe it's because I'm pretty drunk. But I know Leo's ass is looking really good to me. I usually like to be the one dominated, but right now, I'm eager to get my dick in this boy's hole.

Matteo motions me to stand and he turns his brother around, facing him toward me. He moves us closer together until our lips are inches apart. Leo shyly kisses me and our hands run all over each other's bodies. The older brother just watches. I think Matteo is worried he'll cum if anyone touches his cock.

Matteo begins to stroke my dick as I kiss his brother. As an uncut guy himself, he knows how to work my foreskin gently without making me cum. He has his other hand on the small of his brother's back, guiding him closer into me. I feel young Leo's cock, wet with precum, slide up and down my stomach.

Matteo gets close to my ear, "Now you fuck my little brother's ass, Giaco."

In Italian, Matteo tells his brother to turn around and lean against the wall. Or I guess that's what he says since Leo turns around and leans against the wall. Matteo continues to stroke my hard, dripping cock. He pulls me by the dick right up to his brother and guides my cock into his hole. This whole situation has me horny beyond belief! I give a nice push and my cock slides right into little brother's hole. Leo moans. Matteo hushes him by rubbing two fingers on his lips. Leo pretends like he's going to bite them. I pull my cock back a little then push back in, easing Leo into the fuck. He's still really tight around my cock. And it's warm. Most of the guys I've fucked around with are older and love giving my ass a hard plowing. But right now I can't imagine anything that could feel better than Leo's ass wrapped around my uncut tool.

I hear Matteo move behind me. His dick presses against my ass. Fuck! That thing's a monster like… (I can't think of any Italian monsters in my state right now. But if I could, it would be just like that.) I'm having too much fun fucking his little brother to try to stop him. He wraps his arms around my chest and presses his mouth against my ear. His hot breath makes me tingle everywhere. "You like my brother's tight little asshole?" he asks.

"Yes," I pant.

"Buono." Then he plunges into my ass, my hole still wet from Leo's rimming. His balls slap my cheeks. My eyes bulge and his hand flies over my mouth just in time to muffle my scream.

As I should have expected, Matteo is a rough fuck. He doesn't start slow and work up speed. He pulls his cock almost all the way out of me and then slams back in, hitting my prostate hard and sending stars exploding over my eyes. Every move is rough and fast. His violent thrusts cause me to fuck his brother harder than I would have. It's almost like he's fucking us both. But Leo, apparently isn't so shy when he has a man's meat up his hole. He slams his ass back to meet every thrust so hard my balls slam against his ass cheeks. I think I might get crushed between these two brothers. If I've got to die, this would be a good way to go.

I already feel like I'm going to cum. Leo rocks back to meet me slamming into him. And every time I pull out of little brother's ass, I'm pushing further and further onto Matteo's massive Italian sub. My fingers dig into Leo's back while Matteo gets crazy-rough with my nipples. It fucking hurts like hell, but for some reason it brings me closer to my orgasm. I like how aggressive Matteo gets. I like that he's biting my shoulder so hard I might bleed. I go crazy as he pinches my nipple with one hand and squeezes my balls too tight with the other. He's using me as his sex toy and punching bag all at the same time and fuck if I don't want more.

"Più forte," little brother whispers. "Più forte! Più forte! Più forte!"

"My brother is telling you to fuck him harder," Matteo kindly explains. "Like I do to you."

I think I'll break him if I do. Or I'll cum. I'm not sure how much longer I can hold back. Uh-oh. This is it. I squeeze Leo's shoulder with one hand and stroke his uncut cock with the other as I drill harder into his ass. My prick feels like it's on fire. I muffle a scream as I shoot my first load into his taut hole. As I fill his ass with my seed, I feel his cock expand. He softly yells something in Italian that makes me shoot again as his own cock explodes, jizzing all over the floor. Then he shoots again. And again.

Matteo is still ramming into me. He grabs me by the throat and squeezes. "I love how you fuck my brother," he whispers in my ear. He's making me hard all over again. "He likes your American cock. I can tell when my brother likes a fuck." My cheeks heat up, both in embarrassment and euphoria.

My cock is still in Leo's ass. He squeezes his sphincter to drain all the cum he can get out of me. I feel big brother pull his monster cock out of my ass. Fuck! I want his cum in me! What's he going to do? From behind, I hear Matteo let out a loud moan and feel him crash hard into my ass. I remind myself to be careful what I wish for.

He just keeps drilling it as deep into me as it will go. I hear a steady grunting in my ear as I feel the warm wetness of his cum shoot into my ass over and over. It feels so fucking hot, my own cock unloads again into little brother's already-full hole. Matteo just keeps cumming, overfilling my asshole. I feel his spooge run down the back of my leg.

Before I can catch my breath, Matteo pulls out and guides me to the floor. My chest lands in the puddle of my own cum and my face lands in Leo's lake of spooge. I know what big brother wants from me. Even though the floor probably isn't very clean, I don't hesitate. I stick out my tongue and lick every drop of Leo's sperm off the floor. Matteo pulls me up, kissing me deep and hard. His brother's cum flows from my mouth to his and he drinks it down. Leo take his turn and give me a passionate kiss his while Matteo roughly squeezes the last drops of cum from my cock. The two brothers kiss on the lips just a little as they smile and tousle each other's hair.

Is this how brothers are supposed to act? I don't know, but I'm not complaining.

After that, the three of us are just too exhausted to move or clean up. We pass out on the floor of our storage room getaway.

***

Early the next morning, we wake up surprised to be in a storage room. We dress and quietly go back to our rooms, grateful to make it out before the janitor found us. I get myself cleaned up, put on some fresh clothes and gather my stuff. Hoping to see the bros, I make my way downstairs to the lobby. I see Matteo and Leo have already checked out and are waiting for me. Leo puts his arms on my shoulders and kisses both my cheeks before giving me a big hug. Matteo does the same thing, telling me, "It was a pleasure for us meeting you, Giaco."

I'm sad to say goodbye to these two but so happy to have shared the night with them. I really like them both (despite my very sore ass). They're really cool and the sex last night was as incredible as it was bizarre.

"Yeah. You too. Good luck with your trip. I hope you find what you're looking for."

"You too, Giaco"

"Ciao," Leo says as he gives me another big hug.

Then I watch them turn and leave. I check out and make sure I have everything before I head out also. When I step outside, I take a deep breath. I'm at the start of a whole new life and I know it's going to be exciting. I hope Matteo and Leo's new life will be too.

CHAPTER SEVEN
LEARNING TO SERVE

As I walk out of the hostel to the London sidewalk, I'm feeling more psyched than ever about being a spy. I have my assignment and The Agency has me completely taken care of. I have an unlimited credit card and access to cash. Fuck, yeah! It sure as hell beats working in my dad's office over the summer. Life is good.

I make my way among the Brits on their way to work and my mind wanders back to the events that got me here. The final half of my training was intense and unforgettable. Yeah, like anyone could forget the grueling training that made them a secret agent.

***

The bullet ricocheted off the beam, whizzed past my left ear and struck the back wall. It was loud. Really loud. My eyes narrowed as tiny beads of sweat dripped down from my forehead. My fist clenched as I held my breath, waiting for my chance. The room was dark, but I saw a darker spot from where I thought the bullet had come from. I knew I'd only get one shot. If I missed, it would all be over. No second chance. I was pretty sure I had that bastard and I made my move.

I crept my way around the boxes and the crates that were scattered and stacked around the large warehouse room. I didn't breathe and I didn't make a sound. I was close to the shadow as I slowly let my breath out and gently squeezed the trigger. I didn't even feel the recoil. I let my training become instinct and I worked the gun expertly.

The sound of a siren wailed and the room was suddenly bathed in light. Adrenaline was flooding through me. The young man who was the dark shadow just glared at me, his eyes colored with disgust. I'd got the upper hand and I won this round of the training exercise. Ahmed was beyond angry about losing, especially to one of "the queer" recruits. Up until that point, no one had managed to tag Ahmed in our search-and-shoot simulations. The other remaining nine trainees had all tried and failed. None of them had lasted for more than five minutes before Ahmed got them in the vest with the rubber bullet. I was the last up and I took that cocky asshole down.

Ahmed stood there, shocked that he'd been bested. I'd heard him making snarky remarks about me and some of the other gay trainees. But mostly me and my new buddy Kyle. So this defeat must have really stung. Good! The noise of the siren was silenced by Andre, the tall Russian instructor who came up and congratulated me. Ahmed looked pissed and stormed out of the room as the other trainees congratulated me. Despite the sometimes competitive nature of our training, we remaining recruits had become pretty close. We were all happy for each other's victories. Except for Ahmed.

Kyle Mills, another high school-aged recruit, was especially happy to see Ahmed go down. Ahmed was cruelly mocking when he made the shot that set Kyle's buzzer off. Kyle was thinner and more bookish than most of us. Ahmed saw weakness and exploited it. He could be cruel that way, especially when the instructors weren't around. Not only were Kyle and I close in age, he was also gay like me. He was attractive, but a little bit nerdy, with his lanky frame, constantly messy brown hair and those glasses. But he had a great sense of humor and a smile that lit up his whole face. I really liked him.

He had confided in me that he hadn't been with a guy yet, but he wanted to. I found it kind of sweet. I wasn't sure if Kyle and I would end up hooking up since I didn't know if I wanted to be somebody's first. It seemed like a big responsibility and I worried that it might mess up our friendship. But I could be there for him to talk to. And I could be the "faggot" who stood up to Ahmed for both of us.

Ahmed was competitive in a different way than the rest of us. He wasn't used to losing. He was a handsome twenty-year-old born in the Sudan and raised most of his life in Texas. He was straight and made sure we all knew it. He had an appealingly dark complexion, killer cheekbones and dark wavy hair. He excelled in most of our exercises, often placing top among the trainees. But he was a loner. He worked hard and wasn't concerned about making friends. But he was quickly out of my mind. I had won. And a win in this kind of field simulation was making me more confident that I'd make it through training and into The Agency.

Adrenaline was still pumping through my body as I stared at Andre. Or maybe it was more than adrenaline. There was something about the ex-KGB man that got me a little flustered. He had a handsome face, high cheekbones, pouty lips and perfect dark brown hair. Someone told me he was once a model in Moscow. Another guy heard he'd been a lawyer before being recruited by The Agency. And that body! He was so strong and built. It almost seemed wrong that he wore clothes, but he wore them so well. When he put his hand on my shoulder, I almost lost my balance. The guy was strong!

Andre joined The Agency in that sweet spot between the end of the Cold War and Putin going bat-shit crazy. After a few years in the field, he was assigned to train young recruits and assess new trainees like me. His dedication and belief in what he was doing was inspirational. He taught us early on that The Agency wasn't about governments, but about global stability. He told us how our goal would be beyond politics. And I could certainly see that The Agency brought people of extremely diverse backgrounds together. He was the first Russian I'd ever met!

"Well done, my boy," he said, but I barely heard the words. I had it bad for this Soviet stud. Before I could reply, Andre was already moving across the room. Armed search training was over for the day. The other recruits congratulated me on my victory again. They were so happy to see Ahmed taken down, hoping it would humble him a little. The guy was insufferable when he won. I knew he was good at just about everything we were learning, but I wondered if he'd be a liability if he made it into the Shades program. Fortunately, that decision wasn't mine. I was more concerned about my own scores. I knew I had a good shot at making it through but I was concerned about my linguistics skills. The high from my victory faded as I walked with the group into the conference room where our language instructor waited.

Kyle was much better than me in linguistics. He thrived in our crash course in phrases and accents. He may not have been as good as the rest of us when it came to the physical training, but he was near the head of the group when it came to language studies and information gathering. (He also knew where to find the hidden snacks on campus, making him pretty popular with the rest of us trainees.) I was worried that those skills wouldn't be enough to get him through training. At the end of each week, any of us could be called into the office and be sent home with a "Thanks for your service" and a "We'll call you if your particular skills may prove useful." In the three months we'd been secretly gathering, we'd already seen six guys exit. I didn't want to see Kyle go. Training for the Shades program was the most exciting thing that ever happened to him. Hell, it was the most exciting thing that happened to any of us.

Kyle and I were the first to walk into language class and we took seats up front. I couldn't afford to slack in the back. I knew our instructor, Mr. Montgomery, would be advising the recruiters on who had the skills needed to be a Shade. Each of the instructors gave weekly updates and made recommendations. It was important I impress him.

While we referred to most of our instructors by either just their first names or just their last, our linguistics expert preferred to be called *Mister* Montgomery. We found out that he was a professor at Oxford when not working with the Agency's trainees. I was excited to be taught by a real professor from Oxford. In England! For a Texas high school boy, this is big time! No wonder my regular school work became so easy. After a few weeks in Agency training, high school was hardly a challenge. And it didn't hurt that our Agency instructors tutored us in our regular homework. It was essential to them that we all kept up and got a well-rounded education.

Mr. Montgomery was tall, a full six feet, in his late twenties and fairly well built. His skin was light brown and his hair very dark, pitch black and straight. One of our first challenges was to figure out what country he was born in. I didn't have a clue. I couldn't hear any kind of accent. Though he looked exotic to me, he spoke just like any other American guy I knew. He had the ability to take on just about any accent. We even checked the online bios for the instructors at Oxford. No luck. Nothing there. It was only Kyle that figured out, after sessions, that Mr. Montgomery was East Indian. Kyle had researched facial features in various countries and picked up on some slightly uncommon phrasing that Mr. Montgomery used. I wished I'd thought of that. That wouldn't be the last time Kyle was star of the class. Ahmed was pissed that an American queer had beat him to it. That's why he was so rough on Kyle in our more physical training sessions.

Though handsome, Mr. Montgomery was a little nerdy. He often dressed in tan corduroy pants and sweater vests. I don't think I knew anyone who owned a sweater vest before. I suppose it only added to his quirky charm. His shirt sleeves were often rolled up and I could see the dark hair on his arms. It made me wonder how hairy he was all over.

Though nowhere near as physically imposing as Andre, his language skills were beyond impressive. When he spoke French, you would have thought he *was* French. When he said something in German, or even Chinese, with my eyes shut I'd believe a German or Chinese man was in the room speaking their native dialect. He could speak dozens of languages as well or better than someone who grew up speaking them.

It was his job to teach us some basic language skills. It wasn't like we were going to learn a whole mess of foreign languages in our time there, but we needed to be able to figure out if something being said meant danger for us. We were also there to learn to identify where someone was from by hearing them speak, no matter what language they were speaking. And we needed to know a few key phrases for several countries. It was a lot to take on during the few months we were in training. That's why I was stressing.

I knew that if I didn't sharpen my skills, it could be me called into the office one Friday and sent home for good. Even worse, if I did make it through, poor linguistic skills could put my life at risk someday. This wasn't a game with a restart button. We were reminded of that every day.

Three months into training, I decided to seek out the help of my instructor. I planned on letting him know that I was struggling and I was going to ask him how I could do better. Maybe there was some extra credit in spy training he could give me. Hopefully, he'd see my willingness to work hard rather than think I was a lost cause. I would have asked Kyle for help, but his other studies were keeping him busy. I didn't want to drag him down. If he was going to get cut from the program, I didn't want to be the cause.

That evening, after our afternoon of weapons training was done, I made my way down the hall to Mr. Montgomery's office. His door was unlocked and, in my eagerness, I just walked in without knocking. The room was dim, with just a single fluorescent bulb on in the corner. I didn't want to flip on all the lights. The high back desk chair was turned away from the desk and I wondered if my instructor was resting. I was hoping he wouldn't mind the interruption.

As I came in, I quietly called his name, "Mr. Montgomery?"

I walked up to his chair. Empty. He wasn't in it. I figured I'd try him again tomorrow. I turned to leave. But before I was out the office, I saw a large board against the wall to my right. It was a cork board that could be flipped on its aluminum frame, the kind that can be used for presentations. Pinned to the cork, I saw full-face photographs of every one of my fellow remaining recruits lined across in rows. Including mine.

In the dim light, I thought I noticed what looked like a smear or two on my picture. I moved closer to investigate the photos. They were those eight-by-ten photos like I've seen actors use in old movies and TV shows. Is this how Mr. Montgomery was figuring out who would be passing and who would be leaving the program? There were three rows. Kyle's photograph was off to the far right on the top row, clear and clean from any smudges. Several of the photographs were smudgeless but a few others were also marked with the same smearing as my picture. Ahmed's photo had some fluid that had dried running down it. Whatever was on Cole's photo was still a little wet. I put my finger to the picture as my eyes adjusted to the dim light in the room. Fuck me! It was cum! This was getting weird. Certainly there was a good explanation, right? Was it Mr. Montgomery? It had to be. Who else would have been jizzing all over trainee photos in his office?

Before I heard a sound, a hand touched my chest. Then another hand was quickly on me, grabbing me around my flat stomach through my T-shirt. Seeing the brown skin on the hands, I knew Mr. Montgomery found me in his office. I wondered if he was angry. Or was he more embarrassed than I was, knowing that I'd discovered his spank shrine? I didn't know if I was in trouble. It was clear I shouldn't be in his office. I didn't know what to say and I didn't turn around. I waited for a cue from him.

We both stood there for a second or two before he silently removed my olive-green T-shirt, pulling it over my head and arms. He let it drop to the floor behind me. What the fuck? He bent down from behind and removed my shoes and socks. He tossed them to the side of the room. My bare feet felt the coldness of the concrete floor. He unbuckled my belt from behind, then undid my top button. I could feel this furry arms around my torso as my jeans fell to my knees. Then he bent down, pushing my pants to the cold floor. I didn't know why he was doing this but I didn't resist. I stepped out of each pant leg. He stood up and put both his hands on my shoulders. I felt his breath against my neck and I felt so vulnerable. I hadn't even turned around yet and he had me standing in my underwear, with him fully dressed. But not for long. He put his thumbs inside the waistband of my checkered boxers, and pushed the soft cloth down my legs. My already-hard cock sprung straight up.

It seemed like I should object. But what's the point of saying "no" when my dick was screaming "yes" with three exclamation points? I felt his hands explore me everywhere. I loved the way his darker skin made mine look so pale. He squeezed the lean muscle on my arm as he cupped my balls. My pre-cum dripped down my boner and into his palm. Then he brought his hand up and rubbed it all over my chest. I kept forward and stared at the pictures of my fellow recruits. I noticed that some had been splattered by an unusually gener- ous helping of spooge. Some of the photos were high up on the board. Mr. Montgomery must have been quite a shooter! Looking at my own picture I saw how the spunk had hit my likeness twice, once between the eye and once square on the lips.

"I see you found my secret," he finally broke the silence. "This is my office and you don't belong in here. It's not polite to intrude into other people's places, Mr. Parker."

He was right. But I wasn't sure if it was "polite" to jizz all over his students' photos either.

"What is all of this?" I asked as I felt his cock grinding into my bare ass through his Dockers.

"This is my release, trainee. I've always been profession- al. I've never made a move on a student. Do you think that's easy? You're all training to be in peak physical condition and then you come and sit in my class. I'm human. I notice your young bodies and your muscles. It's distracting, to say the least. And it's very frustrating. I have my desires. Over the years some students have even flirted, but I ignored their advances. I couldn't take the risk. I'm the instructor and I have a job to do. I teach you what you need to know and keep my hands to myself. Until lately."

I could feel his cock get as hard as steel as he continued to grind into me. His heart was beating into my back. His arms were wrapped around me. Weird as this was, it felt good to be held by him. Part of me was still nervous and part of me felt very safe.

"I've been using the board and the photos you found to figure out who I'd recommend for the program," he explained. "One night it was getting late. All your faces were staring at me and I started touching myself. It felt good. It felt so good! I shot my load hard and it landed on one of the photos. It was so stimulating that I did it again he next night and the next."

"I've held back for so long, Jake," he whispered in my ear. "But I'm not going to hold back now."

He played with the tip of my foreskin, pinching it over my cockhead. He could feel how turned on I was. I didn't bother to object or invite. I let my body say everything that needed saying. As I continued looking forward at the faces of my fellow trainees, he spread my legs apart slightly, balancing my body as his right hand slowly played with my stiff cock. My eyes moved to the right and I stared at my friend Kyle's likeness staring right back at me. He was smiling that big grin of his and his wavy brown hair hung down nearly touching his eyes. I shifted my body slightly as I heard Mr. Montgomery unzipping his pants.

I felt a pair of hands firmly grip my tightly clenched buttocks, squeezing, exploring and spreading. My instructor handled me like a man starving for touch. I let my body be guided by his strong hands. I didn't look back into the dark room. I just kept looking at my buddy Kyle's still face. It was like he was there with us. Would he have judged me if he were? Or would he have rushed in to join in on what was about to happen?

The hands on my ass shoved and prodded hard, almost making me lose my balance. I could hear that Mr. Montgomery had pushed his pants completely down and then did the same to his underwear. Now his uncut cock was rubbing between my cheeks as I felt his scratchy sweater vest against my back.

My breathing became a bit more shallow as I felt Mr. Montgomery's cock sliding between me like a slippery hot dog that can't stay put in its bun. His dick felt big and torpedo-shaped. I felt his pubes bristle against me. They felt long and coarse. I liked the way they brushed against the top of my ass. Then the motion stopped. He pulled back and I felt a finger between my ass cheeks, massaging my hole. My ass was wet from his pre-cum. I could feel his breath against my sphincter. His face must have been right in my crack. Then I felt his tongue. It explored all around my hole while he pulled my cheeks apart. When his tongue started pushing into my eager opening, it sent me to heaven! I thought I might cum just from getting tongue-fucked.

Kyle's picture kept staring at me. I wondered what he'd say if he could see me standing with my back arched, ass spread wide, getting eaten out by our teacher. Mr. Montgomery wrapped his fingers around the middle of my shaft and stroked. I could feel my balls tighten more. My feet dug into the cold floor, my toes tried to dig into the concrete as I stared at Kyle's innocent face and gave into the pleasure in my hole. I trembled as I felt the tip of a finger poke through my sphincter muscle. The pressure made my body shudder. I closed my eyes and I shoved my hips back to wrap my tight pink hole around the finger. Once it was inside of me, I felt the fluids churning deep in my groin, getting ready to explode. Mr. Montgomery must have felt it too. He stopped stroking me with a "Not just yet, my boy."

My cock nearly exploded. But I took some deep breaths and did as my instructor told me. I felt Mr. Montgomery rise up behind me. He took off his sweater vest and unbuttoned the shirt underneath. When he wrapped his arms around my middle, I could feel his chest hair on my back. I loved the way it rubbed against me. As he pulled me closer I could feel a trail of fur leading all the way to his bushy pubes. Mr. Montgomery's hand dropped from around my waist and I felt it go behind me.

"I'm going to fuck you now, boy," he told me clearly.

"Please fuck me," I whispered back to my handsome Indian instructor, almost involuntarily.

And he did. I felt the tip of his tapered cock push into me. He was so wet with pre-cum, it moved easily as he slowly pushed. I felt it throb and I guessed he was moving slowly more to make sure he wouldn't cum than for my comfort. It hurt, but every inch that filled me felt better than the last. After he was all in, I felt his crotch hair chafe against my ass cheeks. He held his warm meat still inside of me for a minute. Neither of us moved. It was big and it still hurt a bit. I squeezed involuntary to push it out. It wasn't until I relaxed that the pleasure filled me. Once my body made peace with this invasion, I welcomed it in me with everything I had. I reached behind and grabbed his furry ass, pushing him further in. I couldn't get enough. He started pulling out. I tried to stop him, but it was clear I wasn't in control. I was relieved when he pushed back in hard and fucked me, slowly at first, then quickly.

"I've waited a long time for this, Parker," he said grunting.

I wish I could have believed he meant that he wanted me since he first saw me. But I knew he really meant that he'd waited too long to give a student a hard fuck. Right then, I was every student he'd ever wanted and he was making it count. Years of repression violently crumbled away, making my ass its willing victim. He pounded with all of the force of those hundreds of fucks he never had. He rammed into my ass so hard I knew one of us was going to walk away bruised but I didn't want him to stop.

I realized that I'd been fantasizing about my fellow students when Mr. Montgomery first touched me but I was soon only thinking about him. He fucked me like an animal, sloppily and desperately. He must have known it was wrong, but it seemed to fuel him. His hands moved everywhere on my torso and he squeezed me close and hard. He was panting furiously in my ear. So hard. I felt so connected to him.

"I'm fucking you, Parker," he said as if to reassure himself that all of this was real. "I'm fucking you."

"Yes, sir. You're fucking me so good. Please don't stop." I reached my hands back to touch his hair and he kissed my arm. His lips felt warm against my skin.

I heard him groan deeply and he pulled out of my ass. I felt empty and missed his cock. He stumbled beside me, hindered by the pants bunched around his ankles, and we were both facing the rows of headshots. He put his left hand around my shaft and right hand on his own cock. His white shirt was open and I saw his beautiful furry chest and brown nipples. Then I finally saw his dick. It was beautiful, thick and brown, framed with unshaven black pubes that blended into long dark hairs on his legs and stomach. The head of his cock was so pink and wet. It's vibrant color was set off by the light brown foreskin it was peeking out of. I thought of Neapolitan ice cream.

Mr. Montgomery threw his head back like a Pez dispenser as he started to jerk us both in unison. I was so close to cumming and his throbbing, bulging meat looked ready as well. He grunted and moaned so loud I was sure someone would walk in on us. Then he turned his head to me.

"I'm going to cum, Jake." He looked so intensely into my eyes.

He leaned forward on his toes as he fired off a long rope of cum, his other hand still wrapped tightly around the base of my cock. I heard his load splat against one of the photos on the board as I closed my eyes hard. My instructor tightened his grip just below my cockhead causing me to throb and convulse. A tingle ran through my body and I squirt. I felt as if my whole life force was leaving me, released through my cock and my cum. My body shook and trembled uncontrollably as I let loose another milky spray all over the grid of push-pinned photos. Mr. Montgomery fired off another load too. It was like a dam had burst. This one flew and landed very near where the first one did, right on the picture of Kyle's smiling face, right between his big eyes. Another load drenched the entire photo. For a second I felt jealous that it wasn't my picture, but I was feeling too good and the thought quickly evaporated. We silently watched all our spooge drip down the photos, down the cork board and onto the floor.

I looked over at him and we wrapped our arms around each other, leaning in and supporting each other's weight. His eyes stared into mine. I didn't know what to say. I felt so good and this moment felt big. Maybe nothing needed to be said. I quickly kissed his upper lip. Mr. Montgomery smiled then dropped to his knees and drank the remaining cum out of my foreskin. I'd never been with another uncut man before, and the way his tongue worked my prepuce felt so right. He stood up and kissed my forehead, resting his hands on my shoulder.

"I'm sorry for being in your office. I was coming to ask you for some help and the door was unlocked. When I saw the board, I was just, you know, surprised," I felt I needed to explain.

"Considering what just happened, I'll forgive the intrusion if you keep my secret," he told me, glancing at the moist photos on the board beginning to curl.

"No problem, sir. I wouldn't tell. I understand. I'm always horny too. But, if it's not a bother, I really could use some help with my dialect training. Is there anything you can do?"

Mr. Montgomery was sympathetic and gave me a few sessions of one-on-one training after our regular classes. Sometimes he would blindfold me as he played me recordings, asking me to identify what I heard. Sometimes I would spend our entire sessions blindfolded as he quizzed me. But we never had sex again. He changed after our encounter. It seemed like a huge weight was removed. He was happier and smiled more. He just seemed more confident. I really enjoyed our private sessions together. And something must have worked. I aced my dialect and language quizzes.

As the weeks went by, we were down to eight trainees left in the program. Mr. Montgomery replaced the photos of us with new ones. Right up until our last tutoring sessions, I never noticed even a single smudge on any of them.

Kyle had been dropped from the program back in April. It was hard to see him leave. He was feeling down and directionless. He was crushed, but he always knew that most of us wouldn't make it. Still, I don't think any of us were prepared to be dropped. He was kicking ass in high school, but it all seemed flat compared to being a secret agent. I'd asked Kyle to my prom partly to cheer him up and partly because I just wanted to spend time with him. It was good to have a friend like him and knew I might need his support if I got axed. We didn't end up sleeping together that night, but we did get smashed and stayed up talking on the roof of my house. We watched the sun come up and drunkenly told each other that we'd be friends forever. We kissed, but that's as far as it went. I don't know if the alcohol caused the kiss or if it prevented us from going further. I just knew it was a great night and I was happy to spend it with Kyle.

It was June and my high school graduation was two weeks away. I never got Andre out of his clothes, but I wouldn't have traded my experience with brainy Mr. Montgomery for anything. Not even Andre. I even grew to love his sweater vests. By the last week of training there were just five of us left. It was clear that not all of us would be asked to be Shades. We all knew that only fifty young people would be chosen and it was statistically unlikely a tenth of them would have been from Houston.

Our last day of training ended earlier than usual. The five of us were separately called into the office of the recruiters who initially approached me. We each waited alone and our appointments were spaced out. I never saw any of the others enter or leave.

It was good to see the two men who lured me into their van nearly six months earlier. They still looked like Mormon boys to me. They were smiling when I walked in the room. They both stood and each put a hand on my shoulder. My nervousness gave way to cautious excitement.

"I… I made it?" I said sheepishly.

"You made it."

"Fuck, yeah! I'm a goddamn super-spy! I did it! I fucking did it! Whoo-hoo!" I pulled myself together. "Sorry, sirs. I was just…"

"Forget it, Jake. You deserve to be excited. Your scores were great. You did better than anyone could have expected. We've got great plans for you," he reassured me. "We're sending you on a mission this summer. You'll leave in two and a half weeks. Go see Mr. Montgomery. He's got your mission brief and some stuff for you. Then go home, enjoy your graduation and spend a few days just being a regular teenager. You've earned it."

"Wow," was all I could say. "Wow," again and again. I was smiling so hard it hurt.

I made my way across the campus building as it was being dismantled. Soon, there'd be no sign it had ever been here and it would be just another Houston industrial warehouse. I saw Ahmed coming out of Mr. Montgomery's office. I was expecting the worst.

"Congratulations, Parker. It looks like you made it too," he said as he reached out to shake my hand.

Seriously? He made it through also? This guy's been a jerk to everybody for the past five months. Now he wants to be pals? I just stood there.

"I get it, Parker. I was told that I can come off a little abrasive."

"A little?"

"Look, I'm working on it. And it looks like we'll both be Shades. We're the only two that were asked to be agents. I'm willing to try to put any bad blood behind us if you are. Anyway, my acceptance into the team is contingent on me working on my people skills. I find that rather humorous."

"Yeah. Hilarious," I say as I reach out my hand. This guy still seemed like an asshole, but we were both new Shades. A grudge wouldn't do either of us any good. I hoped that being part of The Agency would be good for him and he'd be less of an asswipe. We politely wished each other luck and said goodbye.

I was feeling so happy, not even Ahmed could bring me down. I entered Mr. Montgomery's office and immediately thanked him for the help he gave me. I told him that this wouldn't have been possible without his tutoring. He thanked me for what I gave him, telling me how much that certain afternoon together meant to him. It felt good for him to let go and give into his physical side. He explained that despite his accomplishments, he'd always been intimidated by the muscled, field-trained instructors. But during our encounter in his office, he felt bigger and badder than any of his peers. He confided that it had done amazing things for his confidence. That was obvious but I was happy to hear him say it. He's a brilliant, attractive man and an excellent fuck. He should feel great about himself.

Then he went over some documents with me: a special passport, a few papers that needed signing and a code for an office in London I'd need to memorize before leaving.

"I also wanted to let you know about your friend Kyle Mills," he told me.

"Yeah. The only thing that sucks about this is that he didn't make it. I was hoping we'd be celebrating together."

"Look, Jake. I'm sharing this with you because I know you care about him. I haven't told Kyle yet, but I've arranged for his admission into Oxford where he'll be training in linguistics with me. I think very highly of Kyle's skills. I know he can be a huge asset to The Agency's language and information programs and I plan on working very closely with him."

Maybe *extremely* closely, I thought. These guys could be good for each other. Mr. Montgomery could teach Kyle a lot. And Kyle will get his place in The Agency, the best training and, probably, his first fuck!

***

I smile at the memory and wish Kyle was in England now, but he won't arrive at Oxford until fall. I hope that we'll be in the same place at the same time soon. But for now, I want breathe in every corner of this city and take advantage of my expense account.

CHAPTER EIGHT
ROOM SERVICED

Before I find my next hotel, I want to experience a little bit of gay London. I check my iPhone and find a "left luggage" facility in a train station where I can stash my bag for twenty-four hours for only nine euros. Deal! I grab the tube and make my way to Soho, London's gay district. I'm on boner alert just thinking of all the guys I'll find there.

I get off the subway at Tottenham Court Road and walk over to Old Compton Street. There's something different about the men here. I love American men, but these English guys really do something to me. They're gorgeous, but effortlessly so. They just *are*. A lot of them are very similar to me. They're lean and a little shaggy. And they're uncut, almost every single one of them. I'm so glad my parents left me intact, but sometimes guys back home just don't know how to work a foreskin. My dick isn't an ear of corn and you don't need to shuck it, guys. It's sensitive!

I see some dudes who look like tourists taking in London's gay life like me. Posing for pictures in front of a pub is a big give away. But I'm just as excited to be here as they are. I shoot a smile at every guy I see as I'm walking. Not sure if they all feel my Texas charm or think I'm a freak, but I'm having too good a time to worry about it.

I find a fun-looking café. The building is painted blue with a purple awning hanging over the front door. It's a bright, open restaurant that'll give me a great view of everything going on. I grab a table right up against the front wall, which is made almost entirely of glass. I can see everyone walking by. I love the energy of this city. I've never felt anything like it in the streets or malls of Houston. But with all these gay people around, I feel like I'm home. Not home, like where I grew up, but a bigger kind of home. I wonder if this is how Jews feel when they visit Israel. These bars, shops, cafés, these men are my Holy Land. I belong here.

I know. I'm such a fag. And fuck anyone who has a problem with it!

The waiter comes to take my order and I tell him way too much about how it's my first time out of the United States, how I love London, how I want to see everything and I realize he just wants to take my order. But he's really friendly anyway. And cute. I order a cheeseburger, well-done please, and let the poor guy get back to work. I pull out my iPhone and review my encrypted mission notes. I get butterflies in my stomach. I'm going undercover. I don't want to say that I'm nervous, but this is big. Sure, I played Juan Perón in my high school play when I was sixteen, but this is different. This is some scary shit. Messing this operation up could cost people their lives. That's a way bigger deal than hitting a sour note, or losing my fake mustache in front of a theater full of parents in my junior year production of *Evita*. But I was pretty awesome every night on stage and I'm gonna be awesome when I go undercover. The Agency wouldn't send me out on such an important mission if they didn't think I was ready. Right?

I keep reading. Cody has been training for years, since he was only a child as best as they can tell. I've only had six months. Cody won't know what hit him. I'm going to ace this. I take a sip of my Coke. I miss sweet tea.

I take a deep breath and look up. My eye immediately catches my waiter leaning over the bar. He catches my eye and smiles. Any lingering anxiety about my mission is forgotten. He's gorgeous, with strawberry blond hair and chiseled jaw. He almost looks like old pictures of Prince William. I smile back.

I finish my meal and decide to check out some of the shops on the street. "Come back soon," the hot waiter calls out as I leave. I look back and wave with a smile before exploring all the cool gay shops around. There's a place filled with books and magazines and sex toys. I love this stuff! I get some hot black briefs with cobalt-blue piping there. My first underwear purchase, but certainly not my last. These are going to look great on me! I keep walking around. There's a huge bar that I'll bet gets crazy after dark. I want to come back here one night. There's a theater and sex shops and pubs. I look and flirt and take it all in.

From there I walk everywhere and take pictures like crazy. In Hyde Park I see pale guys sunbathing with very little on. In Trafalgar Square I take a selfie in front of the London Eye. I snap a good one of Big Ben and Little Jake. At Buckingham Palace, I stand next to one of the Palace guards and get a shot of the two of us. I'm giving my biggest smile and he looks like a statue. He probably thinks I'm a complete dork but I couldn't resist.

I arrive at my most important stop: Marks and Spencer. I've read about this store online. British guys love the underwear here. More underwear shopping for me. I pick up a pack of black microskin trunks. Sleek, square-cut, dark and super sexy, the perfect look for the world's hottest twink super-spy. Mom never would have bought underwear like this for me. But now I'll never have to have another embarrassing underwear moment again. Now that I'm an adult, it's time I make my own under-wear choices. My body, my choice. And it's my choice to look fucking hot! I can't wait for a guy to see me in these.

I find a McDonald's with free WiFi so I can send the tourist pictures to my parents and let them know how I'm doing. I type my parents a quick email and tell them about all of the things I've seen today. But I leave out the underwear purchases.

"Love you guys," I write out at the end of my message. "I miss you." And I do. More than I thought I would. I wonder what would happen if I don't make it home. Would my parents ever know what happened to me? I guess I'll just have to make sure to watch my back.

The sun starts to go slowly down, filling the sky with color. I wish I could explore every inch of beautiful London, but it's time for me to find a place to crash for the night. I head over to Charing Cross station where I left my bags. I pull out my phone to find a hotel. I have an Agency credit card and I'm going to make my last night in London a good one. No more youth hostel.

I search for first-rate hotels in the city. Imperial Hotel at London Park Lane looks sweet. One room for one night costs way more than I'd make in a week working a part-time job back home. And that's just a basic room. But tonight, I'm doing it in style. I book the Executive Room and catch a train to get me closer to the hotel.

The second I step inside the hotel lobby, I am blown away! It's huge. Everything is sleek, new and clean. I wonder if I look like I belong here. Fuck that! Tonight, this is home. I find the check in desk and I'm greeted with a warm smile.

"Can I help you, sir?"

Damn, these English guys! I swear, every time I hear that sexy accent, I get a semi. No, I have an accent. He still sounds fucking hot.

"Hey!" I smile. "I have a reservation."

"All right, sir. Can I get your passport?"

I hand it over and he starts typing, looking up the room I just booked. I can see he's surprised that I've booked such a fancy room. I'm loving it! He hands me my key card and writes down what floor I'm on, then tells me to enjoy my stay. He calls for the bellhop to take my bags to my room, but I decline any help. All I have is my backpack and a few shopping bags full of underwear. I manage easily.

I step into the elevator and fall against the back wall. I didn't realize how tired I am. I conservatively estimate I walked a million miles today. Quite possibly a million and a half. I really want to kick my shoes off and get some rest.

I get off on the eighth floor and wander down the hallway, trying to find a match to the number written on key envelope. I find the room at the end of the hall and slide my key. The room is even better than I expected. It's the size of a small apartment. The first thing I see is the living area with a giant beige couch opposite a massive TV hanging on the wall. Behind that is an eating area already set up with a complimentary bottle of champagne. Hello! I wander into the bedroom. Wow! The inviting king-size bed faces another giant flatscreen TV built into the wall. This place is class all the way. I want to move in.

I drop my bags and run to the window. I think the view is my favorite thing about this room. I can see the Wellington Arch, the giant stone landmark in Hyde Park. I see the beautiful sculpture of a winged angel over a chariot led by four horses, sitting on the top of the arch. My dad told me all about the history of the Wellington Arch and the bronze sculpture. It was originally ordered to commemorate the victory of Britain over Napoleon during the Napoleonic Wars. The statue on top is supposed to represent the Angel of Peace descending upon the Chariot of War. I get the strongest urge to call my father and tell him all about my view. I remember the huge time difference. I also remember I'm undercover staying in a hotel room that I shouldn't be able to afford. And my parents think I'm backpacking cheaply across Europe with my graduation money. No call tonight. Maybe someday I'll be able to tell my parents about this trip and this life, but not just yet. Are there books about coming out to your parents as a spy?

I close the curtains and explore the rest of the room. The bathroom is insane. There's a shower and a separate tub made out of the same brown marble as the sink. I decide I need to take a bath. The English love a good bath so who am I to argue?

I get the water to the right temperature and fill the tub with its clear warmth. I sit down on the edge of the tub and take off my shoes and socks. Ouch. I realize how sore my feet are from all my walking. My entire body is coated in a thick layer of sweat that glues my T-shirt to my chest. When I peel it off, the cool air of the room hits my sweaty skin and hardens my nipples. I pull my jeans and underwear down in one swoops and step out of them. The air of the room feels good on my naked body.

I moan as I step in the tub and I feel the water surround me. It's like warm, wet arms hugging me everywhere. I can feel all of the tension in my body flow out of me and into the bath before disappearing into nothingness. I could stay in here all night. I consider having a wank in the tub so I can watch my cum float in strands under the water, but I'm getting hungry. My stomach does not like to be ignored. I towel off from the top of my shaggy head to the tips of my thoroughly pruney fingers and toes. I use the phone in the bathroom to call down to room service. (A fucking phone in the bathroom!) I order chicken satay. I'm not a hundred percent sure what that is, but I'm feeling adventurous. I also tell them to send up french fries and a brownie sundae. And hurry!

I loosely wrap the towel around my waist and check out the bed. I pounce onto the soft mattress and let my head sink into the cool pillows. Fuck, these pillows are amazing! It feels like my whole head is getting a blowjob.

I rest my eyes. Oh, my head feels so good. This bed feels so good. This whole thing feels so...

***

Boom, boom, boom. Where am I? Hotel. I fell asleep. How long? That sound? It's a knock on the door.

"Room Service."

"Oh, shit!" I yell before I jump out of bed and run for the door, flying across the room.

I pull the door open to see a man in his early twenties with a very closely cropped, almost shaved, head. He's young and he looks it. He's dressed in the standard black slacks and crisp white button-down shirt but there's something almost primal about him. It's like he's in a costume he doesn't belong in. I wonder what he looks like when he's not working.

"Your... dinner, sir."

The room-service guy, "Kieron" according to his name tag, is giving me a slight look of surprise while trying to maintain his luxury-hotel professionalism. Is it because I'm too young to be in a hotel like this? Is he getting all judgy with me? His eyes keep darting to my middle and lingering. What is it?

I look down at myself.

"Oh fuck!"

I'm completely naked. Like, no-clothes, my-dick-is-out naked. In my haste to answer the door, I completely forgot about the bath and the nap. The towel, my only hope for modesty, is still lying way over on the bed. Worst of all, I'm hard. I must have been having some great dreams because I'm sporting some massive post-nap wood. Looking down I see a silvery drop of glistening pre-cum spill from the slit at the tip of my cockhead that barely peeks out from its foreskin covering. My entire body goes red in embarrassment.

"Uh, uh," I stammer for a good minute I'm sure.

"I can set this up for you, sir," Kieron tells me, ignoring the 800-pound boner in the room.

"Come in," I step out of the way, trying not to look my server in the eye. I grip my cock in one hand, for all the good it does. The young Brit has already seen everything I've got and hiding it now is completely pointless. Yet, still I try. He gives me a reassuring don't-worry-I've-seen-it-all smile. He wheels the cart into the room, circling around me to set it up at the table. I make a path to the bathroom to grab a robe. I clumsily bump into him as I try to pass. I suddenly feel a hand on my cock.

I freeze. Kieron stares into my eyes, completely unmoving. His eyes are so blue. And maybe just a little scary. His hand is still wrapped around my pole, which throbs with excitement. He doesn't stroke it. He just holds it. There's something so sexual about Kieron's animal look. I feel like anything could happen. He raises one eyebrow as he pulls his hand over my cock and squeezes the tip of my foreskin. I can feel my pre-cum drain into his palm. He brings his hand to his mouth and licks it.

"I'm bloody hungry too!"

Before I know it, his lips attack my mouth. He kisses me roughly and I taste my own pre-cum on him. He grabs the back of my head and pulls me so close. He never takes his hand off my cock as we stand there making out. I'm naked, but Kieron is still in that formal uniform, the costume that seems so wrong on a guy so rough, so sexual. Now I'm experiencing the real Kieron. He keeps rubbing my shaft, slowly and deliberately. My foreskin rubs over my wet and sensitive dickhead. I think Kieron knows that if he goes too fast, I'll explode. He knows exactly how to work my cock. I'll bet Kieron knows a lot about cock.

I guide him, still attached by the mouth and cock, toward the bedroom. Light headed with excitement, we both fall to the ground before we can make it to the bed. We separate, but only long enough to get that unfortunate uniform off Kieron's body. There's a thin sheen of sweat across his skin. He smells wonderful, like a man who's been working all day. So natural.

I stare down at his body. He has a light dusting of hair across the front of his pale skin. He's thin but toned. He's got the kind of hot body that doesn't get built in the gym, but by working hard and skipping meals so he can afford drinks and cigarettes. He wears a chunky metal chain around his neck that dips down to his chest. Tattoos scatter his body including a large block of text on the center of his back. But I'm not up for reading right now.

I rub my hand over the light reddish-brown fur on his chest. A dark patch leads down to his belly button and then to his crotch. His soft pubes are unshaved but there's not a massive amount of hair there. The best part about his body is definitely his cock. It's as big as mine, but with a longer foreskin. He has so much foreskin. I feel jealous and turned on.

"I hope you're enjoying your stay, sir," Kieron says, smiling right at me. "It's a pleasure serving you." He looks rough, but sweet at the same time. I'm very interested in the rough part.

"Then fuck me," I tell him. My cock is painfully pulsing. My body needs to feel his dick inside of me. "Fuck me!"

We roll on the floor and I'm on top. I push our dicks together, squeezing them and letting our pre-cum run and mix down our long shafts. I moan deeply.

His smile widens as he rolls me over on to my back. "Only if you stick that bloody-huge fucking American cock deep inside me fucking hole first."

I moan again. If he keeps talking, he won't have to fuck me. I'll cum just listening to his voice.

Kieron pins my hands with his and kisses me hard. I feel the stubble from his face. Everything about him is so rough, so wonderfully unpolished. He's certainly not the kind of guy on those fancy British tea-and-tophat shows my mom loves to watch on PBS. He's the type of English guy who probably knows all of the dirtiest parts of London. And they all know him. I just want to drink everything about him in. I've never experienced a guy like this in Texas.

We get up and stumble to the bed, guided by our bouncing boners. I playfully push my new Brit buddy down on the bed and kiss his thin lips, then his tightly cropped hair, then his earlobes. This drives him crazy.

"Bloody fuckin' hell!"

He lifts his legs and tightly wraps them around my waist. Then he reaches through his legs and guides my cock to the tip of his hungry English hole.

"Fuck me fucking arse," he commands.

His face scrunches up like he's in pain as my pre-cum lubed poker pushes through his sphincter muscles.

"Should I stop?" I ask concerned, hoping he says "no" because I really, really don't want to.

Kieron laughs. "If you do, I'll bloody kill you!"

I chuckle with him. Then I plunge deep inside his tight hole. Kieron barks, throwing his head back. His hands reach out and grab fistfuls of white sheet. I don't know how long I'm going to be able to last like this. Seeing this beast underneath me at my control is turning me on more than I would have ever expected. I fuck him hard. Nothing I can do is enough to satisfy his hunger for my cock. His legs keep me locked in place. His hands squeeze my ass, pulling me harder into him. I pound my torpedo further into his chute, giving him the fuck he's begging for. He pulls at my shoulders, my ass, my neck, anything he can reach to force me to fuck him harder. His eyes never pull away from mine as I fuck.

"Harder," he pants. "Fucking deeper!" Kieron lifts his ass higher and grinds into my hips. My cock feels like it's on fire, buried deep inside his snug walls. I've never fucked anyone like this before. I feel like I'm going to shoot Kieron full of gallons of my nut if I don't stop. Like now.

I freeze. "My turn."

Kieron smiles wickedly at me. "Mate, you're going to get a fucking you'll never bloody forget."

Without missing a beat, he uses his hold on my waist to flip us over so I lay on my back, still buried deep inside of him. As he lifts that perfect ass off my member, I almost regret my decision.

"I'm gonna give you the kind of fuck I learned in the dark rooms of London bars that would make a pussy little tourist like you wet your trousers and go crying to your mum."

Why is he being so rude to me? Why is it turning me on so much? I hope he doesn't stop. He lifts my thighs onto his shoulders and lightly rubs his tongue along my boyhole. I throw my head back into the pillows and I relax my ass. I want to feel more of that tongue inside of me. But he's finished.

"Meow," he says, rubbing the cat's paw-shaped birthmark on my right butt cheek.

He spits on my hole three times before he drops my legs and sits back up. He pins my wrists down above my head with one hand while using the other to guide his enormous cock and foreskin into my tight hole. I don't think I could get away if I wanted to. But I don't want to. I want him to fuck me so bad. But as he starts pushing into me, I have my doubts that I can take all of Kieron. I grit my teeth and growl in a mix of pain and pleasure.

"Fuck! That's big!"

Kieron smiles a cocky smile as he looks down at me. But he doesn't ask me if I'm okay or if I want him to stop. He pulls out all way out of me and then slams back into my hole, smashing his cockhead deep into me. I squeeze the sheets with my fingers and let out a muffled scream. I can barely take it. It's so big and he's so rough. He slams into my ass over and over again with a cruel grin on his face. Then he sweetly kisses my forehead.

He's such a hot mess of beautiful contradictions. With every thrust I feel like I'm being torn apart, but I can't find the will to tell him to stop. With every stab into my prostate, the pain lessens and my pleasure increases. It's starting to feel right. Now I'm thrusting back into his every strike, swallowing his cock with my ass. His attack increases with such a strength, it feels like he's trying to fuck right through me. And I want him to. I begin to understand what an excellent fuck Kieron is. He fills me with as much pain as I can take before allowing me this intense pleasure. He plays my body better than I play Xbox and he knows it. He has instincts like an animal. This must be what it feels like to get fucked by Wolverine.

"Fuck me!" I yell while I try to pull my wrists from his grasp just so I can touch him. "Fuck my hole hard and don't stop!"

He gets on his knees and lifts my back off the bed, my legs still around his shoulders. In this position, he's completely in control. I'm just his puppet now. He pulls me down onto his cock as he thrusts forward, allowing him deeper inside of me. He grabs my cock with his rough hand. He's strangely gentle with it, a complete contrast to the relentless pounding my backside is taking. He knows how to work a boy. He moves two fingers and his thumb up and down the base of my shaft, keeping me on the edge. He knows that I've been on the verge of jizzing my load ever since he first grabbed my cock. An overly eager stroke could pull my trigger.

But I know he can't hold on much longer either. I can feel Kieron's hooded meat-missile swelling and throbbing inside of me. He slams into my prostate and it's too much. He's barely touching my cock, just working his thumb and forefinger at the base, causing my foreskin to glide over my wet cockhead. My balls go completely tight and my cock pulses with heat. I explode! My cum shoots out of my tapered tip and drenches us both. At the same time, Kieron growls and I feel the warmth of his fiery release fill my damaged body. It fills me up and starts oozing out of my hole as he keeps pounding his seed into me. There's so much and it doesn't feel like it's ever going to stop. I don't want it to. I want all of him inside of me.

Kieron's head drops to his chest as he finally finishes emptying his heavy ballsack in me. He pulls out, lowers himself to my crotch and licks my cock clean. His tongue swirls around the inside of my foreskin, squeezing my shaft and licking the salty cream from the sheathing. I stay rock hard. Kieron's tongue moves like a cat's as he licks me completely spoogeless.

He takes one final tug on my foreskin before standing up. "I bloody better get back to work or I'm gonna fuckin' lose me job." He grabs his clothes, but his eyes never leave my naked body. He smiles again. "But it'd be bloody worth it if I did!"

He gives me a deep, long kiss. I can taste my cum in there. I enjoy the flavor of my own sweet jizz as my tongue probes his mouth. Before he can grab his bright red underwear from the drab pile of his uniform, I give Kieron's foreskin a tug. It's so long, and hangs so far below his cockhead, you could fit a Prius inside of it.

He pulls my hand away from his foreskin, calls me "cheeky" and finishes getting dressed. He gives me one more scratchy kiss before he leaves me alone in the room. I'm spent, exhausted and hungry. I don't bother getting dressed. I just grab my cold chicken satay off the room service cart and shove it in the peanut sauce. Best fucking dinner ever!

CHAPTER NINE
THE EXPERIENCE HE CRAVES

My eyes open and the room is bright. I check the clock. It's late. Really late. It's after noon. But I feel great. I'm glad I asked for a later checkout. Last night wiped me out. But in the best way possible.

I enjoy the shower in my fancy room. It feels great but I almost regret washing Kieron's smell off of me. I wish I could enjoy it a little longer.

I throw my things together quickly and take in my surroundings one more time. Goodbye, beautiful room.

I take the elevator down, pass through the ornate lobby and check out. Goodbye, beautiful hotel.

I bum around London for a while. I grab a sandwich near Trafalgar Square and watch the people. I browse through some local comic book shops and tell myself I'll be back to London soon. I head down to the Liverpool Street Station. I play some games on the iPad while I wait for my train.

Ninety minutes later I'm in Harwich. I see the ferry. It's lit up like Christmas. It reminds me of the ship my parents took me on after sophomore year for our cruise from Galveston through Mexico. But this one's getting me to Holland. And no parents. I'm on my own and everything's different.

I board the ferry and make my way to my sleeping quarters. I have a small cabin. It's no Imperial Hotel Executive Room, but it's nice. It's bordering on cramped but it has a bed and a shower. And it's mine.

I get comfortable. I throw on some basketball shorts and a black Superboy-logo T-shirt. The shirt hugs tightly and I like the way it feels. I look in the mirror and I like how it makes me look even better. Being away from home and on my first adventure makes me feel like a super boy. And it feels good.

I grab a bite to eat in the a la carte restaurant while browsing through some comics on my iPad. I found these gay porn comics online and I'm in heaven. Class Comics. They're fun, colorful and the superheroes have big dicks. I mean, really big dicks. And foreskins. And they get fucked. By guys. Who also have big uncut dicks. I may never go back to The *Justice League* again.

I head back to my room, ready to relax and have a wank to some of these comics. After all the wild sex in London I worry that a solo session might be a little bit of a let down. But then I feel a bit of a spring in my dick and remind myself that all orgasms are good orgasms. And I'm an expert at slinging my own meat.

I wander down the hall distracted with thoughts of colorfully clad super heroes saving the world and hungry for horny rewards. Then *thud*. I bump right into a guy.

"Oh, man! I'm so sorry!" I try to apologize.

The man smiles.

"Don't worry. That happens in narrow hallways. American?" he asks with an American accent, West Coast if I'm not mistaken.

He's older, maybe middle fifties. He's got gray hair, receding a bit on top, and a white goatee. He's thickly built with just a bit of a belly, but solid. He's wearing shorts and a light blue short-sleeved button-up shirt, the vacation uniform for older American travelers. He gives me a big, friendly smile.

"Yeah. Is it obvious?" I smile back.

"No," He laughs. "I heard you ordering back in the restaurant. Hi. I'm Rich."

I introduce myself. This guy is really charming. As much as I'm loving my time away from home, I'm surprised by how comforting it is to chat with another American.

He asks me if it's my first time in Holland. I explain that it's my first time out of the United States.

"I've come to Europe every year since college. I love it. I'm heading to Antwerp," he tells me.

"Amsterdam for me," I reply.

Rich doesn't respond. He's just kind of smiling at me. He gives me a little chuckle. His glance lowers to my crotch and he raises his eyebrows. Did I say something wrong?

"Uh?" I ask, giving him a confused look.

I look down. I see my shorts tenting. Maybe these shorts weren't such a good idea. My boner is at a right angle, hard and pointing forward.

"Fuck!" I'm mortified.

"Looks like you're having a good night," Rich teases with a grin.

I'm so embarrassed. I'm so hard, but I'm so embarrassed. My boner is uncontrollable. It decides when it wants to play and never thinks to consult me. It's like having an unruly demon in my pants, but one I couldn't live without. Or want to live without.

Rich laughs at my obvious embarrassment.

"When you're my age, a hard-on like this is a reason to celebrate," he says to comfort me. "There's nothing to be embarrassed about."

Rich takes a glance behind him and then reaches right in my shorts. He just sticks his hand in. Right there! He doesn't even ask. His fingers close around my hard cock. I feel a surge of wonderful warmth shoot through me. Maybe these shorts were a good idea.

I can feel his hand getting wet. My pre-cum is really flowing. The front of my shorts are getting wet too. But he doesn't let go. He's very forward and nervy. I like this guy.

"Any interest in taking this back to my room?"

I just look at him and smile. He pulls his hand from around my cock and puts his arm around my shoulder as he leads me down the hall to his room. It's not far. I walk in first and notice that his cabin is a lot bigger than mine. And very fancy. As I'm taking it in, he has my Superboy shirt, my London-bought underwear and my shorts off in a flash. He's got some mad undressing skills. He puts both hands on my chest and rubs in circles, feeling my firm body. Then he licks my right nipple very gently while he strokes my cock. I just stand there. He's enjoying my body and I'm enjoying him enjoying it. I let him explore me. His hand rubs the small of my back and lands between my ass cheeks before moving between my legs. It tickles my ball sack and my cock throbs. I can hear the sound of my cock, getting wetter and wetter as he strokes me. He drops to his knees and licks the tip of my dick. It's torture and pleasure. He squeezes my cock and pulls all the foreskin forward, looking at it and taking it all in. More of my pre-cum spills, falling onto his shorts. He plunges his face into my cock and swallows the whole thing down his throat. I feel a shock of electricity run through me and I moan loudly. He's so good at this! I'm sure he's sucked a lot of cock in his life and his experience shows. He moves down to my balls and he massages them gently with his lips as he rubs the sides of my upper legs.

"Nice cock," he tells me, taking a momentary break from pleasuring my nuts.

"Thanks," I shoot back, not quite knowing how to respond. I mean, it's not like I've put any work into making it the fine cock that it is. But I'm happy to take the compliment anyway. I'm so turned on, he could probably insult me and I'd be grateful.

He stands up and kisses me, wrapping his hairy arms around me. His silver goatee scratches against my face as we make out. It's wet and salty from my pre-cum. He pulls me close and our crotches meet. I'm sure I'm leaving a huge wet spot on the front of his shorts as my pre-cum continues to flow. As he rubs his cock against mine through his cargos, I push back into his. I put my arms around him and reach up the back of his shirt. I rub his body. It's wider and softer than mine. But I don't need a hard body to feel good. I'm so turned on by the aggressive kisses and the firm grip of his arms around me.

I realize this clever man has me completely in the buff while he hasn't dropped a single thread. I pull away and throw myself backward on his bed. I land with a bounce and lift myself to my elbows.

"Now strip for me," I order him.

He smiles. "Anything you say, boss!"

I love his playfulness. Sex feels fun with this guy. My dick springs up as he unbuttons his shirt and drops it to the floor. He has a spattering of white fur on his chest that trails down to his belly. He looks his age, but he's attractive. He's a good decade older than my dad. I wonder if this is wrong somehow, but that only turns me on more. A bead of pre-cum drops from my stiff cock on to his bedspread.

"Take it all off!" I command.

Rich unbuttons his loose shorts and they fall to the ground with a light thud. He's wearing black briefs with a white waistband. They come off in a blur. Then he pounces on the bed, right on top of me. He kisses my neck and it sends a tingle through my body. His cock is hard and it rubs against mine, pulling my foreskin back and forth over my slick cockhead. I can't tell if he's pre-cumming or if I'm leaking enough to drench us both. Either way, the result drives me crazy.

Rich's cock is smaller than mine at about six inches, and he's cut. It jabs at my cock with every thrust of his hips, like a little dog fearlessly yipping at a Doberman. And the result is just as delightful. It feels good! We roll on top of his bedspread exploring each other's bodies. He's smiling the whole time. His silvery goatee enhances his grin, making his face light up. I can tell he's thinking about how big he's scored. I can feel his excitement in the way his fingers move over my tight body and the way he growls as he licks my firm stomach. It tickles. I realize I'm smiling too and I can't stop. His happiness is contagious. I slide out from under him so I can suck his cock.

Then I hear the door handle turn.

Fuuuuuuuck!

I instinctively cup my cock and balls with my hands. A man quickly opens the door. He's also in his fifties, with a military style haircut, brown on top gray on the sides. He's an imposing man, thick and heavier than Rich.

"What are you doing with my boyfriend?" he barks.

Oh, fuck fuck fuuuuck!

I look at Rich wide-eyed and confused. My heart is racing. What have I got myself into?

Is he going to freak? Is he going to hit me? I stiffen slightly. I may need to call on my training to make a hasty retreat. But I don't want to draw too much attention to myself.

The man starts laughing. "I'm just fucking with you, boy!"

"Jake, meet my husband Doug," Rich says through a chuckle. "Sometimes he thinks he's funny."

My heart is still racing as the new guy reaches out to shake my hand. We all laugh at the absurdity of the formality as I take his hand, sitting naked next to naked Rich.

"What're you guys getting up to here?" he says, not really asking, as his sits down next to us on the disheveled bed.

"I met this fine boy in the hall and he followed me back to our room," Rich explains, giving me a wink.

Doug responds by rubbing my chest and my stomach as if he's inspecting a new purchase.

"Nice!"

Then he firmly grabs my cock, causing all the pre-cum to spill out of my foreskin and run down his hand.

"Looks like you guys have been having fun."

I like where this is going. Two cool older guys for the price of one! I enjoy the way more mature men treat my body. They worship it. They act like they're lucky to land a hot young guy. I like to let them think that. But the truth is they know how to work my body better than anyone. I like their skills and experience. And I love the attention. I love the way they work so hard to please me and the way they explore every part of me like I'm some long sought-after treasure found in some exotic pyramid or something. I wish I could play it cool with these guys and make them work even harder. But my cock gives me away.

Rich wraps his arms around me from behind while his bearish spouse tugs on my foreskin. He starts sucking my cock while Rich turns my head and kisses me.

Doug releases my dick, stands up and undresses: first his short-sleeved button-up, then his Dockers, his short socks and his boxers. Though broad shouldered, his tan and rounded body probably wouldn't impress anyone, certainly not most body-conscious gay men. But I like the look of his salt-and-pepper chest fur, his slight belly and his cut cock that looks so similar to his lover's. Neither Rich nor Doug look gym-sculpted but they're fit. And there's something manly in the way they seem to embrace their softer bodies confidently, and seem unashamed of their bellies and fur. I'm excited and eager to play.

We all make out. Doug isn't hard yet but I'm ready to do something about that. I kiss him deep and stroke the shaft of his cock. I rub the tip of his mushroom cockhead and feel a little moisture, just a bit of pre-cum. I rub it around his cockhead with my palm and it gets a little wetter. I use that moisture to stroke his cock and he's as rock-hard as I am. Then I pull my foreskin over the flared head of his cut cock. I see his eyes widen and I wonder if he's ever docked before. His circumcised cock throbs with approval as he's covered in my prepuce and drenched in my pre-cum.

Both men rub my body and kiss my neck. I pull Doug's dick out of my foreskin and grip both their cocks. But mostly I just experience the sensations of their hands and lips on my body. It feels warm and charged in between this couple.

They lay me down and kiss me in unison down my chest, down my stomach and to my cock. They kiss my shaft from both sides. My cock throbs as they tease me. Rich moves down and gently takes both my balls in his mouth, licking my smooth sack with his tongue. Doug sucks my cock. His tongue explores my foreskin. Despite having a cut husband, this guy knows how to work an uncut boner. I don't think having a partner has kept him from keeping his skills sharp. The dual sensation gives me a head rush.

They lift my legs high and Doug rims my hole. Rich watches his husband's expert work and assists by holding my legs so Doug is free to stroke his own cock. They work so well together. I'm certain I'm not the first boy they've shared. Rich tells Doug to stand up. Doug pulls himself away from eating my ass and does as he's told. He's rewarded as Rich drops to his knees and sucks his lover's prick. Doug throws his head back and growls. I watch them interact the way they've probably done for years and years. It gives me a voyeuristic thrill. Then I'm pulled back in as Rich grabs his partner's wet cock and guides it toward my still-moist hole.

"Fuck him," Rich tells his man.

I'm being offered up like a gift. I feel like an object. And it only makes my rod harder.

Doug plunges his cock into me and the two men kiss. His cock feels good in me and watching them kiss only gets me hotter. I'm in the middle of their very private moment, a part of it, but also just a prop in it. They kiss each other differently than they kiss me. There's less passion, but more warmth. I wonder if one feels better than the other. But I am certain that this hairy daddy's cock feels great hammering at my ass.

Rich moves to the side of the bed and kisses me on the lips. Then he rises, rubs the back of my hair and feeds me his cock. These guys are giving it to me from both ends. I'm their vacation fuck toy!

Rich rubs one hand over my smooth pecs and one hand through the dark fur on his husband's chest. I know he's loving it because his cock is so hard in my mouth. His hand moves to support my head as I enthusiastically suck his cock. I cup his balls while I give him a blow-job he's going to remember long after their vacation is over and all the duty-free alcohol bottles have been long-emptied from the recycling bins.

"Uuuuuugh! His fucking hole is so tight," Doug moans, holding my ankles in the air.

"Fuck that ass, baby. Fill this little fucker's hole up," Rich tells his partner, breathing heavily.

It's nice to see a couple communicating like this.

Our moans and panting fill the room. The cocks in both my holes fuck faster. These guys aren't going to last much longer. Neither am I. Doug heaves into my ass and I feel his cock throb right before I'm filled with his warm wetness. He's pounding the last drops deep into me as my mouth fills with Rich's creamy load. I bury my face in his gray pubes, drinking every drop of his daddy sperm. He hold the back of my head for support. Though untouched, I feel my own cock about to blow. My cock fills with a powerful load of spunk and I spasm and spray. Both of my hot daddies pull out of me and watch my gusher of jizz. I feel like it's never going to stop as my body thrashes and shakes with pleasure. Once the gusher ends, I realize I've cum all over my new friends. They'll be pulling pieces of my jizz out of their chest hairs for a while.

"Damn, boy! What a mess." Rich tousles my hair and we laugh.

My cum is all over me. It's on them and all over their bed. Instead of giving me a towel to clean up, both men pounce on me and engage me in a three-way kiss. I feel someone's hand squeeze my still-hard cock and drain another squirt out of it. They move down to my chest, licking all my spooge off like they're jungle cats cleaning their offspring. Rich goes all the way down and licks my foreskin cum-free.

They both crawl up and meet at my lips for an aggressive kiss, filling my mouth with the taste of my owns spunk. I love it. And I love the warm feeling as I'm smothered between their soft furry bodies. I feel like a cub, warm and safe. My eyelids get heavy and I drift to sleep in I their arms.

***

I wake up in the morning and thank my hosts with matching blowjobs and hugs and kisses. Travel souvenirs seem so unnecessary compared to experience like this. They've got another stop, but I need to get off the ferry. I rush to my room and quickly gather my stuff and brush my teeth. I disembark and I'm in Amsterdam!

CHAPTER TEN
GETTING SCHOOLED

After a day exploring Amsterdam, checking out its pot cafés and getting into a little bit of sexual adventure, I'm on a short flight to Saba, an island in the Caribbean Netherlands. I stare at myself in the small airplane's bathroom and try to shake the exhaustion out of my head. Amsterdam was definitely an awesome experience, but the effects of the edibles are lingering. I stare in the mirror and mess up the shaggy look of my hair. I pop the collar of my polo shirt. I put on a pair of expensive sunglasses and smile at myself. I think I may be pretty good at playing the part of Jake Reilly, a rich private school snob.

I return to my seat and order another drink, to the dismay of the flight attendant. I can tell he thinks that I've had enough, but I have a part to play. He needs to believe I'm rich and spoiled. Also, these drinks are fucking awesome. He brings me a drink and I toss him a tip. He instructs me again that gratuities aren't necessary and tries to hand it back. I pat him on the ass and stuff a few euros down the front of his pants. He walks away saying something about ugly Americans under his breath in Dutch.

I let out a satisfied "Ahhhh" as the taste of alcohol spreads through my mouth and down my throat. I ignore the seatbelt sign and push up the armrest between my seat and the empty one closer to the aisle. I kick my feet up, pull the blanket over top of me, pop in my earplugs and pull down my eye mask. I slowly drift... off... to...

"Sir. Sir!"

I faintly hear a voice pulling me out from my slumber. The warm arms of sleep try to pull me back in. I feel someone shake me and my training kicks in. Without sight or hearing, I instinctively locate my aggressor and have him pinned to the floor. I hear gasps around me. I keep the assailant pinned with my knees and remove my earplugs and eye mask with my free hands. I see the shocked looks of the flight staff all around me. I notice that the rest of the plane's passengers have departed. Major oops! I quickly jump off of the cute male flight attendant.

"So sorry, bro. I was having a nightmare," I apologize with a grin.

I pat the airline steward on the cheek and help him up. He flinches at my touch. Poor guy! I decide that a quick exit is probably the best idea. I reach up to the luggage cabin above me and grab my suitcase and my jacket. I quickly depart the plane to the tiny runway and breathe in the beauty of Saba. I'm surrounded by blue water to my right and luscious greens to my left. This island will be my home for the next few weeks.

I'm greeted by a suited driver, standing in front of a black town car, holding a sign that reads "Jake Reilly." I nod toward him and he opens the rear door for me. I toss my bag in, give one last look at the gorgeous scenery and hop into the back of the shiny car.

"Directly to the academy, sir?" the limo driver asks.

I try not to laugh. I'm not used to having people call me "sir."

"That's right. Make it quick," I respond, a little concerned how easy it is to play the role of entitled private academy brat.

The car speeds forward and we begin to make our way toward the all-boys academy that I've been sent to infiltrate. I guess it's not that much of a stretch that I'm undercover as a first-year college student attending a summer semester abroad. I check my phone and stare at a photo of Cody. He's young, handsome and deadly and he's the reason I'm here. I'm on my own on this one. This island is too small and too remote for backup and any communications from the campus may be monitored or intercepted. I'll need to go into town and use a hard line if I need to reach anyone. This won't be easy but I know The Agency has faith in me. More importantly, I know I can do this. I find Cody and find out what his mission is. Then I get out and report to The Agency. A simple job. Then everyone will know what an awesome spy I am.

The driver's voice pulls me from my thoughts, "Is this your first time on the island, sir?"

"Yeah. My parents think spending my summer vacation with books in my face is a good idea. My dad's pissed off that I wrecked his favorite Bentley. I think this is my punishment. I just hope there's some fun to be had," I respond casually.

I've done my homework. Saba is a small island, just five square miles and a population of less than two-thousand, including the boys at the academy. It's technically part of the Netherlands and it's mostly mountain. Fortunately for me, most people speak English here.

"We're about to start up Mount Scenery, sir. You never know when it'll explode."

I take a look up and marvel at the sight of this potentially active volcano. With no eruption in almost four-hundred years, it seems pretty unlikely. But it's a great story for the tourists. And it's beautiful. The school sits almost at the peak where it's been for over two-hundred years, a modern Mount Olympus for the sons of the rich. The dark car starts its climb up the narrow road to the top of the mountain. I look out the window and watch the trees fly by as we climb higher and higher. I can understand why this private school is so exclusive. It's built on top of the volcano and houses less than a hundred students at a time. But since it's the summer session, there's only going to be about fifty of us or so.

When we pass the school's gates and stop in the driveway. The driver opens my door. I grab my bag and bounce out with a "thank you." I hand him a sizable tip as we shake hands.

I walk up to the front doors and I'm immediately swarmed by a number of students racing out. Many of them are shirtless and I can't help but smile at the sight. They look like they're off to play some kind of game. Rugby? Squash? I'm tempted to join them. Well, to be honest, I'm tempted to pants a few of them and start a welcome-to-school orgy. Since the school attracts students from all around the world, I see hot Italians, Finns, Danes, Greeks and Brazilians running through the field. Someone drops a soccer ball and I can hear the guys playfully shouting at each other in English thick with accents. It sounds like foreskin to me.

Distracted, I turn and bump into two tall guys. Both look a year or two older than me. One is definitely Dutch, with pale blond hair and blue eyes. His white tank top hangs from his skinny, tall frame. He introduces himself as Joost. Standing next to him is a sexy, athletic Spaniard who tells me he is called Esteban as he reaches out to shake my hand. Staying focused on my mission is going to be a challenge while I'm living at the International House of Hotness.

"Welcome, Jake. The Academy sent us here to greet you," Esteban explains, putting his arm around my shoulder. "We're so pleased to meet you. We'll take you on a quick tour and then you can settle into your room."

Joost takes my bag from me.

I smile back and say, "Where to first, guys?"

The pair show me around the classroom area, the dining hall and the sports field. There are spectacular views all around since we're up so high on the mountain. I ask questions and act like I'm taking it in for the first time, but I've already been on a virtual walkthrough of the entire facility. The Agency's tour provided me with details about this place that would stump any student or faculty member here. As we tour the library, a sexy older professor walks by and Joost grabs his attention.

"Professor Hawkins, I'd like you to meet a new summer student. Jake, this is Professor Hawkins."

I do my best not to stare. Professor Hawkins is a Scottish man, in his early forties, with reddish-brown hair. He's surprisingly built for a literature professor. I notice a shock of fur coming up from his white button-up shirt. I want to rub my fingers through it, but I settle for a handshake.

"Welcome to the Drake Academy for Young Men, Jake. I look forward to seeing you in class. Are you a fan of literature?"

"I love the classics, sir," I say trying to impress. "I'm looking forward to your class."

Professor Hawkins notices my flirtatious tone. As he shakes my hand, he lingers for a few moments. I watch as Joost and Esteban exchange glances. I start to wonder if the rumors about all-boys schools are true. Could it be that without a female in sight, the students and staff indulge their urges with one another? Is it like prison but with better food and fewer ugly religious tattoos?

The professor makes his goodbyes and we leave the library.

"Did you have an eventful trip?" Joost asks?

"Well, I did tackle this one flight attendant guy."

They laugh, not sure what to make of me, and we continue on with the tour. I meet a number of other teachers and students. I quickly realize that Joost and Esteban are two of the more popular guys at the school. I can see why. Both seem friendly and are very good-looking. It doesn't hurt that their respective parents are very rich and very influential. I learn that Esteban's two older brothers also attended the Academy.

Both boys have attended school here the past two years. While most of the guys go home over the summer break, the Academy offers specialized training over the summer for returning students and some basics for visiting students. Joost is spending his summer learning to paint and Esteban will be trained in fencing.

We take the spiraling stairs two at a time and arrive in the dorm area. Doors stretch further than I can see down the long, red-carpeted hall.

"You'd think for the fees that our parents pay that we'd get our own rooms. But the Academy believes that part of the experience here is about bonding. We've been roommates the whole time we've been here," Esteban says cocking his head in Joost's direction. "He snores."

Joost smacks Esteban in the head. "Ignore him. He loves having me as a roommate. We were strangers when we got here. Now we're inseparable."

I notice how Joost's fingers gently graze Esteban's back and then quickly drop. I figure that these two are more than roomies. They make a hot couple! I thank them for the tour and promise to catch up with them after I've had a chance to settle in. I close the door and note that there's no lock on it. Goodbye, privacy.

The room is nice. It's a good size, enough space for two queen-sized beds, a vanity with sink and mirror, two large desks with high-end, modern office chairs in front of them, two chests of drawers and a small sofa. The antique furniture is strong, made from quality dark wood. Some of it dates back to the early years of the Academy.

The thick walls are decorated with framed photos of the Academy's history and old maps of the island. It looks like Hogwarts for the most privileged of wizards. This wouldn't be a bad place to really attend school.

Before I settle in, I have a task. I rush across campus to a building at the far end of the school. It's the auditorium building that houses the ballroom. The large structure is completely empty, making it easy to do what I need to do without anyone noticing. I rush up the stairs and pick the lock to the roof entrance. It's a beautiful view from up here. This building faces out over the mountain. It's stunning, and just a little scary on the rooftop. I remove the parts of my gun from my shoe and assemble it. Then I tape it inside the metal air vent with silver duct tape. There's nearly no maintenance staff over the summer session so no one is going to find it. And it'll be here if I need it. I can't risk Cody finding it in the room, concealed or not.

I race back to the room without being spotted. Just as I catch my breath, there's a knock at my door. I open it and see an attractive young Nordic guy standing on the other side. He's wide, with a rugby player's body and dark blond straight hair. He fills out the school uniform of burgundy sweater and black shorts quite nicely.

"I'm called Anders," he says. "Welcome package for you."

"Hi. I'm Jake Reilly. Thanks," I smile back at him. He hands me the box with a large grin on his face. I lift the lid and see it's clothes, my own uniform. I unpack the box and find black shorts, black slacks, a burgundy jacket with white trim and the school's crest, two sweaters with the same crest, several white shirts and a black tie. There are also exercise clothes: shorts and tank tops in the school colors, maroon and white.

"It's the standard issued uniform that everybody wears here but everything is custom fitted to your measurements. Summer dress code is a bit more casual. You can wear a white T-shirt under the sweater to class. But a shirt and tie is always required for dinner," the handsome Swede explains. "It's all in the manual in your desk,"

"Thanks for bringing this. Much appreciated," I tell him. I could have picked this up downstairs myself, but I have a feeling he was eager to check out the new boy. A lot of these guys have been here the past year and the other newbies have already arrived. I'm the last one.

Anders smiles. "Dinner soon. Everyone must be in uniform by then," he says as he walks away.

I look at the time and realize I'd better start getting ready. I shut the door and stash my new clothes in a drawer and hang the jacket. I throw tonight's outfit on the bed. It's time to become one of the boys and get into my uniform. I lift the green polo I'm wearing over my head and catch a glimpse of my torso in the mirror. I throw the shirt on the floor and rub my hands over my abs. Looking good!

I undo my belt buckle and undo the top button of my jeans. I pull down my zipper and let my pants fall to the ground. I check myself out in the mirror to see how I look in my white trunk-cut boxer briefs. Not bad. There are so many good-looking guys here, but I feel like I measure up. I hook my fingers into my underwear and pull them down just as I hear the doorknob turning.

The door opens open before I'm able to cover myself. Blush!

"Hi. I'm Cody Lionus," my new roommate coolly tells me.

Still crouched, I spring up and shuffle over to him, my underwear around my ankles. I reach out my hand.

"Uh, I'm Jake," I reach out my hand, totally embarrassed.

He's completely unfazed. He takes my hand and shakes it firmly. I've made official contact with my target. The mission is on.

"Welcome to Drake. Is that what you're wearing to dinner? You might want to check out our dress code," he gently mocks with his slight Greek accent as he pulls a tie out of his drawer.

Wow. This is Cody, the guy I've heard so much about. And he's using "Lionus" as his last name? Could that be his real name? More likely, it's an alias. Now that I meet him, he seems like a regular guy. Okay, kind of a snarky guy, but an attractive snarky guy. He seems very close to my age with a similar build and roughly my height. But his hair is dark and short and his skin is a deeper tan than mine. He's handsome, though he wears his entitlement on his face. I'd almost say we looked alike if I didn't know that we were opposites in so many ways.

"Too casual?" I ask him jokingly, holding my arms out wide at my side.

I notice the corners of Cody's otherwise stoic lips curl as he takes in the sight of me in the buff. His eyes move down to my cock as he sizes me up.

"Better get dressed. We all need to be at dinner or else it doesn't start. You don't want to go through the kind of hazing these guys give the boy who makes them wait for dinner," Cody explains.

He manages a perfect knot in his tie as I rush into my new uniform. Anders was right. It fits well.

"I'm all set. Shall we go?"

"Just don't embarrass me at dinner, new guy, and I'll let you sit with me," Cody says walking by me and out the door.

I race to catch up. This Cody is a more interesting guy than I'd imagined. There's a real charisma buried in that snottiness. And his smooth legs look so good in those uniform shorts. It's a shame that my new buddy is an international terrorist and totally evil.

We hurry down to the dining hall and sit down at a table with Esteban and Joost. I catch the eye of Anders at another table and I wave. He winks and smiles back. The headmaster gives a speech, welcoming new and returning students. He tells us to be the fine men he knows we are and to honor the students who have walked the halls of this school before us. He reads a poem by Walt Whitman then advises us to get enough rest before the first day of instruction tomorrow. I quickly devour my tasty meal as the other guys talk about European soccer. If only all school food could be this good! After a dessert of Czech Bubble Cake, I excuse myself from the post-dinner activities explaining that I'm exhausted from my flight. Everyone nods knowingly. The rich seem to find luxury exhausting.

I head up to my room, strip out of my clothes, wrap a towel around me, grab a robe and head to the showers. As I enter, I see another student toweling off. He looks up and I recognize that it's Anders from earlier today. I can't believe my luck. I wanted to see him naked and now he's just standing there in front of me. His shoulder-length blond hair and his entirely smooth body are still wet from showering. He dries his firm pecs and broad shoulders. He has thick large nipples and I wonder what he'd think if I licked them. He dries his back while making direct eye contact with me. He nods toward me with a smile and continues drying off with no attempt to cover up. He looks good. I glance down below his wispy patch of blond pubic hair and see he has a pretty small uncut cock, well below average. He's got more foreskin than shaft. He reminds me of the Greek statues that I used to spend hours staring at in my junior high history textbooks. Those were some of the first naked men I even saw and their cocks, modest as they were, were the hottest things I had ever seen. Those ancient beauties imprinted themselves in my brain and gave me some of my first boners.

"Hi, Anders," I say, announcing my presence.

Anders, my Swedish Kouros, smiles and makes no attempt to cover his compact endowment as he finishes drying. Instead, he seems to radiate a certain confidence as he dries his taught balls and skinny shaft. I always thought small guys were supposed to be ashamed. He seems totally self-assured, kind of saying "Yeah, I got a small cock. Got a problem with it? Fuck you, then." His good looks and fearlessness are making me very small-curious.

I set my toiletry kit by the sink as Anders wraps his towel around his waist. I stall taking off my towel, because I can feel my cock is almost fully hard.

"Enjoy your shower," he says smiling as he walks past me.

"Thanks," I smile back.

I shed my towel and stand in front of the wall of mirrors over the sink stations. I see the reflection of my semi-hard uncut cock. I think about Anders' much, much smaller cock. I cover up half my dick and wonder what it would be like to be so small. Would guys still be into me? Would I manage to be as confident as Anders? Or would I be self-conscious and stay covered up, worried about what people would think? It's a boost to my confidence knowing that I'm much larger than the average guy. But Anders doesn't need a big slab of meat swinging down between his legs to give him his swagger. It makes me wonder how much of my personality is tied to my cock. I like to think I'm more than my dick size.

I notice in my reflection that my big club is now completely hard. I like the look of my cockhead poking out of my tight foreskin. Hello, little guy. It's safe to come out.

With everyone else reading and playing games downstairs, I'm pretty sure I have the showers to myself. It's nice to have some time alone. I'm in the mood for a wet wank. I'll hear anybody coming. I can always turn toward the wall to hide my erection if someone shows up.

I move into the large tiled shower room. There are no individual stalls, just a large communal shower with roughly twenty-five faucets. I wish these shower heads could talk. I take my place under a faucet head in the middle and I turn the handles to get the temperature just right. I let the hot water pour over me and my hair falls in front of my eyes as the steam rises around me. Feels good. I know that this mission is going to be tough. But right now, I just want to rub out a big fat load. I clear my mind. I think about all the hot students that I saw today. I think about the cute flight attendant from earlier and how his body felt under mine. I wonder how he would've reacted if I had planted a kiss on him. I soap up my armpits. I wonder if he would have kissed me back. I lather up my torso. I close my eyes and see all those international guys running past me, so many different shades of shirtless skin. I soap up my legs and I picture Esteban, Joost, Cody and naked Anders.

I step in something. What? It's gooey. Fuck!

Oh! Anders must have shot a big load out of his little cock. Not all of it made it down the drain. If I showed up here five minutes earlier I would have seen him stroking his little monster. I wonder how he would have reacted if I got in the shower with him. What would he have done if I pulled our cocks together and compared sizes? Would it turn him on or piss him off? What would that little cock have felt like in my mouth as I swallowed his entire shaft and mini-balls? Would it drive him crazy? How quickly would that dinky dick have shot it's sizable payload in my mouth? Maybe I'll get the chance to find out.

I get a good lather going before I start to stroke my cock. I savor this moment and I think about seeing handsome Professor Hawkins earlier. He has all the trappings of a bookish lit professor on the outside, but that patch of red-brown chest hair coming through his shirt hinted at something manly and primal. I lather up my cock and it's quickly throbbing in my hand. I slowly soap it and stroke it, imagining Professor Hawkins approaching me from behind in the shower. I picture his wet, hairy body against mine. His arms tightly wrap around me. I can feel his rough, full red bush brush against my lower back. He kisses my neck and thrusts forward and his thick cock slides between my cheeks. He's a decisive man and he doesn't waste time. He tells me that he knew he was going to fuck me before I even told him my name. His cock throbs and bobs between my cheeks. He tells me I'm just another piece of ass for him and I'm only here for his pleasure. Yes, I tell him. That's all I am. He teases me by not making contact with my hole. I whisper, I beg him to fuck me. He puts two fingers in my mouth to shut me up. I suck them like I was sucking his uncut cock.

I have to stop stroking my cock. I'm going to blow if I don't. I feel good and I want to enjoy it. I lather up my right hand with soap and begin to play with my hole. I quickly insert a finger, then another, and imagine that it's my imaginary lover, Professor Hawkins' thick cock plunging deep inside of me. I lean forward and pretend that he's roughly pushing me into position. I hear him tell me to bend over so he can use me and drive his cock as deep into me as it can get. I force my own fingers further and further inside of me. Faster and faster. I imagine the sounds of his strong grunts echoing off the tile of the shower room, blending with the noise from the wet spray rushing past my ears. I feel the hot water pouring down my back and wetting his front as he fuck only for his own pleasure. He thrusts faster and faster, picking up the pace with each forward motion. His cock is the perfect size to fill by eager ass, or maybe just a little bigger to give me some challenge. Our wet skin creates a smacking sound and his grunts deepen and intensify. I know that he's on the verge of cumming hard and I'm there too.

My phantom lover pulls out and my body feels empty. He allows me to beg for a minute. Then he shoves his cock all the way inside of me. Hard. And I feel complete again. He does it again. I despise the moments he's not in me. He does it again and makes me beg again. Please, Professor. Please fuck me. He catches me off guard and slams all the way in. But this time he doesn't pull out. He quickly and forcefully humps into me like a jackhammer. I know my fingers are simulating these motions, but in my head it feels like the professor is truly right behind me. He's selfishly pounding away at my hole, using my ass like he's used so many students before me. He's grunting loudly and recklessly, getting me more turned on than I thought I could be. He grabs my hair and pulls my head back and unleashes a massive load that explodes in my gut. I'm breathing so hard. I'm taking in water from the shower and I don't care. I stroke my cock with super-speed, foreskin flying back and forth over my cockhead. The fingers of my other hand dart in and out of my ass, but I let myself believe it's the professor still filling me with his seed. I open my eyes and look down at my cock in time to see it spray load after load of thick white cream. I watch myself squirt four large loads in quick succession. It lands right on the spooge puddle left on the tiled shower floor by Anders. As each load flies out of me, my boycream blends with his and I wonder what he was fantasizing about as he emptied his nuts.

I remove my fingers and turn the shower head toward my ample load. The stream of hot water pushes the Anders-Jake hybrid jizz puddle toward the drain. I slump down to the floor and take a few deep breaths. I pull back my tight foreskin and stroke my cock a few more times. A small squirt of semen spills out and I collect it with my fingers, bringing it to my tongue so I can sample the taste. It makes a fine dessert.

Just as I'm about to turn the water off, I hear the sound of someone scampering away. Was someone watching me? Who? Could Anders have snuck back to see me naked? I'd like that. But part of me hopes that Professor Hawkins came in and caught me. I would love to turn that intense fantasy into a reality. I rush outside the shower to investigate. But nothing. Whoever it was is already gone. I grab my towel and dry off. I put on my comfortable Academy robe and head back to my room. I'm not sure I'll ever know who was watching me but I hope they enjoyed themselves.

I get back to my room and Cody's not there yet. I hang my robe up and drop heavily to my bed, naked. It hits me how exhausted I am. I feel sleep overtaking me. Tomorrow I have a job to do, but right now I'm drifting to sleep, fantasizing about Professor Hawkins' auburn-furred arms wrapped around me.

CHAPTER ELEVEN
KEEP YOUR ENEMIES CLOSER

I've spent the last two weeks getting to know Cody. I try to be at his side most of the day when we're not in classes. Things go pretty smoothly as we settle into life at the Academy. Cody seems at ease around me now. He even shows me around a bit. He was here for a few weeks before I arrived so he knows his way around and where the best off-campus food in the area is. Best of all, I'm sure he doesn't think of me as anything but the son of a wealthy Texas oil executive. We spend so much time together that some of the other guys call him my "brother from another motherland." A bit of his snootiness has even faded around me. Sometimes it's almost like he's flirting with me. Could he be?

It's sometimes hard to remember that he's the enemy when we're on our bikes, racing down mountain roads into town together. It's possible we could be friends if we weren't on opposing sides and he wasn't working to destroy the free world. But he is. If The Agency's intel is correct, Cody's been with SATYR since he was a child.

We're not sure if his parents brought him into the organization or if he's been coerced somehow. I wish I could ask him how someone who's barely a legal adult could become involved with an evil global cabal run by the world's power brokers, heads of corporations and even an ex-vice president. It's not like troubled teens are uncommon, but this guy is rumored to have made his first kill at twelve. That's all the more reason to stay focused on the mission and remember that we won't BFFs.

There is a downside to spending all of this time with Cody, though. We've been together so much, I haven't had a chance to search his things without him around. The guy takes insanely short showers and is a very light sleeper. During one of my first nights in our dorm room, I tried to search his phone while he slept. He woke out of a sound sleep, grabbed my wrist and pushed my arm away before I even touched it. I told him I was drunk and thought it was my phone. He told me not to let it happen again and went back to sleep. I need to get into that phone. If he has any information, I have a feeling that's where it'll be.

I have managed to search around the school and go through their records. But I haven't been able to find out who or what Cody's here for. There's nothing unusual about the staff or the faculty. Sure, they're all some of the best in their fields, but there doesn't seem to be anyone useful to SATYR. The students all come from wealthy families, but other universities around the world are filled with the same type of kids. I haven't made the connection yet. So I keep my eyes and ears open. And I wait.

Today, Cody and I have been roommates for two weeks and one day. I'm pulling on my sweater and I hear Cody yelling from his bed.

"Fuck! I'm going to be late for class." He springs out of his covers wearing a snug pair of black trunk underwear. "Why didn't you wake me up?"

"Dude! I tried waking you. You were really out," I tell him as he stumbles out of bed and grabs his toiletries and some clean clothes.

"I cannot get kicked out of this school. They'll kill me!" he says, still adjusting to being awake.

"Your parents sound as strict as mine," I tell him.

"You don't know the half of it," he says, running out the door.

We were drinking last night. I thought it might loosen his tongue and something I could use would slip out. No luck. This guy's a pro.

Minutes later Cody comes out of the bathroom fully dressed. His dark hair is still pretty wet. It's rare to see him anything but perfectly styled. He drops his worn underwear into his hamper and grabs his jacket. He rips open the door and leaves the room before I even have the chance to say goodbye, rushing off to the science lab.

I make my way to lit class. I see a few students standing around the door. Why aren't they going in? A few of the guys seem to be reading a note on the door. Professor Hawkins had to leave the island for a family matter. He'll be gone all day. Class is canceled.

Hot damn! Three free hours. This is my chance!

I walk briskly walk up the stairs and back to my room. Part of me hopes I won't find anything on Cody. Even better, I'd like to find out he really is just a rich Greek kid with strict parents and an attitude. As I've got to know him, I've questioned if the Agency may be wrong about the guy. When we chat, he seems like an okay guy. I never feel like I'm talking to a teen terrorist. And he's just so fucking cute. Can cute guys still be evil?

I take a deep breath to gather my focus. The clock is ticking and I have to find something.

I walk into our room and it's empty as expected. I look over to Cody's side of the room and find a nice surprise. He was in such a hurry to leave he forgot to grab his cell phone. It's still sitting on his nightstand plugged into the charger. Whoo-hoo!

I just stare at it for a second. I can't believe my luck. The Holy Grail! Cody keeps that thing in his pocket everywhere he goes.

I snatch the phone up, making a detailed note in my head of exactly where I found it. I glance over at the door. What if Cody realizes he's missing his phone and comes back to grab it? That's probably not going to happen. You just don't walk out of class here at the Academy. Still, I put a chair against the door. I can alway tell him I'm doing drugs or something. I hope it doesn't come to that though.

The four digit password isn't hard to crack. Any first-month Agency trainee could get into a cell phone. Twenty-seconds and I'm in. I start scrolling through everything. Nothing unusual in the call history, mostly guys from school. All of his texts are school related too. There's some syllabi, orientation materials and some music on the hard drive. All Euro dance pop. Is this the Hi-NRG soundtrack of the sinister? I flip through his pictures. He's got some nice shots of Saba, various locations around the school, the blueberry pancakes from Saturday's breakfast and… a dick pic? And a naked selfie? And another dick pic? He's even hard in this one! Nice! Cody's been so private. I haven't seen him in less than his underwear. I've hit the jackpot!

It's an awesome dick. It's long, uncut and tapered like a thick, fleshy candlestick. I can't pull my eyes away from these beautiful pixels. *Focus!* I shake my head and slide over the picture. There doesn't seem to be anything incriminating here. Well, except the dick pics.

I keep searching through the phone, not finding anything useful. But there's a whole other level of snooping to be done. Any phone or computer can hold data that's invisible to anyone without good espionage training. Fortunately, I'm prepared. The Agency gave me a search and decryption device during my briefing in London. It looks like a simple body hair trimmer, but the plug has several connection options hidden away. The device's body contains a hard drive and advanced decrypting software. I plug it into the USB port on Cody's phone and it downloads all the hidden files. I also download the dick pics as a little bonus for me. With the encrypted files on my device, I unplug from Cody's phone and return it exactly where I found it.

I can see in the shaver gadget's display that it's working through the encryption and it may take a few hours to get these files done. As I put it back in my shaving kit, it hits me that there's been no mistake about Cody. I'm not sure what's on those files yet, but regular kids don't have files with that level of encryption on their phones no matter how rich or secretive they are. I'm disappointed but I have no reason to be surprised. I get out of the room. I don't want to be seen in here if Cody comes back.

***

Cody and I are in the dinner hall, eating and chatting with a bunch of the other summer students like we've done every night for the past couple of weeks. But everything's different now. I didn't realize how much I was starting to like this guy. Does he like me at all or is this all part of his cover? Who knows? Fuck him!

Cody excuses himself after dinner saying he has an errand in town. I ask him if he'd like me to join him and he abruptly tells me I'd be bored and that he's fine alone. I can only imagine what he's up to. I'd follow him, but I need to check on those files.

When I return to our room, Cody has already left. I check my decryption device. The light's gone from red to green. It's scanned all the files and decoded everything it can. I plug the device into my phone's charging port and begin to see what I got. Not everything was decrypted. What I have is very spotty and still a little vague. SATYR's covered their trail very well. The files were written in code and then deeply encrypted, making it very difficult for me to get any solid information. At first, there doesn't seem to be anything particularly threatening: maps of the school grounds, faculty lists, profiles on the students, nothing I haven't seen already. In one of the last files I can read, I see something that makes my stomach drop. Cody is here for an assassination. For several assassinations, actually.

I read that the Drake Academy is going to host the next session of the Tomorrow Talks, the gathering of the world's most inventive and effective people. They call it a "brainstorm of the brilliant." Total Tony Stark stuff! Due to the exclusivity of the event, they only announce the location two weeks in advance. And this one won't go public until the end of the week. But SATYR seems to know all about it. It looks like Cody's targets are several guests that will be presenting at the Tomorrow Talks: inventors, innovators and people who want to change the world for the better through technology and ideas. But some of these new ideas and innovations would cut into someone's profits. Looks like someone isn't thrilled about the next electric car or life-saving medical advancement.

"Fuck me," I whisper.

He's going to kill the people trying to improve life on the planet. How can anyone be this greedy and corrupt? I run my hand through my hair.

"Fuck," I say again, this time louder.

The location for the Tomorrow Talks will be announced to the public in two days. Two weeks after that, this place is going to be filled with the world's best and brightest. It makes sense they'd have the Talks here. It's a beautiful location and plenty of room since there's so few students and faculty on campus over the summer.

So much for my hope that Cody isn't the guy I'm after. I may not like the situation, but this is what I signed up for. First thing tomorrow, I've got to get into town and get this info to The Agency. It's over, Cody. You've met your match.

As a reward for my good work, I think I'll take advantage of being alone in the room. It happens so rarely, I'd be a fool to let it go to waste. I flick the light off, strip my clothes off and climb onto my bed. It's fairly warm, so I don't bother getting under the covers. I check out the dick pics I lifted from Cody's phone and transferred to mine. Why did he take them? Was he sending them to someone else or does he just get off on looking at himself? Yeah. That's probably it. That cocky little fucker is in love with himself. Asshole. But I can't stop flipping through the three pictures again and again. His cock looks big, at least as big as my own fine tool, but it's hard to tell from a photo. I grip the phone tightly in my left hand as I stare at the picture of Cody naked in the bathroom mirror. It cuts off right at his nose, but there's no doubt it's him. His body is tan, lean and tone. His dick rises straight up from his nest of dark pubes. My right hand trails down my body and grasps my already-hard cock. I think it's been stiff since I saw these photos of my roommate earlier today. I couldn't get them out of my head. I'm lucky I didn't shoot a load in my pants at dinner.

I pull my foreskin back halfway over my cockhead. Pre-cum leaks out of the tip of my penis and dribbles down the side of my shaft. The air hits it, turning the slick liquid cool as it travels from my moist tip, down the shaft. My cock throbs. Fuck, that feels good. My finger dances around the inside of my foreskin, gathering the pre-cum and spreading it across my cockhead.

A shiver goes down my spine. I pull at my foreskin with slippery fingers, stretching it out over my cock, then pulling it back again. My eyes never pull away from the glow of the phone and the image of Cody preening. I think about how much I want to taste his cock and how good it would feel to have it push inside of me. I groan as I think about Cody bending me over and fucking me.

Suddenly the door opens and the light comes on. My eyes adjust to see Cody standing in the doorway, his finger still frozen on the light switch. I turn off my phone and covertly stash it under the mattress. I'm lying exposed, completely naked with my hard dick still in my grip. I pull my hand away from my boner but it's too late. Pre-cum runs down from my foreskin. My mind races like a supercharged computer to figure out what to say to minimize my embarrassment.

Before I find words, Cody shuts the door and moves across the room. He sits down at the end of my bed and furrows his brow. "What's this?" he asks, giving away no emotion, not pointing at anything at all.

"I, ugh...," I stammer, still completely unable to think of anything to say. There really nothing I can say. I'm still naked, my cock is still rock hard and he's looking right at me. The Agency never gave me training in being busted in mortifying masturbation situations.

"Uh, hi?" I blush and smile weakly. I smell a hint of booze on Cody's breath. He's been drinking, but he doesn't appear to be drunk. My guess is he's just feeling good.

Cody smiles a little. I don't know what he's thinking. He never gives much away. He hasn't said much, but he isn't moving away or telling me to cover up.

Suddenly, he grabs the base of my cock and lightly strokes it up and down with small motions. I breathe deeply as more pre-cum oozes out of the tip of my pole, through my foreskin and onto Cody's hand. Without taking his eyes off of mine, he licks the salty fluid off the back of his hand. He lets out the slightest moan as his eyes close. I think he likes the way I taste. He stands up and pulls off his sweater and shirt. I take him in. Cody is glorious. He looks even better than in the small selfie. There's something elegant about his physique. His body is a lot like mine: athletic, but not bulky. He has hints of dark hair in all the right places. The slightest bits of black fur accent his chest and tempt me to lick them. I want to bury my face in the patches of ebony hair sprouting from his armpits.

He grabs at the top button on his dark uniform shorts. My mouth waters. My cock gets even harder. Slowly, he pushes his pants off his hips. Naughty boy. He's already hard inside his snug fitting black square-cut briefs. He looks beautiful standing in front of me in his underwear, hand on my cock. How can anyone this glorious be so evil?

He releases my cock and pulls down his underwear, keeping them in his hand. His boner bounces hard and stiff as it's released. I see his pre-cum bubbling out of the tip of his tight foreskin. I take another deep breath. That's definitely the dick in that picture that got me so worked up.

Suddenly, I'm surrounded by black. My heart is beating so hard I hear nothing else. Cody is shoving his underwear into my face hard. I can barely breathe through the fabric. Is he trying to kill me?

"Smell me," he orders.

And I do. I breathe deeper than I've ever breathed. I smell the sweat from his crotch on the fabric. I smell the scents of every move he's made today. I smell the odor left by his balls and his foreskin and pre-cum. I smell *him*.

He pulls his underwear out of my face and my vision is again filled with black, this time the darkness of his pubes as he shoves his cock into my mouth. I smell his musky crotch as I suck him. His cock becomes the center of the room for me, and… fuck, the center of the whole world at this moment. I swallow it down. It's so much better than I could have imagined looking at those pictures. I want to make him shoot his cum down my throat as he fucks my face. But before I can cause him to nut, he pulls out.

He grabs my hips and flips me over onto my stomach. My dick twitches against the bed. I'm exposed and vulnerable. Cody can do whatever he wants to me. Fuck! I want him to do everything to me. He rubs my hard ass cheeks and bites down on one. His teeth gently nibble the skin. He's driving me crazy.

He pulls away from my butt and I feel his body cover mine. His cock rests between my ass cheeks, but he doesn't push inside of me. His arms keep mine prisoner as he kisses the back of my neck. I feel his roughness of his tongue rubbing circles across my skin. I feel his teeth ever so gently nibble on my shoulder. I close my eyes and moan. My ass pushes back against his cock, hoping to get it inside of me.

"I knew you wanted me," he whispers against my ear before taking my lobe between his teeth. "I've wanted you since I first saw you in this room, standing there like an idiot with your underwear around your ankles." He laughs.

Again, I smell the hint of alcohol on Cody's breath. I want to breathe in every bit of him. I want to get drunk off of Cody. It's so wrong. All of this is so very wrong. But our bodies fit together so perfectly. He shoves his cock below my asshole, down between my legs. His foreskin wetly kisses the back of my balls. He knows how to play my body like it was his own. I need to stop this but that just makes me want him more.

I twist my upper torso around, my lips searching for his. His tongue plunges into my mouth roughly. He assaults my mouth as I feel him grind his cock between my legs. He rubs his moist foreskin upward and his cock is at the gate of my sphincter. It pushes to get in, hooded and wet. I push my hips back and spread my legs wide to help him. I want him to infiltrate me and go deep undercover.

I can feel the liquid drizzle out of his cock and fall warm onto the ring of muscles around my hole. He's spilling as much pre-cum as I am. The tip of his knob locks in on my hole and he pushes, using only his pre-cum as lube. His left arm grabs my hip to keep me still and his right goes around my neck.

Cody pushes harder on my ass. I arch my back and groan. His grip on my hip tightens and, with one final shove, buries himself inside of me. I want to scream in agony, but I manage to stifle it. All I let out is a small yelp. It hurts so much. Cody isn't kind to my body. But it starts to feel good. So good. I'm not sure he cares. He fucks me selfishly.

"Tell me you want my cock," he orders.

"I do. I need your cock," I beg back.

I try to kiss him, but he won't let me.

"Tell me I own your ass!"

"My ass is yours, Cody. Fuck me hard," I tell him. "Use it. Use me."

I tell myself this is wrong. I can't be doing this. Every logical part of me is screaming out. Stop this! Cody is my enemy. He's about to commit murder. I have the proof now. I don't want to tip him off that I know anything, but this is more than that. I really want him to keep fucking me. His body feels so right inside mine, like we were made for each other. So how can I end this? What excuse could I possibly make when it's so obvious that every cell of my body wants to be filled by him?

The room is on fire with the passion between us. Sweat is pouring down from my hair to my eyes as he drills into my ass. Cody's grip on my neck loosens as our skin becomes wet and slippery. I can feel Cody's uncut dick move inside of me. I can feel it moving in and out of its sheathing. I can feel it touching deep inside of me. I've never had my ass pleasured so perfectly or pounded so hard.

Cody's fucking is so rough. The entire bed is slamming hard off the thick, solid wall. My cock is crushed between my body and the sheeted mattress. Every time Cody thrusts into me, I feel my boner rub over the bedding and my cockhead darting in and out of my wet foreskin. It feels like I'm getting the best blowjob of my life without even being touched.

Again, I tell myself I shouldn't be doing this. I have to tell him to stop. I can't do this. *This is so wrong*. It's six-billion kinds of wrong.

"Please, don't stop," I groan. "Don't ever fucking stop!"

So much for self-control. I'm supposed to be focused on my job. Getting fucked by Cody wasn't part my mission briefing. But I never want his amazing cock out of me. Wouldn't it solve every problem if he and I never leave this bed, if his cock never pulls out of my ass? Fucking and cumming over and over again. Like Prometheus but with boners and jizz. If he never stops fucking me, he can never do anything wrong again. If only it could be.

Cody pulls his arm out from under my neck. Using the hand on my waist, he flips me around onto my back and throws my left leg over his shoulder. His cock never leaves my ass. He's masterful. I try to pull him down on top of me. I want to taste his lips again. I wrap my arms around his neck to keep him locked in place and shove my tongue deep down his throat. My leg is bent at an awkward angle that hurts like hell, but I don't care. I kiss him deeply as his cock slams into my prostate and his abdomen rubs my stiff cock. My fingernails dig into the skin on his back. I want to hold him like this forever.

He pulls away from my mouth and grabs my hair tightly in both hands. My head jerks back. He laughs.

"You like that, little American!"

"Yes, I do," I tell him, whimpering. He's rough but I want more.

Then he pulls his cock almost all the way out of my ass and slams it back into place with all of his might. Again and again. This should be tearing me apart. But his cock… it fits so perfectly in my hole. And knowing I'm getting the fucking of my life from my nemesis just makes this hotter. I'm so turned on. And, apparently, so fucked up.

My free leg wraps around Cody's waist and pulls him closer. I throw my head back and cry out in pleasure. But Cody grabs my face and forces me to look at him. His steely smile lets me know that he's making the rules.

I see so much of myself as I look in his face. He's like a dark, distorted carbon copy of me. Is he the Joker to my Batman? The Magneto to my Xavier? I smile. It's almost like getting fucked by myself. Except I doubt if I could even fuck me as well as Cody can. He knows my body better than I do. He's so dominant, borderline violent and sadistic. Hardly surprising. He's taken complete control of my body and I've completely let go. Geo-political warfare can wait until tomorrow. Right now I'm getting the best fuck of my life.

My cock rubs against his tight stomach and throbs as he continues wrecking my ass. It feels so good to be dominated by Cody, to be a hole for him to fuck and use. I feel his pre-cum flow wet in my ass. He slides in and out of me easily. "Harder," I beg. I pull my leg off his shoulder and wrap it around his waist to pull him even closer into me. I push my ass up into the air to see how far I can get him inside of me. I want him all. I despise every gap that's between us. I want his body to merge with mine.

I'm going to explode. I reach for my throbbing cock. It's begging to be touched. I think I may go off the second my fingers make contact, but I can't ignore it any more. It needs to be touched. It's hurting to be touched.

Cody slaps my hand away.

"No," he lets out in between grunts, very calm, yet still firm enough that I know not to try again. "Your cock is mine and you don't touch it until I tell you that you can."

"Yes, Cody," I say shocked at how easily I submit.

He grabs my wrists and pins them above my head. He keeps his body away from my aching hard-on, but his right nipple lands close to my lips. I reach forward to try and take the tiny nub into my mouth. Cody denies me that pleasure as well. He grabs my face with his free hand and kisses me. His assault on my ass intensifies even more as our lips come together. I didn't think it could be more intense. I feel his cock plump inside me and his breathing becomes heavier. Three more hard, severe plunges into my throbbing hole and I feel the heat of Cody's cum shoot inside of me. It's so hot, like lava is shooting from his cock. I think I may burn up from the inside out as he fills me up. More and more and more. I feel it running out of my hole. It's more than I can contain.

Every nerve in my body suddenly tingles. My cock, untouched, goes off like a garden hose. I can't control it and I can't make it stop. I shoot my cum all over Cody's body and face. Then it shoots onto the ceiling and drops back down and lands on my face.

I laugh lightly. Did this all really happen? What I just felt was unbelievable. I've never cum like that before. I've cum big, but not paint-the-ceiling big. Cody leans over me, laughing himself. I want him to kiss me, but instead his tongue darts out and roughly licks away the cum from the tip of my nose. He runs two fingers over his spooge covered chest, picking up as much of the creamy liquid as he can, then he brings his fingers up to my lips. I pull his fingers into my mouth and suck them completely dry.

He scoops up another glob of spunk off of the headboard and feeds that to me too. Then he leans over me and sucks the boy-juice off of my chest. He can't get enough of my cum. Or of feeding me my own spunk. Fortunately, I've shot more than enough for both of us. He kisses me with a mouthful of my own load. I swallow it all as we kiss. My cock throbs and I wonder if I'll ever be soft again.

Cody lays a final, gentle peck on my lips before resting his head on my chest. He lies on top of me, spent. We become a messy pile of limbs and jizz. We don't say anything. There's nothing to say. And we fall asleep.

CHAPTER TWELVE
NAKED TOWARD TOMORROW

I sit on the side of my bed staring at the floor trying to get myself centered. So far it isn't working. Today is the kickoff for the Tomorrow Talks. Tonight, actually. The opening reception is being held in the grand hall of the Drake Academy. Sometime during the next week, my roommate is going to murder several guests at that seminar in the hopes of causing chaos and destroying the global economy. And I'm going to have to stop him. Alone.

I've known about Cody's mission for the past two weeks, but I haven't told The Agency. I should have. I know that's the first thing I should have done when I found out about the assassination plot. My instructions were to tell my contacts at the Agency once I knew why Cody was here. This should have been strictly a recon mission. I'm supposed to get information, bring it back to them, and get out. Instead, I've waited around for two weeks, full of guilt when not getting my brains fucked by a trained killer. I never should have let him have my ass in the first place. I know I screwed up. But I know I can make this right.

I keep replaying that first night over and over in my head. I should have stopped Cody when he first grabbed my dick with an "I have a headache, Cody." Or even when he took his clothes off. I should have stopped him, but I didn't. I wanted him so bad, more than I've ever wanted anyone. It was so wrong and yet so good, so satisfying. I get hard every time I think about it, which is often. And every time I think about it, I desperately want to feel Cody's cock deep inside of me again.

I take a deep breath. Now I have to fix this. I'm going to redeem myself to The Agency. The Agency? They don't even know what happened yet. No, I need to redeem myself to me.

I pull myself up from my bed. First, I have to retrieve my gun. I hid it on the roof of the auditorium when I first got here. I couldn't risk having it in the room, not even concealed in my shoe. Not with Cody here. I couldn't take the chance. I thrown on my uniform sweater and head over to the building. I'll get my fire-arm, stop Cody in the act and then I'll take him to the authorities. I'll contact The Agency and I'll be a hero. I'll forget all about sex with Cody and everything will be right. Simple.

I make my way to the auditorium, staying calm and focused. Some of my new friends try to stop and chat. I nod with a smile, but I don't stop. I don't want to blow my cover and I don't have a minute to waste. I keep moving so I can get to my gun before I run into Cody.

I take the stair three at a time and make it to the roof. The auditorium building is at the edge of the campus with a view that faces out. From the rooftop here I can see the town at the bottom of the mountain, looking tiny below us. In the opposite direction is the vast ocean that seems to just go on forever. It's beautiful, but I'm not here for sightseeing. I head to the heating vent where I carefully hid my weapon. My hand reaches for the gun, which should be concealed and taped to the inside of the vent. I only feel cold, flat sheet metal. What the fuck? I reach all around with my hand even though I know exactly where I left it. The pistol isn't here. Fuck! This is where I left it. Am I going crazy? I glance around, hoping to find something. My heart and my mind are racing. Then I hear something that makes me freeze.

"Looking for this?" I'm asked in a Greek accent. It's Cody. He's smiling and casually pointing my gun directly at me. He's leaning against the only door on this rooftop.

Shit!

He must have been up here before I was, hiding. I should have checked my surroundings better. That's a rookie mistake.

Cody isn't wearing his school uniform. He's in a pair of black jeans that hug his legs and a snug black knit turtleneck. He looks so good, but I don't think he's here to ask me to the school dance. My roommate may be sexy, but he also homicidal. And he has a gun. A gun that's currently fixed on me. My gun! I'm busted.

"Stand up."

Cody motions the gun upwards. He moves away from the door and approaches me. He's cool and casual. I'm intentionally slow to my feet. I look around for a weapon or a way out. Cody's blocking my only exit and the only thing even close to a weapon are some tiny stones that cover the roof. I could probably pelt him to death if he just stood still for about a month.

I glance behind me. We're standing on the roof of a building on one of the highest points in The Netherlands, thousands of feet up. There's nowhere to go. I realize I might die up here.

I turn back to Cody. The gun is now held tight in his right hand and his left hand rests on his belt. He arches an eyebrow at me in smug amusement.

"What are you doing?" I ask quietly. "I don't understand." My only chance is to play dumb.

Cody just chuckles. "Forget it, mate. I know everything."

I tense. Cody's smile widens. "I've known all along who you really are, Agent Parker." He grips the gun tighter. He looks me up and down. "Now strip."

"Uh… what?" I ask.

I'm stunned. Surely, I heard him wrong.

Cody rolls his eyes.

"Strip: the act of removing one's clothing," He laughs. "I figure you'd be an expert at that by now."

He doesn't sound like he's messing around. My dick twitches. I tell it to calm down. I hate that Cody can still have an effect on me when threatening my life. There was something between us, a real passion. I know he's thinking about the nights he fucked me, and getting just as turned on by it as I am. I can see it in his pants.

"Hey, buddy," I stall for time. "There's got to be some kind of mistake here. Maybe you should put that gun down and we can talk this over."

He doesn't budge. "Do it. Now. Or get shot." He cocks the gun to emphasize his point. It's now pointing directly at my head.

"Cody, you don't have to do this. If they're forcing you, I can help you!"

"Nobody's forcing me to do anything," he screams. "You're the fool! You're the one doing nothing but defending the status quo and your soft, privileged life. You know nothing about this world. You're weak. You're the puppet!"

Wow. He's angry, so full of rage.

"Okay. We'll do it your way," I say to calm him. I grab the bottom of my uniform sweater and pull it over my head. I toss it to aside. I toe off my shoe, then the other one and kick them away. One of them rolls off the side of the building. And down the mountain.

"Keep going," Cody orders.

"You sure you don't want to talk about this?" I try again.

He just glares, pointing the gun.

I pull my white T-shirt off and feel the late afternoon air on my bare torso. Then I quickly discard my socks. I grab my belt and start to undo the buckle. Can I use this? My mind runs through a dozen scenarios and I lose in every one. Gun versus belt is a no-go. Not with Cody. We're too evenly matched under the best of circumstances. Armed Cody definitely has me beat.

"Look, you don't want to do this." I know it's foolish to try and argue with my adversary, but I don't know what else to do. Talking Cody down is my only chance.

"I wouldn't be doing any of this if I didn't want to," he tells me with a very serious look on his face.

Damn it. I close my eyes and push my uniform pants down. I'm now standing on the roof wearing nothing but a pair of striped gray and black boxer briefs. I stand up tall and try to look like I'm not scared.

I don't know what his game is. Is he trying to embarrass me before killing me?

Cody lowers the gun, pointing at my undies. He flicks the gun impatiently. "Off!" he shouts.

I jump, one hand going to the band on my underwear while the other goes up in surrender. "Okay, okay." Slowly, I remove my boxer briefs and kick them away. I'm completely naked and exposed. The wind is starting to kick up and I feel it everywhere on my body. My cock is starting to stir. I better not get a hard-on. I think I'd rather be shot.

"Move," Cody says, gesturing to the edge of the roof with the gun. I raise my hands up over my head and back away. There's only about half a foot between me and oblivion. There's no railing around the edge of the roof, just a border a few bricks high. I look down. It's a long fall. There's no way I could survive that fall. No one could. It looks like Cody's planning on throwing me over. He might even make it look like a suicide. My body gets tense. My heart pounds hard in my chest while my stomach twists into a million knots.

Then I remember my training. It's okay to be scared. Acknowledge it, move past it, stay clear. I take a deep breath until I feel in control again.

"I don't understand, Cody." I shrug my shoulders. "How did you know who I am? How did you know about the gun?"

"You may have been prepared to stop me, but I was better prepared," Cody scoffs. Hell, I'm just better than you, asshole. I knew who you were the minute I saw you."

The color drains from my body. He knew who I was this whole time? Even before he fucked me?

"How? I didn't do anything to give myself away. How could you know?"

Cody throws his head back and laughs like I just said the funniest thing he's ever heard. It takes several minutes for him to calm down long enough to finally say, "I'm your brother, you blind idiot. Your twin brother"

My breath catches in my throat and my jaw drops. Cody spreads his arms open and points at himself. "What? You didn't see the resemblance?" He drops his hands to his sides, chuckling. "And you call yourself an agent."

What the fuck? I've noticed a similarity between us, but what he's saying is ridiculous. I don't have a brother, much less a twin. That's just impossible.

"You've made a mistake, Cody," I tell him. "Somebody's been telling you lies."

"You're a fucking retard!" Cody shouts, his calm washes away. Now he's just angry. And the more he speaks, the angrier he gets. "You're the mistake! Being taken away from you and those fucking idiots you call parents was the best thing that ever happened to me." He sounds manic now, like he's really losing it. He's screaming. Spit flies as the words leave his mouth. I've never seen him like this.

"I was told The Agency might send you, you know." He laughs again. "Killing you is going to be the sweetest part of this assignment."

I've never seen Cody this emotional before. He's always seemed so collected, so above it all. Nothing ever seemed to faze him. I look at his hand holding the gun. It's shaking. What could he possibly be talking about? I'd know if I had a brother, wouldn't I? Cody must be crazy. Maybe he's trying to shake me up, or maybe SATYR filled his head with this crap. I don't know. But I don't have time to worry about it.

Cody calms down a little. His face brightens with mischief. "But you were a great fuck, bro. Really, that was a pleasure."

Oh, damn. I feel my cock start to stiffen at the memory. Cody's eyes fall to my cock. His eyebrows raise. I can see his mind working. Then he raises his gun again.

"Wank it."

"What the fuck?" I let out. I must be hearing things. He couldn't have said what I thought he said. That would just be crazy.

He raises the gun again. I almost take a step back until I remember I'm at the edge of the roof.

"It's going to look like you came up here to have a toss and slipped. 'Oh, that sad Yank boy,'" he mocks with a fake Dutch accent. "'Tragic. Couldn't keep his hands off his own willie and he fell from the rooftop. Someone should have told him that playing with himself would be the death of him.'" He laughs.

"Nobody's ever going to believe that." It's terrifying enough that Cody is planning on killing me. The idea of getting away with it like that is even worse. I take a step forward.

Cody instantly stiffens up, raising his gun to my face again. I freeze.

"Take your cock in your hand and stroke it," he says slowly and deliberately. "You're already hard anyway."

"What?" I look down. Sure enough, my cock is rock hard. Fuck! What is wrong with my dick? A silvery string of pre-cum drips off the tip of my pointed, fore-skin-covered pole. Why the hell is it hard right now? Of all the times I could get a boner, why did it have to happen when a psycho twink has a gun pointed at my head? Whose side is my cock on? Traitorous prick!

Could part of me be getting off on being dominated by Cody? I've never been as vulnerable to anyone as I am to him right now. But what if Cody is really my brother? That's some sick stuff, dude. You know that, right? My mind and my dick seem to be at war on this.

Cody gestures at me with the gun again. I don't have much of a choice. I better do what he says. At least it will buy me some time. It won't be a lot of time, but a few extra minutes can't hurt. Slowly, I reach down and grab my foreskin between my fingers. My tool throbs. I'm so hard. I involuntarily let out a small moan. I know I should be trying to come up with an escape plan, but all I can think about is how bad I want to cum.

My head fills with memories of Cody fucking me. My body remembers exactly what he felt like inside me. The muscles in my sphincter tighten and loosen as if it's trying to recreate the feel of his uncut cock entering me. I knew at the time it was wrong, but I had no idea just how wrong. Cody may be my brother? It hasn't escaped me how similar our bodies are. He knew what turned me on better than I did. His cock felt like it belonged in me. It fit inside of me so perfectly and touched me in all the right spots. But it's impossible.

My hand moves up and down, stroking my cock. My dick gets harder the more I think about my nights with Cody. I try to think of anything else, but I can't. I manage to maintain a slow rhythm. I don't want to cum now and give Cody that satisfaction, but I'm so close. I don't know if I can stop it. I pull my foreskin all the way back and palm my moist dick tip. Then I pull my loose skin forward until it completely covers my cock. I slide it between my fingers, massaging the moist flaps of flesh. My hole cock throbs as I give me needy foreskin loving attention.

"Finger your hole," Cody orders. "Go deep inside yourself. Remember how I fucked you."

I lick my fingers and do as he says. I feel my pointer finger moving into my sphincter. I push it in and out. Then I insert my middle finger too. They feel so good moving inside me. I keep the slow strokes going on my cock with my other hand. I'd be in heaven right now except for all the impending doom and stuff.

Cody watches. I can see his cock tenting in his jeans. He's enjoying the show.

"Hurry up, I don't have all day," he insists. "I've got people to kill. And this family reunion is starting to bore me."

Cody tries to look impatient, but the growing bulge in his black jeans keeps him honest. He's as hard as I am. As the light catches the front of his pants, I notice a wet spot. He's pre-cumming up a storm! My eyes lock onto his stiff, denim-covered member. It turns me on even more. It won't be long now until I cum. I get an idea.

"Oh Cody," I moan.

I think about him fucking me hard as I finger my hole. I remember those nights he wouldn't let me touch my own cock, but made me cum just by pounding my ass. I focus on the way he used my body and filled my insides up with his massive loads of warm seed.

I stroke my cock faster and faster. Warmth floods through my body as I look right into Cody's beautiful eyes. My balls draw up and my cock pulses. With cock in hand I take aim. Massive white lines of my seed shoot out the tip of my cock. I'm spraying like a fountain. I aim my cock like a marksman and my spooge hits Cody directly in his right eye. Perfect shot. Then the left. Again and again.

Cody instinctively reaches for his eye. "God damn it! It stings."

He still has the gun in his grip, but I know this is going to be my only chance. I rush forward to tackle him. My cock is still hard and cum is dripping onto the rooftop. I jump into Cody and grab him around the waist, pushing him right off of his feet.

Cody hits the roof with a loud thud. The gun flies out of his grasp. I can't see where it landed. Before I have the chance to look, he smashes his fist into the side of my head. I'm disoriented long enough for him flip us over. He's on top of me. He tries to pin my arms down. I twist out of his grasp but it hurts. He's every bit as strong as I am. The stones press hard into my back. I wrap my legs around Cody and roll him over again. I'm on top now. Cody thrusts his hips up to distract me. I can feel his rock-hard erection even through his jeans. My own exposed cock hasn't softened at all.

I try to punch Cody in the face but he grabs my arm and pins it against my chest. His fist comes barreling into my nose before I know what's happening. Contact. Pain! I roll us over again, but then I remember that we are high on a roof on top of a building built way up a mountain. Well, technically, it's a volcano. But I've got my own natural disaster to worry about.

I stop us mid-roll, too close to the edge. Cody grabs my throat and pushes me away. I roll toward the drop off. My head is hanging over the edge, but I manage to catch myself before I fall off. I turn around and jump to my feet. Cody quickly gets to his feet as well. We're so even-ly matched that I consider, just for a second, that there might be something to this "brothers" thing.

I move away from the rooftop edge. Cody's face is pure rage. This isn't looking good. If I don't figure out how to end this fight soon, I'll end up dead. I'm completely naked and vulnerable here. And I'm really starting to feel those punches to the face. But at least he hasn't been able to kill any of his Tomorrow Talks targets.

Cody spins around on his toes and kicks me in the face. His shoe is cruel on my face. I tumble down spitting blood. Cody brings his foot down to strike me again. I barely manage to roll out of the way and stand up. His foot smashes hard into the rooftop.

I need to remember my training. The Agency taught me to find whatever weakness an opponent has and exploit it. I need to find what advantage I have, no matter how small.

Cody resumes his attack. I'm barely avoiding his blows, and he has me on the defensive. Every time I try to strike, he throws his forearm into my fist's path. I'm surprised he hasn't shattered his arm, or my hand, by now. He throws a right hook aimed at my jaw with powerful force. This one looks like it could knock my jaw clean off. I lean back. Cody's middle knuckle barely grazes my cheek.

Even that light contact sends me flying back. If my he makes contact again, I doubt I'll be as lucky. I need that advantage, but I can't see anything! I'm fucking exposed, on a roof with my dick swinging free.

Free.

Free from clothes.

Unlike Cody.

I have to get in close. I charge at him. His fists are flying at my face and sides. I hurt everywhere. I shut the pain out and move my hands to his middle. I grab the bottom of his turtleneck and pull the shirt as high as I can until it gets caught at his arms. The shirt covers his face blinding him and leaving his arms flailing. While he's distracted, I pull his jeans and underwear down to his ankles. He struggles to keep his balance as he pulls his turtleneck off. He throws his shirt off and it flies off the side of the building. He's still off balance, now shirt-less and pantsed. He's stumbling but his dick is hard. I don't know if it's me or the violence that's causing his erection. Part of me still wishes we were fucking and not fighting. But we are fighting. I'm fighting for my life and the lives of everyone gathering in the auditorium below us.

I wind back and put all of my weight into my fist. This has to count. I punch forward, making contact with Cody's handsome face. He stumbles back, his ankles in knots of black jeans and black underwear. He's off bal-ance. He's moving quickly toward the edge of the roof.

I race forward.

"Cody!" I scream. My arms reach out. I have to save him.

My opponent was trained well. Somehow he manages to stop mid-stumble right at the roof's edge. He kicks off his pants and underwear, freeing himself. I breathe a sigh of relief. But I know he's about to come at me. I don't have any more tricks and I don't know how much more of this I can take.

Then I feel something cold under my toe. I look down and feel luckier than I've ever felt in my life. My gun is right there, right next to my bare feet. This is where it landed. I drop like lightning and it's in my hands.

"I'm taking you in, Cody." My words don't come out as strong as I intended. They're filled with more sympathy and exhaustion than I intended to show. Over these last few weeks, I developed feelings for Cody despite how complicated the situation is. I'm a little sad for having to arrest him. Even though he just tried to kill me. And a bunch of other people. And he's a total lying psycho.

He just stands there frozen, glaring. It's the coldest look I've ever seen. No rage, just ice. I can feel how much he hates me, but he doesn't seem at all angry. He looks back over his shoulder, down at the mountains below us. He looks at me again.

"Fuck you," he says with eerily calm.

He staggers.

"Cody!" I yell. I'm too late. He falls backward over the side.

I run forward and drop to my knees at the edge of the roof. I look over the ledge, frantically searching for him. It's a long fall down the building, then a horrible drop down the mountain. It's starting to get dark, and I can't see anything. He's down there, somewhere, but I can't spot him anywhere.

"Cody!" I scream at the top of my lungs.

I didn't hear him land. But I guess I wouldn't. It's hundreds of feet down the mountain. I stand back up, completely stunned. Stunned about so many things. I have no idea if Cody just fell or if he jumped. Did he hate me so much that he'd rather die than have me take him in? Did he hate me so much that he would tell me those lies about being my brother just to hurt me?

I wipe blood from my bruised face and shake my head to clear it. Four-million things are running through my mind. Should I go searching for Cody? There's no way I can scour the entire mountainside in the dark? Is he alive? No. There's no way. The fall off the building would be enough to kill him. And this side of the building faces down the mountain. No one could survive that.

Did I see a birthmark on Cody's right butt cheek as he fell? I think I did. Did I imagine that? No. I did see a flash of a birthmark. I've never see his ass when we were together. He was always on top of me. Could he have the same cat's paw birthmark? Could he actually be my brother? But how? It can't be possible! But he's still in my head. My mind feels at bruised as my body.

I search for my clothes. They don't seem to be up here. Damn, did they get blown off the roof? Did they fall off during our scuffle? All I know is that they're gone. Left with no other choice, I make my way down the stairs, in the buff. The only way out is through the auditorium. The Tomorrow Talks are just kicking off and the opening night reception is in full swing. I nearly crawl down the stairs. My body hurts everywhere. I open the door at the bottom of the stairs to see an entire ballroom full of some of the brightest minds in the world. The man in front of the room stops speaking when he notices me. Everybody turns around to stare at me and my exposed junk. I'm naked and battered, but still looking pretty good, even if I do say so myself.

"Don't mind me," I smile, embarrassed. I feel every eye on me as I continue to make my way across the back of the room. I don't even cover my dick as I head for the exit. After what I've been through, having a room full of people get an eyeful of my uncut pecker is the least of my worries. I even get few smiles and a wink! I make it out of the hall and race back to my room.

I have to put some clothes on, treat my cuts and call The Agency. I'm not looking forward to that. But it's time to face up to everything and let some healing begin.

CHAPTER THIRTEEN
DEBRIEFED BY MY SUPERIOR

I'm sitting in the London office of my commanding officer, Colonel Jason Anger, telling my story. After what went down in Holland, I contacted The Agency and briefed them on Cody's plans. I told them that I made the decision to stop him myself and how he had fallen off the auditorium building after our scuffle. They immediately sent security agents to retrieve me while other agents covertly scoured the mountainside for Cody's remains. Last I heard they hadn't found anything.

The Agency made up a story about Cody and I being attacked by rowdy gang of drunk tourists while visiting the nearby village of Windwardside. An agent posing as my father told the Academy he was pulling me out of school and that Cody's parents had already come to bring him home. They'll never have to know what went down at their school and the nightmare that could have happened.

I've already written up my full report, which is currently crumpled in Colonel Anger's fists. Apparently I also have to be debriefed orally as well. I've been dreading this.

I don't bother lying and I don't leave anything out. I tell Colonel Anger everything from the moment I arrived in The Netherlands until the minute The Agency pulled me out. And I mean *everything*. I explain that the first time I met Cody, my pants were around my ankles. I tell them about how I managed to seemingly win his friendship. I even admit that I knew about Cody's assassination plot for two weeks, but didn't inform The Agency because I was ashamed we'd had sex. The only thing I leave out is Cody's claim that we were brothers. This is something I need to deal with on my own. And I still don't believe it could be true. It's a horrible lie that should die with Cody.

Colonel Anger stares at me completely silent while I talk. I know he's not happy. His face is purple and his hands are shaking with rage. I know the only reason he's quiet now is because he's waiting for me to finish before he tears me a new one. Part of me wants to keep rambling on for as long as possible so he won't start screaming at me.

But I did make some bad decisions and I need to accept the consequences. It's probably better to just let him yell at me and, hopefully, move on. Maybe it won't be so bad.

"I told Cody I was taking him in," I explain. "At that point, he glared at me and went over the side of the building. He either fell accidentally or he jumped. I don't know for certain. Then I made my way back into the building and called The Agency."

I stop talking and take a deep breath, bracing myself for the dressing down I'm about to get.

"So," Colonel Anger starts. Surprisingly, his voice is quiet. He's furious, I can tell, but he's not yelling yet. His quiet fury is more terrifying. I think I'd prefer him to yell.

"You're saying that you put the Tomorrow Talks guests' lives in jeopardy to cover up getting shagged by a SATYR operative," he confirms, his voice is deep and measured. Being scolded by someone with a British accent stings worse than I could have expected.

I swallow the lump in my throat. "Yes, sir."

I can't deny it, that's exactly what I did. I look Colonel Anger directly in the eye.

"You were thinking with your dick, Parker!" He shouts. He stands up and slams his fist down on his desk. To my surprise, I don't jump. "You put this mission in jeopardy. You risked the lives of who knows how many people for a quick fuck."

"Well, technically, there were several fucks involved, sir, but…" His glare cuts me off.

He continues screaming, calling me an unprofessional spoiled child who should never have been recruited by The Agency in the first place. I want to argue. Now, more than ever, being a Shade means everything to me. I continue to stand straight and I keep my mouth shut.

"You are cocky and unfocused!" He walks around his desk until he's in my face. "You're undisciplined and reckless!"

My ears are ringing. He's screaming directly in my face. I feel his warm breath as tiny bits of spit fly in my face with every outburst. But I continue to take it without complaint. "You should be let go from The Agency. Or worse!"

I stare at him, open mouthed. He can't possibly mean that. "Sir, while some my actions may have been unwise, I handled this mission to the best of my ability. I made choices, but the results..."

He cuts me off. "If this is the best of your ability, I'd hate to see what happens when you half-arse a mission."

I grit my teeth. I know I shouldn't have argued with him. He just freaked me out by suggesting I should be cut from The Agency. He has no idea how important this is to me. It's who I am now.

The colonel keeps yelling in my face, going over and over how badly I screwed up. It feels strangely good. Somehow healing, like he's washing my failures away. I almost feel redeemed as his rage washes over me like a tidal wave. Almost.

"I should have you taken out of here, stripped of your place in the Shades program and brought up on charges," he barks.

My heart sinks. A drop of sweat runs down my forehead.

Colonel Anger sighs heavily through his nose.

"I should, but I'm not. Ultimately you accomplished your mission," he says leaving me stunned.

He's calmed down. I haven't seen him this chill since I arrived back in London. Was all the rage an act? Was the screaming to make a point? To scare me? If so, it worked.

He backs away and leans against his desk. "You have potential. It's very rough, but it's there." His eyes narrow at me as if to say I'm still not completely off the hook. He crosses his arms over his broad chest. "You successfully blended in at the school and you discovered your target's mission. The Tomorrow Talks went on without a single casualty or even anyone knowing they were in danger. And a dangerous SATYR operative has been terminated."

I allow myself just a hint of a smile. He glares at me.

"Most importantly," he says begrudgingly, "you may have saved our economy." He goes silent, as if his next words were hard to get out.

"All in all, a good job," he says turning away. "But I'm keeping a close eye on you," he adds quickly. "A very close eye."

Pride swells in my chest. Getting yelled at for forty minutes is worth it for that small bit of praise. Colonel Anger isn't a man who's loose with his compliments. I allow myself another small grin.

"Wipe that smirk off your face, agent!" He shouts, back to business. "Just because you got lucky once doesn't mean you're off the hook. Looks like I'm going to have to make you my special project."

Was there a hint of playfulness in his voice? What does that mean?

I let it go. My place in The Agency and the Shades program seem safe for now. Looks like I'll be fine.

"What's going on here, agent?" The colonel asks, motioning with his eyes for me to look down.

I look down. Holy fuck! I'm rock hard and my pants aren't doing much to hide it. How much trouble can my dick get me into? I don't know if it's hard from the dressing down or the praise. Around Colonel Anger, it could go either way.

I can't even look at him, I'm so embarrassed! I keep my eyes lowered. Wait! What the fuck? Colonel Anger's cock is also bulging his tight slacks. I'm shocked. It looks like all of this tension has had a similar effect on both of us.

"We're not quite finished here. I'm going to need you to remove your clothing immediately, agent," the Colonel orders. He folds his arms over his chest. "Then drop and give me fifty."

He sounds both serious and playful at the same time. It makes my cock pulse.

"Yes, sir!" I immediately pull my shirt over my head and toss it away. My eyes stay glued to Colonel Anger as he undoes a few buttons on his shirt. He watches me rip off my socks and shoes. I unzip my jeans, bending over as I push them down to the cold floor. He's definitely got a hint of a smile as I stand in front of him in nothing but my loose fitting, plaid boxers. They barely contain my hard dick. The front fly is spread open revealing my shaft and pubes. The wetness of my pre-cum starts spreading over the soft, thin fabric.

"Everything, Parker," Colonel Anger barks. His right hand is in his pocket.

Could this really be happening? I walked in here thinking I could be fired from The Agency. Or end up in some secret prison in Eastern Europe.

With a huge smile across my face, I turn around. I slowly push my underwear down without bending my knees. My ass sticks up in the air invitingly. I look over my shoulder at Colonel Anger sporting an erection through his pants. I can't believe this! I kick my boxers into the pile with the rest of my clothes. Colonel Anger points downward, reminding me that I haven't completed my task.

I drop down into push-up position, completely naked. The cement on the floor of Colonel Anger's office is cold on my palms. But the heat from my cock is giving off more than enough warmth. And motivation. I lower my upper body down until my firm chest hits the floor and I pop back up. The Colonel circles around me, inspecting. He removes his shirt and throws it on my back. I can smell his scent on it and I breathe in deep. I give him push-up after push-up, smiling the whole time. My ass is tight and my cock slaps against the floor every time I go down. I add a clap as I come up.

"You think you're pretty hot stuff, don't you, agent?" he asked sternly as he leans over me. I can feel the heat of his breath on the back of my neck.

"Sir! Yes, sir!"

I continue my impressive push-ups. I've almost lost count at this point. The colonel moves behind me out of my sight. What's he doing? I feel his index finger massage my tight hole. An electric shiver runs down my spine. My body freezes in the up position while he continues to explore my sphincter.

"Did I say you could stop, agent?" He yells, slapping my ass.

"No, sir!" I moan.

Doing these push-ups feel so much better with his finger in my hole. He's knows just how to motivate me. My legs inch farther apart to give him better access to my ass. His finger slips through the tight ring of muscles. I come up hard on my push-up and I swallow his finger deep inside of me. I moan again but I don't stop moving.

Another finger joins the first inside of me and they twist around. He kneads my insides. He knows what he's doing. It feels so good. I slow down with the push-ups. My ass lifts into his hand, not wanting to dip down anymore.

"Twenty-five more, Parker," he orders.

My arms are starting to weaken. I'm still healing from the horrible beating I took from Cody on the rooftop. And my ass is hungry for whatever the colonel has planned me. But I can hold out for twenty-five more.

Twenty-four. Twenty-three. Twenty-two. He adds a third finger. He feels so good inside of me. I glance behind me and see his furry, bare torso. My pre-cum drops to the cold floor. Twenty-one. Twenty. My tempo increases. Boom, boom, boom. Only ten more. My cock is so hard. I barely feel the ache in my arms. Instead, I focus on the expert way Colonel Anger's fingers are fucking me.

Nine. Eight. Seven. Six. I hear the colonel undoing his pants with one hand. Fivefourthreetwoone. I drop down on the floor. My cock presses between my body and the puddle of pre-cum on the cold cement. My arms feel weak but I embrace the pain. The colonel's fingers are still inside of me. He pushes deep. So deep. I gasp. I'm so tight back there. And he didn't lube me up before he pushed inside of me. The pain is excruciating. I let it wash over me and I'm turned on even more.

My cock throbs against the cold floor. My dickhead moves in and out of my foreskin, lubed by my steady flow of pre-cum. I'm so close to shooting already. I can feel it building up inside of my nuts and wanting to explode out. I want to feel the colonel's hard cock inside of me, but I don't know how much longer I can hold back. I'm on the edge. My muscles tighten up. If he pushes inside of me one more time, I'm done.

Colonel Anger pulls his fingers out of my backside just in time. My eyes shoot open. I roll over onto my back and stare up at him. He stands over me on his knees, staring down at my young body. His shirt is off. His pants are open, but still on. But not for long. With his eyes fixed on me, he slowly gets up and removes his shoes and socks. He pushes on my tight balls and hard cock with his bare foot. His big toe pokes at my asshole. I almost cum. He removes his pants and lays them on his desk, taking time to carefully fold them. He's wearing nothing but the whitest Y-front trunks as he stands over me with his feet on either side of my waist.

I love his body. It's wide and strong, classically manly. There are scars scattered all over. Each one, I'm sure, a trophy of a dangerous adventure. His legs, like his chest are covered with dark, thick fur. Occasional gray hairs mark his age and experience. His cock pokes up over the band of his underwear, straining to get out. It's a monster.

I slowly reach up to remove his briefs, wondering if he'll stop me. My hands get to the waistband and he doesn't voice any objections. I pull the last bit of his clothing down to his feet as his fat, uncut cock is freed with a bounce. It's an amazing cock. Possibly the most imposing I've ever seen. It's as solid and strong as he is, with cords of thick veins running through it. A full, dark bush of thick, unruly pubes frame his mighty member. I feel high breathing in his masculine scent. The masculine smell almost makes me splooge on myself.

He's intimidating and sexy when he's completely clothed. Naked, he's even more intimidating. He's a total alpha-male. As fit as I am, he looks like he can rip me in half with his muscular arms. He's pure strength and power.

"Suck my cock, agent," he orders like the commanding officer he is. "All of it."

I look at his giant fuckstick again and gulp. I don't know if I can take the whole thing in my mouth. But I never back away from a challenge. If this is part of my punishment, I more than gladly accept it. I lift to my knees and steady myself by gripping the sides of his strong, furry legs. I lick his warm cock up and down. It stiffens and throbs. I can smell the sweat that's gathered under his foreskin. It's intoxicating. I want to bottle it and never be without his sharp scent.

My tongue circles his cockhead, half covered by his fleshy hood, and I lick his piss slit. The salty taste makes me light headed.

Colonel Anger lets out a deep growl. He wraps his hands around my head and forces his giant cock into my face. I choke. My mouth aches as it stretches far wider than

I ever thought it could. I tightly grab his legs to let him know I'm struggling. He doesn't let up. His relentless attack on my mouth intensifies. My survival instincts urge me to push him away, but I take him all down. I need to. I have to take everything he gives me. I want him to know that I don't back down from a challenge. My jaw is straining and sore, but it feels so good.

He's feeling good too. He moans deeply and gutturally. I look up into his face. His eyes are closed and his mouth is slightly parted. All of his considerable strength is in his hips as they pound at my face. I grab onto his tight ass. It's firm and unyielding, all hard muscle. My grip does nothing to slow his bucking thrusts. He's far too powerful in every way. All I can do is give into his assault.

My balls draw up again. I grind my own cock against the Colonel's leg, coating his skin and hair in my pre-cum. It mats his fur with it's slick wetness. My cock throbs against his strong leg. I'm so hard. I can feel the cum boiling in my cock, begging to be released. My mouth has finally adapted to his giant cock and I'm no longer choking on each thrust. I enjoy how absolutely delicious it tastes. I want to be filled with his seed.

The Colonel pulls my head off of his cock and holds me still. His mushroom tip is hard and throbbing, wet with my saliva. I need his cock back in my mouth. I try to push free from his grip to no avail. I try to break his hold with my hands so I can keep sucking him off. He just won't budge.

Instead, he lifts my body up in his strong arms, then quickly drops me down on his desk. His phone falls to the floor with a loud thud. Papers stick to my sweat-moistened back. He pulls me far enough forward so my ass is dangling off the edge. He stands between my spread legs, his dripping cock aimed my eager hole. My hands clutch the sides of his desk. With a single thrust, he shoves his engorged cock deep inside of me. He's not gentle when he pushes and fills me. I cry out in pain.

"You can do this, Agent Parker."

I'm reassured by his deep, authoritative voice and my ass muscles relax. I trust him. His fucking feels good now. So good. He rubs his palms over my chest and I want to purr. His rough hands charge my nerve endings everywhere they touch.

"Fuck me, sir. Fill me up with your cock, sir!"

His hands move down to my groin. He runs his fingers through my pubes while the other hand toys with my balls. It's pure heaven.

He slows his fucking, moving deliberately in and out of me. I think he's on the brink of cumming. I know I am. He grabs my legs and pulls my ass at his cock. I slide down the desk, pulling files and paper with me. His cockhead slams into the back of my inside. He's all in. He freezes, his only motion the throbbing of his cock inside me. He holds in me for minutes. We are motionless, overwhelmed by the pleasure of our bodies joined together. I'm breathing hard, trying not to cum, trying to make this moment last.

The colonel lowers his head toward me and kisses me on the lips. Just once. It sends a rush of warmth through my entire body. Then, with slow and shallow thrusts, he begins to fuck me again. He grinds into me, never pulling out all the way. I can feel his breathing, hard and hot. His head is still close to mine and he fucks me slowly. My cock is sandwiched between us, rubbing against his tight, hairy stomach.

He's taking his time, trying to prolong our fuck. But I feel his cock nearly ready to explode inside of me. He keeps me on the edge of orgasm, but I hold back with everything I have. Our eyes stay locked as we both moan. I wrap my legs around him and pull him close with everything I have. He cups the sides of my face in his hands as his thrusts start getting deeper. He fucks me faster now, never pulling his eyes from mine. His stomach smashes against my cock as I take his pounding.

Gripping the desk, I push back on his thick slab of meat, taking an active part in my fucking. I slam my ass against his cock again and again. His face contorts. He goes completely wild, fucking me without abandon. I howl with pain and pleasure. His large balls slap hard against my smooth ass. My fingers grab his shoulder blades and dig into his skin. He groans and fucks me even harder.

He's going to bring this home. I spread my legs wider, letting him go deeper than I ever thought anyone could. I feel his cock bulge, then the warmth and wetness of his hot load fills me beyond capacity. He fucks his seed deep into me. My uncut cock moves between us as he continues wrecking my ass, gliding in the wetness of my pre-cum. He kisses me. I can't take anymore. My cock explodes, shooting my jizz up our bodies, between our chests, all the way to our kissing mouths. We don't break the kiss. Colonel Anger opens his mouth wider to lap up every drop of cum as it shoots in our faces. I drink as much out of his mouth as he lets me.

I release load after load as my commanding officer continues to fill me up. His cum drips out of my body when I'm too full. I clench my ass, trying to keep every drop in while shooting the last of my load between us.

Colonel Anger pulls my face forward and into a deep kiss as the last squirts of his warm seed surge into me. His kisses are aggressive. He fucks my mouth with his tongue as I wrap my arms around him. The colonel's cock flexes inside of me to force the last of his orgasm out. Our bodies press together and my cock spits out the last of its creamy filling.

I look into the eyes of this rugged man. I see the lines around his eyes and the gray at his temples. I feel his strength and authority. I want to be with him and I want to be like him. I wish he could fill me with all of his experience along with his cum.

He releases my mouth and starts licking the cum off my neck and chest. His cock pulls out of me and his lips move down my torso, lapping up every bit of my boyish jizz. He licks my stomach clean. He takes my cock in his mouth and sucks it like it's a straw holding the last drops of a milkshake. He even licks his own excess cum off my tender hole. I smile at how greedily he drinks up my young spunk. It makes me feel proud and worthy. I imagine that as much as I want to be filled with the Colonel's wisdom and experience, he wants to drink up my youthful impulsiveness and energy.

He stands up and helps me off the desk. With a smile, he gives my cock one final tug before he releases it. He gathers his clothes from where they've fallen and dresses quickly. He takes his place behind his desk.

"Dismissed, agent," he says firmly.

I look at him.

"I said 'dismissed.'"

I guess that means we're done.

I grab my underwear from the pile on the floor and pull them on as quickly as possible. I try to catch Anger's eye as I put on my jeans and shirt. Nothing. He doesn't look at me. I hobble as I pull on my socks and shoes while standing. As I open the door, I glance back at the colonel, eyes buried in a file. I can see the ghost of a smile on his lips. Hot damn! I light up as I walk out the door.

I leave his office with renewed confidence and filled with optimism. Despite everything that happened, my very first mission is one for the win column. I'm an agent with my first (mostly) successful mission behind me. And the good, deep fucking from my commanding officer is the highest commendation he could have given me.

I can't hold back a big smile as I make my way back out onto the streets of London.

EPILOGUE
POUNDING MY WAY HOME

The plane speeds down the runway, slowly lifting into the air. I look out my window and see London getting smaller and smaller. I miss Europe already. I stare out and watch the clouds pass by. Goodbye, London. Goodbye, sexy uncut British guys. Goodbye, adventure.

Summer is almost over. In a couple of weeks, I'll be a college student. Everything is changing. I've changed.

A very handsome man is sitting in the seat next to me on the plane. He's slender with dark blond hair, flawlessly swept to the side, and dark blue eyes. He looks older than me, maybe twenty-six or twenty-seven. His body is lean, but I can tell he's toned through his tight polo shirt and snug navy shorts. When we sat down he acknowledged me with just a hint of a smile. I flashed a friendlier one back.

"Are you originally from Texas?" I ask now that we're up in the air.

He shakes his head. "Originally, I'm from Ukraine. But now I live in Los Angeles. I'm just stopping off in Texas on my way home." His accent is strong, but his English is flawless. Had I heard him speak, I wouldn't have needed to ask.

He grins at me. "What about you?"

His angular features and his smooth tan skin are beautiful. I won big in the seat-mate lottery. And I've never a Ukrainian before. I love the way his words roll off his tongue. It give me a bit of a chubby.

"Yeah. I'm from Houston," I reply.

He nods quickly then starts looking back down at his men's fashion magazine. I try to keep him talking.

"So were you in Europe visiting family or..." I trail off.

He shakes his head. "I was working." He smiles bashfully. "I was doing some modeling there."

How exciting! A real model! But not so surprising by the look of him. With his angular features and high cheek bones, he belongs in magazines. Or on the runway. Or whatever models do. He looks like he just stepped out of an ad. I place my pillow on my lap to better conceal my growing erection.

I hold out my hand. "I'm Jake. Jake Parker."

"Dean Cocteau." His grip is firm.

I try to engage him, but Dean doesn't make it easy. There's nothing rude about him. He's very courteous, but not at all chatty. Maybe it's just cultural. Maybe that's just how models are. I've never met a Ukrainian or a model so I wouldn't know. Maybe he just wants to be left alone. I'm sure he gets hit on all the time. I had hoped there could be some under-blanket groping during the flight when I first saw him. I don't think that's going to happen. He seems invulnerable to my Texas charm.

Maybe it's for the best. After everything that's happened recently, I'm not in the mood to make up cover stories about my trip. I recline my seat back and close my eyes. Everything that's happened since my last flight comes flooding into my head all at once. Am I still that kid who sat around in his underwear all day getting high and playing video games with the pizza guy? I don't think I am. I almost died just a few days ago. The world looks different to me. Who am I now?

I've spent the last two weeks in London recovering from the beating I took. The Agency didn't want to send me home to my parents looking like I'd been hit by a truck. It would raise too many questions. And I didn't want them to worry. All they have to know is that I saw some great places in Europe, met a whole lot of interesting people, tried some new foods and took some pretty good pictures. Thanks to The Agency's medics, they'll never know I had a scrape on me.

I wonder when I'll be called on another undercover mission. Where will I go? Will there be retaliation from SATYR?

And what about Cody? I can't stop thinking about him. What happened to my "twin?" Could I have done something to save him? Could I have changed him? Was anything about our connection real? I certainly felt something. Is there any chance he could have really been my brother? I want to believe he made up the story to throw me off guard. It's the only plausible explanation. I mean, I think I'd know if I had a brother.

I wish I knew more about Cody's life. The Agency had so little hard intel. In some ways he and I were incredibly similar. But the rage I saw in his face at the end scared me. What could have happened to twist him, to make him so angry and dangerous? It must have been something horrible. Is it possible he was just born evil? If our roles were reversed, and Cody grew up in Texas with my mom and dad and I grew up... however Cody did, I'd like to believe I'd still be the same person I am now. But I can't be sure. It's hard to ignore the importance of my parent's love and the faith in me.

I think Cody really did a number on my head. I keep reliving that evening on the roof. I see him falling again and again when I try to sleep. I keep seeing flashes of a birthmark on his butt cheek. I try to slow down the movie in my mind to see if what I saw resembled my cat's paw-shaped marking. But I can't ever make it out clearly enough. I also find myself wondering if he's really dead or not. I know there's no logical way that he could have survived that fall. But The Agency searched the mountainside for days and didn't find his body. There's a lot of area to cover and there are wild animals that could have got to him. But finding his body would have put any lingering doubts to rest.

A pretty female cabin attendant walks by the aisle handing out small bags of pretzels and offering beverages. I get a Coke, while Dean asks for a coffee. He barely even raises his head from his magazine to give her his order.

I wonder if The Agency knew more about Cody than they told me. Did they have more reason to send me after him than my skill set and proximity to his age? I didn't tell them about Cody's claim to be my brother, but did they already know? If I want information, I'll have to find it on my own. I'm going to find out everything about this mysterious "brother" of mine and I'm going to do it without anyone's help.

I'm working myself up for no reason. This was a good trip. Well, except for that whole almost-getting-murdered-on-a-roof-naked thing. But a good trip nonetheless. I take a deep breath. For now, I'm just going to enjoy the flight. Soon, I'll be back home with my family who I miss more than anything. Except for maybe sweet tea.

I pull my eyes away from the clouds. Dean is passed out in his seat with his magazine lying on his lap. Now that he's asleep, I can openly stare at him. He's so gorgeous. His clothes are all designer and he wears them well. I don't think I could ever look as put together as he does. His salmon polo doesn't have a wrinkle and his navy shorts look almost formal. I'm not sure I understand the idea of formal shorts. Shorts are meant to be casual, right? But they look so fine on my new Ukrainian friend.

His shorts rode up a bit during the flight to reveal more of his tanned and toned legs. They're surprisingly hairless. He must shave his legs. I wonder at what point on his body he stops. Is he completely hairless, or does he leave a few patches around his body? It would be nice to find out.

I stare at his crotch. (Please don't wake up and find me like this.) The dark blue fabric has bunched up around his crotch. What mysteries are you hiding, shorts? What kind of dick are you concealing? Small or big? Thick or thin? Smooth or hairy? Cut or uncut? I suppose his dick would have foreskin like mine. I don't think Ukrainian guys are circumcised.

Do models universally have big dicks? They seem so confident and cocky on TV and in photos. Do you need a monster cock to be confident? What is your dick like, Dean? There's really only one way for me to find out. I have the skills to break into most locked buildings and rooms. I'm sure I can easily reach over and unzip his shorts without him ever knowing. Purely a fact-finding mission.

I laugh to myself. That could lead to an awkward situation if I got busted. I wouldn't want to have to explain to The Agency why I got put on the sex offender registry or the no-fly list. Or is sneaking a peek at a guy's cock mid-flight considered air piracy? I just can imagine the air marshall yelling, "You! Young man! Step away from the zipper."

No. You and your willie are safe, Dean. For now.

But thoughts of Eastern European boners have got me all worked up. I adjust myself in my seat. Oh fuck me! I have a very noticeable boner propping up my shorts like a tent. A wet spot of pre-cum is already visible through the fabric of my Khaki cargo shorts. Fuck. It's spreading. If there's enough pre-jizz to leave a patch through my underwear and shorts, I can only imagine how much I've actually leaked. I'm tempted to reach in and find out. That's probably a bad idea.

Then again, most people on the flight are either asleep or have their eyes glued to their iPads or laptops. And the lights are pretty dim. Nobody's paying any attention to me. "Fuck it," I mumble to myself as I quietly undo the top button on my shorts and slide my hand into the waistband of my underwear. My fingertip finds the opening in my foreskin. It feels like there's a warm ocean in there. My finger is completely drenched in pre-cum.

I pull my hand out of my shorts and lick my wet finger. I love the salty taste of me and I do it again. I'm reminded of playing in the ocean when I was a kid. I loved the taste the salt water left in my mouth. And I love the taste of my own pre-cum. I suck my finger dry as I get lost in the intoxicating flavor.

I'm about to reach into my pants for another taste when I notice somebody standing in the aisle. My hand drops away from my mouth. Oh fuck. As the figure comes closer, I'm in shock.

"Hey, kitten," he says. "What are you up to there?"

It's the very same purser who fucked me on my way to London all those weeks ago. His smile is so big that it makes his eyes squint. He looks as happy to see me as I am to see him.

"Tim!"

He looks so distinguished in his dark blue uniform, silver wings pinned on his vest. His arms are folded behind him. Did he see that whole episode? My face burns red. Really red. His wicked grin lets me know he saw the whole episode.

"Can I get you anything to drink, sir?" he says with that huge smile.

My eyes move down his body. Seeing his athletic legs in those thin slacks does nothing to calm my boner.

"No thanks. I think I'm covered."

I want to leap over the Ukrainian model, undo Tim's zipper, gobble his cock and drink down the contents of his balls. I'm so horny.

Tim leans closer to me and whispers, "Give me seven minutes." He winks, then walks away.

Jackpot!

I'm so excited. Seven minutes crawl by like seven years. I don't see Tim. I stand up and make my way to the back of the plane. Most of the other passengers are sound asleep. Tim comes up behind me and shoves me into a small restroom.

His hands are immediately on me, grabbing me everywhere. The bathroom is tight, forcing us close together. The tiny room can't contain the desire between us. His hips frantically grind against mine. I can feel his cock press hard against the side of my own throbbing member. My fingers wildly try to pull his belt apart and shove his pants down. I can't get them off quickly enough! I want to rip them! His heavy breathing fills the room as his pants finally drop to the floor. His thin, soft boxers follow quickly with no problem.

Fuck the in-flight meal. I need to get that dick in my mouth now!

I drop to my knees and swallow his meat whole in one gulp. Tim falls back against the sink and moans. My tongue massages the underside of his hard cock while my lips knead his shaft.

"I didn't think it was possible, but fuck, you're even better than last time!" Tim tells me between moans.

I smile around my mouthful of cock. His compliment turn me on. Tim is over twice my age. I'm sure he's had some very fine blowjobs in his lifetime. I want to be the best cocksucker he's ever had. I pull my mouth off and run the flat of my tongue from the base of his cock near his balls, then up the shaft to his slit before swallowing him down again. I can taste his pre-cum flow into the back of my mouth. I can't imagine anything tasting better.

I work the knob at the end of his six-inch cut cock and suck more of his pre-cum into my mouth. Then I stand up and shove my tongue down his throat. I love making Tim taste his own sex fluids. It totally turns me on.

"I want to see all of you, boy!" He tugs at my clothes to get them off of me. He's so rough in his excitement, he stretches and tears the neck on my T-shirt. It just makes me hornier. He unzips my shorts and they fall hard. His hand rubs up and down on the front of my pre-cum soaked underwear as he stares into my eyes. I want him to rip them off of me. He's teasing me and making me want him even more. I want him to make me naked. I'll beg if I have to. He just keeps rubbing and rubbing, playing with me.

I put a hand on his chest and spin us around, pushing him against the wall while I lean against the sink. I kiss and lick his neck as I pull down my own black trunk-cut briefs. I rub them rub them over his face before dropping them on the floor. He laughs and kisses my nose. Our hard cocks meet and my whole body tingles.

Wait. What's that sound?

Oh fuck! The outside latch fidgets for a second before the door loudly folds open. I hold my breath. There's nowhere to hide in here and I'm completely naked, my pre-cum dripping onto the cold linoleum floor. I see the intruder's face. It's my seat neighbor, Dean! He stares at us from the open doorway. Tim can only stand there in shock with his pants around his ankles.

Dean smiles wolfishly. "Room for one more?"

He slips into the tiny bathroom and closes the door behind him. He look up and down at our sweat-glazed bodies before locking the door. "Amateurs!"

Oh fuck me! How could we forget to lock the door? We all share a quiet laugh.

There isn't really room for three people in this tiny bathroom. We're packed in tight as our hands try desperately to grope each other's bodies. Dean pulls his shirt over his head and drops it into the sink. He's thin, but so fit. The lines of his lean muscles all seem to point down to his beautiful groin. Tim undoes the new guy's belt and pushes his formal shorts to the ground. Dean isn't wearing any underwear. Fuck, that's hot. If only I'd known that back when I was sitting next to him!

Like the rest of his body, his dick is lean and hard. It's roughly seven inches long, tapered and pointed straight at the sky. Just like I suspected, he's intact.

"I saw you guys slipping off and I thought I'd investigate," he says quietly. I didn't think this flight could get any better until I heard that accent again.

The three of us stand in a tight circle, our backs pressed up against the walls. Tim takes control by grabbing onto both mine and Dean's dicks. Dean has a drop of shimmering pre-cum on the tip of his pointed foreskin. Tim scoops it up with his finger and gives it a tastes. "Mmmmmm!"

Tim may have the most compact penis at just over six inches, but he takes control so naturally. He pushes Dean and I together, making us kiss as he strokes our uncut cocks. I shut my eyes and kiss Dean with everything I have. He gives it right back. I feel a finger slide into my foreskin and slide around my cockhead.

My eyes open to see Dean move his pre-cum moistened finger out of my cock hoodie and put it in his mouth. His eyes close as he sucks every bit of my cockjuice. I'm about ready to cum right then.

Tim seems to know how close I am. He takes his hand off my dick and sits himself on the sink. He spreads his legs wide, inviting us to feast on his meat. Dean and I scramble down to get a taste of his boner. Our tongues meet on Tim's shaft. We take turns exploring the flared knob at the end of his circumcised cock. It fascinates me because I've spent most of my life just playing with my own hooded tool. Tim's cock feels strange and exotic to me. I'm guessing Dean feels the same way from the way he's all over Tim's pole. In between sucking and licking, we share kisses. I can't tell what tastes better, Tim's cock or Dean's mouth. With all this cocksucking, it's hard to tell the difference. We slide up and down, holding our shared flesh-toy between our lips. We take turns swallowing the head. I get hornier with every gulp.

Dean nuzzles Tim's hairy balls while I work his mushroom head. Then we switch. Tim is so much hairier than either Dean or I. We both love the trails of black fur and run our hands up his legs, up to his ass, up his firm stomach and around his hard chest. Dean twirls his fingers through Tim's dark pubic hair. He buries his face in it while he swallows Tim's stiff shaft. I look down and notice Dean's pubes are all shaved off. Completely gone! His cock is as bald as a baby's.

I gently nudge Dean aside and swallow Tim's cock down to the base. He barely manages to quiet his groan. Tim grabs onto the back of my neck at the base of my hairline. He isn't rough. He massages my head warmly as I take his cock into my mouth. I feel it pulse and throb. My hips thrust forward as my cock fucks the air. I'm so hard!

Dean's face is inches from mine. He smiles as he grabs onto my cock. He'll never know how badly I needed that. He handles my foreskin like an expert. My eyes roll back in my head.

Tim pushes me off of his cock, jumps off the sink and tells me to stand. I obey. He gives me a passionate kiss and turns me around. His hand cups my butt cheeks and pulls them apart. Is he going to fuck me? With Dean watching? My cock throbs and spills a shimmering rope of pre-cum. Then I think of something.

"Wait. I have an idea."

I turn around and shove my tongue down Tim's throat. Then I gather my foreskin in my hand and slowly roll it over Tim's cockhead. His eyes roll back in his head as I move my foreskin back and forth over our dickknobs. Dean shoves his tongue in Tim's mouth to quiet his grunting.

Then Dean slips behind me and wraps his arms around my torso. That boy saw an opening and went for it! I feel his cock glide between my ass cheeks, like a hot dog in a bun. He massages my ass with his dick, slicking my hole with his flowing pre-cum while Tim's and my juices flow together in my foreskin.

"Is this what it feels like to be uncut?" Tim asks.

"Fuck, yeah!" I tell him. Tim grabs hold of our connected cocks and starts stroking them, his cockhead never leaving my foreskin. Our knobs glide together inside my fleshy hood. It feels so good!

Dean starts to get bolder behind me. I can feel the tip of his cock press against my hole trying to gain entrance. He doesn't even ask if he can fuck me. He's so cocky, so entitled. That runway fucker probably has people throwing themselves onto his dick everywhere he goes. I'm sure he can have whatever he wants, whenever he wants it. Why should my ass be any different? It's not. I love the way he takes what he wants. And his invading cock pounding on my hole gets me so turned on. I'm light headed. All the blood that should be going to my brain is flowing and throbbing through my hard-on.

With a deep moan, I shove my hips backward and impale myself on Dean's cock. He gasps in my ear. My knees buckle. I'd probably fall over if Tim and Dean weren't holding me up. Dean's arms wrap tighter around my body. His teeth finds my earlobe. He pulls his cock out of my hole before slamming back in. I feel his cockhead glide in and out of his foreskin inside me. His tool hits my prostate like a heat-seeking missile over and over. I'm so close to cumming. I try to hold back and make this last.

I rock my hips back and forth, meeting every thrust Dean pounds into my ass. My cock rides Tim's hand as we continue to dock. Our boners are so wet that Tim's dick slides out of my foreskin. He quickly slides it back in. I don't know that he's ever felt anyone's foreskin wrapped around his cockhead before, but I can tell he loves it. He's groaning loudly. I don't think he can hold back much longer either. Dean notices too. He unwraps one of his arms from my torso and puts a finger in Tim's mouth.

"Uuuuugh," Tim lets out.

His entire body clenches. He grabs my shoulder and squeezes so tightly into me. His body shakes. His cock explodes with a massive load of cum. His warm load fills my foreskin up like a balloon.

Dean's fucking gets rougher and faster. He's breathing heavily right into my ear. He slams his meat torpedo inside me hard and deep one final time. I feel the wet heat explode in my ass. He thrusts again and more of his seed flows and fills me past capacity. His cum runs down my leg. It's all too much. My muscles tighten up, my head drops onto Tim's shoulder in front of me. I feel hands all over my cock, rubbing my balls, fingering my foreskin and stroking. My ballsack tightens. I start to shudder everywhere. Oh, oh, ooooooh! I shoot my massive load of jizz straight into the air. It sprays Tim's face and chest. The guys keep at my cock and balls, milking another huge shot out of me. This one flies behind me and covers Dean, his perfect skin becomes a milky mess. He purrs and then licks his face. Tim drops to his knees and sucks our mix of out of my foreskin.

The Ukrainian model circles around and joins Tim for a drink out of my semen-filled sheathing. I'm still hard as a rock. I'm still so turned on. I wonder I'll ever be soft again. The two beautiful men lick my cock so eagerly. I tremble all over.

"Watch out, guys!" I say shakily. "Uuuugh!"

I cum all over again. Right in their faces. I'm so drained and it feels so good. I watch Tim and Dean lick the cum from each other's handsome faces. Then they kiss. It makes me smile hard.

When they stand up, I pull them into a three-way kiss. I can taste my boy-spooge on their tongues. I love the way I taste in their mouths. I swallow down all the cum I can get.

We are miles above the ground, flying through the clouds. Our bodies and tongues tangle together, cramped and close. I feel an overwhelming sense of camaraderie, of brotherhood. This is a Heaven I can believe in.

Dean is the first to break away. He grabs his polo shirt out of the sink and slides it over his head. But before he's completely covered, I kiss his left nipple. I saw a bit of my cum there begging me to taste it.

We dress quickly. It's very challenging in this cramped space. Dean is the first to leave after giving Tim and I each a final kiss. After cleaning up some of my stray spunk with a paper towel, Tim also takes his leave. I'm the last to exit, careful to make sure enough time passes before stepping out of the airplane bathroom and down the aisle. Dean winks at me as I rub past his body and into my window seat. Tim comes by and gives us both cold bottles of water.

I lean back on my headrest. A giant smile makes it's way to my face from deep inside. I'm definitely not the same kid I was at the beginning of the summer. I've changed and grown. I spent my first summer on my own, triumphed over evil and fucked around with some really hot guys. I saved the world and I looked great doing it. Not a bad summer vacation. I'm going home a completely different twink. And the twink I've become is pretty fucking awesome.

The plane finally starts to make its descent into Houston. As the wheels hit the ground, I'm filled with confidence that I can handle whatever is thrown at me next. Bring it on. Agent Jake Parker is ready for anything.

.

Jake Parker will be back for more adventures.

FIFTY SHADES OF FORESKIN AND HIV

You may have noticed that Jake Parker has sex in this book. A lot of sex. Sex with older men. Sex with guys near his age. Sex with brothers. All kinds of sex. Sometimes the sex is warm, sometimes it's rough and sometimes it's both. But none of the sex involves condoms or even a discussion of safe sex.

"Isn't that irresponsible?" you ask.

It would be. But Fifty Shades of Foreskin is set just slightly in the future. Maybe a year. Maybe three years. Maybe even less. In this future, there's a vaccine for HIV and there are treatments to eliminate the viral loads of people with HIV. There's no safe sex or barebacking. Gay men are free to be intimate and playful with each other without fear.

But today, HIV is real. We all need to educate ourselves about how the virus is transmitted. If we are negative, we should find out how to stay that way with safe sex and/or preventative meds. If we are positive we should take good care of ourselves. We've come a long way and living with HIV isn't what it was just a few years ago. If we don't know our status, we need to find out. Knowledge is our best weapon against the disease.

And above all, we need to treat each other with kindness and respect. There is no "clean" or "dirty" when it comes to HIV status. There are only people.

Jake Parker doesn't have to worry about HIV in his world. If we educate ourselves, love each other and support our doctors and scientists, we may be living in Jake's world very soon.